Adrian McKinty

THE SUN
IS
GOD

A complete catalogue record for this book can be
obtained from the British Library on request

The right of Adrian McKinty to be identified as the author
of this work has been asserted by him in accordance
with the Copyright, Designs and Patents Act 1988

First published in this edition in 2015 by Serpent's Tail
First published in 2011 by Serpent's Tail
an imprint of Profile Books Ltd
3 Holford Yard
Bevin Way
London WC1X 9HD
www.serpentstail.com

ISBN 978 1 84668 984 0
eISBN 978 1 78283 052 8

Text designed and typeset by Tetragon, London
Printed and bound in Great Britain by
CPI Group (UK) Ltd, Croydon CR0 4YY

10 9 8 7 6 5 4 3 2 1

It is when we try to grapple with another man's intimate needs that we perceive how incomprehensible, wavering and misty are the beings that share with us the sight of the stars and the warmth of the sun.

JOSEPH CONRAD
Lord Jim (1900)

The sun is God!

J. M. W. TURNER
reputed last words (1851)

AUTHOR'S NOTE

The following story is based on true events. Emma Forsayth, Bessie Pullen-Burry, Governor Hahl, Doctor Parkinson, August Engelhardt *et alia* are real individuals who lived in, or, in Miss Pullen-Burry's case, visited, German New Guinea in the years 1906–7.

Kabakon Island lies in the Duke of York group between the large Papuan islands of New Britain and New Ireland, roughly 1,500 miles north of Brisbane and 200 miles west of the Solomons. In the decade before World War I, Kabakon was the *Heimat* for the extraordinary society who called themselves 'Naked Cocovores' or '*Sonnenorden*'. The mysterious deaths that took place on Kabakon during this time remain unsolved to the present day.

There are several fictional characters and many fictitious elements in this book; where the interests of the novel and strict historical accuracy have collided I have put the demands of the former first.

THE SUN
IS
GOD

Massacre on the Groot Hoek River

Lieutenant William Prior should never have been on duty that night at all. The war was nearly over and Will and three other officers of the Military Foot Police had been on their way to a saloon in Bloemfontein. On the track down from the camp a starved lioness had launched an attack on Lieutenant Rigby's horse, a shot in the air sent the skinny creature scurrying into the bush, but Rigby fell and broke an ankle. Riding double with Rigby, Will reached the field hospital just after nine where he surrendered his friend to the efficient hands of Harry Douglas of the Royal Army Medical Corps.

A breathless enlisted man ran over to Prior. 'Lieutenant Prior, sir, lukin for thissin, sir, trouble at Camp Z. T' kaffirs. Blow up, sir, or as near as makes na matter.'

Sergeant Black was a Yorkshireman from some hamlet in the North Riding and while few in the regiment could follow anything he said, Will could understand him perfectly. Will had grown up in Leeds and as the son of a popular doctor he had come into contact with every social class in the county.

'Who is supposed to be in charge of Camp Z., Sergeant Black?'

'Lieutenant Ashcroft, sir but he's legged it, sir. Drunk, sir.'

'What sort of trouble is it?'

'Know nowt, sir. Corporal Townes comes running t' camp, sir, screaming about t' kaffirs and Lieutenant Ashcroft, sir.'

'All right, let's get over there, sergeant, and see if we can't sort this out between us, eh?'

Camp Z. was across the valley on the other side of the Vaalkop about three miles from the field hospital. Both men got their horses from the stables and rode together across the barren wasteland that had been rich wheat and barley fields until the previous winter when they'd been torched on the orders of General Kitchener.

The sky was cloudy and moonless and the two men could see virtually nothing. Bats flitted above the horses' ears and great moths the size of small birds collided with man and beast.

As they got closer to the Groot Hoek River they could hear the sound of gunfire and yelling. Will nudged his pony into a canter and Sergeant Black followed suit.

Camp Z. was a 'concentration camp' for African prisoners who had worked in some capacity for the Boers in the Orange Free State. The condition for most inmates in the British camps had improved since the findings of the Fawcett Commission and the noisy campaigns of Emily Hobhouse and David Lloyd-George. Before Hobhouse's polemics in the liberal press, thousands of Boer women and children had perished from malnutrition and disease while their menfolk were shipped to prison camps overseas. Over the last year, however, the Boer camps had seen ameliorated food supplies and the establishment of prison hospitals, but the truth was that almost nothing had been done to better the lot of the native African prisoners. No one in England or Germany or anywhere else got terribly worked up about the well-being of inmates in the 'kaffir camps'.

As they neared Camp Z., Will and Sergeant Black saw the

first escapee, a boy of about eleven, running blindly towards the town with blood pouring from a head wound.

Sergeant Black raised his rifle but Will shook his head. One runaway child didn't amount to much. As they climbed the *kop* they passed another half dozen boys and one old man jogging up the hill. 'Doesn't look good, sergeant,' Will said.

'Nay, sir,' Black agreed.

They followed the curve of the Groot Hoek River and galloped to the camp entrance, where they found the situation parlous in the extreme. Seemingly the entire population of around a thousand men, women and children was attacking the small Military Foot Police garrison who were lined up in two rows in front of the camp gates. Three of the MFP soldiers were already injured but a corporal was holding the nerve of the remaining men. Some of the prisoners were escaping over the barbed wire and others were in the process of ransacking the aid station and supply shed, but by far the biggest danger was the mob at the gate. If the line of a dozen military policemen broke, the entire camp could run off into the South African night.

Will was in his dress uniform, armed with a six-shot revolver and a cavalry sabre. He dismounted, unsheathed the sword and ran to the camp entrance. 'Lieutenant Prior assuming command!' he bellowed.

A terrified private let Sergeant Black and Will inside the gate and it was at that moment that the Africans surged forward again. Two volleys from the soldiers kept them back but Will could see that several dozen African men had ripped the corrugated iron roof from the storage shed and were preparing an assault from behind these improvised barriers. If the prisoners all charged at once they would certainly overrun the position.

'Sergeant Black, go to the guardhouse, find the bloody Maxim gun and bring it back here!'

Sergeant Black saluted and ran to the guardhouse. He did not ask the obvious question: what if Camp Z. did not possess a Maxim gun?

'Does anyone know how this kicked off?' Will asked the soldiers.

'They've had no food or medicine for four days. The supplies haven't come through,' a Scottish corporal told him. 'We've been taking the dead ones out in carts, sir.'

Will marched in front of the line of military policemen and addressed the mob. 'Return to your tents at once! We will not hesitate to shoot if you attempt to escape!'

He was well aware that few if any of them spoke English but he hoped that his uniform and sword would at least have a visual impact. The mob jeered and someone threw an improvised spear at him which missed.

'Return to your tents at once! The food situation cannot be addressed until order has been restored!'

A skeletal woman dressed in rags ran to him from the mob and fell at his feet. He was horrified by her miserable, hollow face and bony outstretched fingers.

My God, were all the prisoners like this? He looked beyond the woman to the other inmates and from what he could see in the lamplight it was the same story: half dead, naked, brown stick-like figures with weeping sores and great gaping eyes.

For almost his entire time in South Africa he had been on standard policing duties in captured Boer towns or in the British garrison. He had heard the stories, of course, and even read the reports in the *Manchester Guardian* but he had expected nothing like this. He stepped away in horror and backed towards the British line.

'If you return to your tents I will make sure that food arrives tonight from the British commissary!' he yelled, but as he had expected, none of the prisoners moved. He could see that many of the young men had armed themselves with rocks, stones and spears that had been manufactured from wooden joists and sharpened tent pegs. And all at once assorted missiles began to fall among the soldiers.

'Do any of you speak Dutch?' Will asked the men.

One of the privates raised a nervous hand.

'Tell them that I will personally guarantee the arrival of food tonight from the commissary at the Vaalkop!'

The private raised his voice to shout to the mob in Afrikaans. Although many of the prisoners did understand what he was saying the situation was too far gone for further British promises.

More spears and stones and one of the soldiers went down hurt.

'Sergeant Black, tell me about the Maxim!' Will bellowed.

'Maxim ready to fire, sir!' Black said in the stolid Yorkshire burr that gave Will confidence.

'Excellent. Now, who is the best rider among you men?'

The soldiers looked at a short blond private at the far end of the line.

'All right, you take my horse, ride over to the Vaalkop, find Major Potter and briskly apprise him of the situation. Then ride to the field hospital and tell Lieutenant Douglas that we are in need of orderlies and medical assistance.'

'Yes, sir!' the young man said, relieved to be getting out of here with his life.

Will addressed the nervous men. 'Now lads, this is nothing to be alarmed about. We are British soldiers and they are unarmed African civilians who should pose no threat to the likes of us. We shall fire a warning volley in the air and then we'll advance by squads and drive these people back into their tents. Sergeant Black will cover us with the Maxim at the gates, and I think I can safely say that—'

A heavy stone struck Will on the head, knocking off his pith helmet.

He was only unconscious for a few moments but when he came to he saw that the gates had been opened and half his command had deserted and were running for it. The mob was racing towards what was left of his men with their improvised weapons and corrugated iron shields.

A spear hit the Scottish corporal next to him and a private took a half brick in the head. Then Sergeant Black opened up with the Maxim gun. It didn't sound like much. Like water coming out of a drain or a fast pair of workmen hammering metal plate. It was not an unpleasant noise at all. Its effect, however, was devastating. Flame spat from the barrel and row upon row of Africans began falling to the ground. Will watched in awe and stupefaction. He had never been in a battle. He had never seen anything like this. Still they kept coming and Sergeant Black kept mowing them down like barley under the scythe, until, finally, the mob began to understand what kind of a machine the Maxim gun was.

'Cease fire!' Will commanded.

Only one minute had passed since Sergeant Black had begun to shoot. One minute and all was changed. Africans were dead and dying in row upon row. Sergeant Black had undoubtedly saved the lives of the remaining soldiers, but at what cost?

Will walked back to the military policemen who had gathered round the Maxim gun in amazement. Its brass was searingly hot and the holy words 'Deutsche Waffen und Munitionsfabriken, Berlin, 1898' glowed in the darkness.

All around them the air smelled of blood and gunpowder and death.

Presently a detachment of Australian troopers showed up with a group of MFPs from the Vaalkop. No one could believe the slaughter. When Lieutenant Douglas appeared and attempted to examine Will's head wound Will pushed him angrily away. 'Not me, you fool! Them! Treat them!'

Nineteen had been killed outright. A further sixty-five were wounded. The incident at Camp Z. did not merit a mention in the *Manchester Guardian* or *The Times* or even in the fervently anti-British Dutch and German papers. The dead, after all, were only kaffirs. Will was not criticized by anyone. Quite the reverse. His actions were widely praised. He was mentioned in dispatches to General Kitchener and a month later he was informed that he was going to be awarded a DSO. They normally didn't give the Distinguished Service Order to anyone under the rank of Major but since Will had been the acting commanding officer at Camp Z. it had been deemed appropriate. The citation said: 'For gallantly leading his men in the face of the enemy.'

He didn't react when he heard the news from Colonel Wilson, but when he saw his name in the *Gazette* a month later he was physically sick.

2

The Duel

T he nightmares began a week after the *Gazetting* and two days after Will's company had been transferred to the Lime Kiln barracks in Cape Town. The war was won, of course, and the prisoners had all been set free, but Will's troop of Military Foot Police weren't going home. Their orders were to wait at the Cape for their new destination. There were fires all over the Empire that needed dampening and where the British soldiers went to put out the flames, the MFP went to dampen their ardour for plunder and rapine.

Will's nightmares were so vivid and terrifying that the young captain he had been billeted with moved out after the second day.

Often the nightmares were a simple replay of the incident at Camp Z., but frequently they involved Will's own violent death. They had a vividness which he had never experienced in a dream before and when he awoke sweating or sometimes crying in his cot he had trouble convincing himself of the veracity of the comparatively tranquil waking world.

Initially, the one sure method of staving off the night terrors was to get blind drunk, and fortunately in Cape Town there were many places where that could be accomplished cheaply on soldier's pay. But eventually even the local brandy lost its power to charm the demons.

Of course, he could tell no one of these dreams. It would be out of the question to write to his father or mother and apart from Adam, who was a junior doctor in his father's practice, his other brothers were all military men who would scoff at his weakness. May was another matter. They had been close in age – the two youngest of the family – but May's proud, happy letter to him on learning of the DSO had, he felt, removed her too as a potential source of consolation.

The syphilitic mollies and whores on Waal Street could not be relied upon either. They would listen to him but they did not understand and after a few incidents of night terror in the more respectable brothels Will felt it best to keep himself away from such places.

He feared to sleep but he could not keep himself awake.

His days were long and brimming with misery and his nights were worse.

As the weeks dragged without an onward destination for the regiment, Will began to see the inklings of a solution. He must leave the army. He must leave the army at once and in as ignominious a way as possible so that his conscience would be placated and so there could be no possibility of ever rejoining in the event of some national emergency or other contingency.

A court martial would be the quickest and easiest route and to Will's troubled mind, the most honourable one. But courts martial were tricky. You had to grade your offence in such a manner that you would be dismissed from the service but not imprisoned or subject to capital punishment.

Fortunately, as a military policeman, he knew the Army Acts and Kings Regulations backwards but he also knew that military courts were harder on MPs than on other officers. Firing-squad crimes included: delivering up a garrison to the enemy; casting away arms in the presence of the enemy; misbehaving before the enemy in such a manner as to show cowardice; sleeping when acting as a sentinel on active service; causing a mutiny in the forces; disobeying in such a manner as to show a wilful defiance of a superior officer; striking a superior officer; deserting HM service.

Offences that led to cashiering included: the negligent discharging of firearms; occasioning false alarms in camp; fraudulent enlistment; assisting a desertion.

There was some overlap between the crimes and misdemeanours and the more Will thought about it, the more he saw that striking an officer of the same rank as himself could be the answer. If Will provoked the quarrel it would almost certainly lead to a penalty of cashiering but, because he was a DSO, probably not penal servitude or imprisonment.

He was still very much in the planning stage when an opportunity presented itself at the Kings Arms on Victoria Street. Albright, a tall blond moustachioed officer from the Horse Guards was abusing a small dark Welsh lieutenant from the engineers. Will knew Albright. He was from Somerset, the third son of an Earl, but not a bad fellow at all. Will and he had played billiards together on several occasions and even in defeat Albright had displayed humility and a measured temper.

Will had no idea what the dispute with the engineer could have been about but he knew that this was an excellent chance. Albright had the little Welshman around the throat and was muttering something about 'Nancy'. Nancy could have been a horse, a girl, or even one of the boy mollies for all Will knew or cared.

He got up from his table, strode across the room and interposed himself between Albright and the quaking lieutenant. 'Steady on, Albright, do you always have to be such a confounded bully!' Will said and shoved Albright backwards into the long bar.

Albright was amazed but unsure how to proceed next. Was Will on duty? Was he acting in his capacity as a member of the Military Foot Police?

'Get up man! Get up and face me! You've always been a coward and a bloody cheat!' Will snarled.

Albright was propelled forward by one of his friends.

Everyone in the saloon bar had stopped to watch the action now. There would be plenty of witnesses: Lieutenants, Captains, and even a Major or two. Will took the measure of Albright's startled face and threw a punch at it. Albright easily dodged Will's punch and had hit Will twice in response before he knew what was happening.

'Get him, Ally!' someone yelled and Albright punched Will again: a gut strike that doubled Will over. When Will recovered and saw Albright waiting for him in a boxer's stance he understood the nature of his mistake. He'd probably learned to box at school. Will wiped the blood from his lip.

'What's the matter, Prior? Don't like a fight with a white man, eh?' Albright said.

Will understood the implication only too well. He was seething now. He hated Albright. He hated the army and he hated South Africa and every bastard in it. Most of all, of course, he hated himself.

He took a step away from Albright and straightened his uniform. 'My friends shall contact your friends. I trust that you are a man of honour, sir!' Will declared.

Albright's pale, furious face lost its colour at once. 'You cannot be serious, Prior,' he said.

'I am serious, sir, but if your Lordship does not wish to fight then I shall accept a full and complete apology in the presence of these witnesses,' Will said.

All heads in the saloon were now turned upon the hapless

Albright. The sensible little Welshman, Will noted, had long since gone. The establishment was so quiet that they could hear the call of the fishmongers on the wharves a half a mile away.

'So be it, madman! My seconds will call upon you this afternoon,' Albright said, his voice trembling with rage and confusion.

Will's second, Lieutenant Blakely, a Scot and something of a damned fool, arranged the whole thing. They were to meet at Scarborough on Table Mountain at dawn, which meant that they would all have to get up at four in the morning.

Word of the duel, of course, had spread throughout the colony. No one had been called out in Cape Town in ten years. Duelling was both illegal and, worse, unfashionable. And so, despite the hour, when Blakely and Will arrived at Scarborough they found a small crowd waiting for them.

Albright's second was Lord Donnybrook, a Captain in the Grenadiers, an excitable young man who thought the duel 'a fine wheeze'.

Donnybrook and Blakely consulted for a moment and Will was surprised to find himself looking at a box of antique single-shot duelling pistols.

Will examined the grey sky and the pale, milky sun rising over False Bay. It was almost like the heathland of the East Riding. Not a bad place to die at all. Yes, this was the way to go. To finish it one way or the other. Will smiled at Blakely. 'Let's get on with it and if he kills me, please tell Albright that there were no hard feelings and that the whole thing was my fault,' Will said and marched to a position on the moor that was well away from the chattering crowd of officers, civilians and, scandalously, one or two ladies.

Donnybrook marked out twenty-five paces from where Will was standing and Albright assumed his position on the ground.

He had taken off his hat and jacket and was holding both pistols, cocked and ready.

The seconds retreated and a hush went over the small crowd of spectators. Albright's shirt billowed in the light breeze and his golden hair flowed freely behind his head. Without further ado Albright immediately raised both his pistols and before Will quite knew what was happening he saw a cloud of pistol smoke and heard two reports. One of the balls whisked so close to his left ear that he felt its hum in passing, but the other came nowhere near him.

When the smoke cleared he saw Albright's pale, amazed face. Will displayed both his arms Christ fashion to demonstrate that he was unhurt. Albright nodded, began to tremble and after a quarter-minute pulled himself together and stood to attention, facing his potential assassin. Will could see that the poor man was terrified. Even third sons of Earls loved life and hated death.

Will grinned and discharged both his pistols into the earth. When the smoke cleared Albright looked at him with wonder. The seconds reloaded the pistols and the men were moved five paces closer. Albright cocked his duelling pistols and pointed them at Will.

A hawk was rising on a thermal. The sea was turning a deeper shade of blue.

Yes, Will thought, *come on, man, do it!*

Albright saw the gleam of acceptance in Will's eye, held the pistols horizontal for a moment and then shook his head.

'He wants to die, Donnybrook, he wants me to kill him, to save himself the trouble. I will not give the damned fool what he wants!'

Albright began walking back to his horse. 'Come back, you coward!' Will yelled.

Albright ignored him.

'Stand your ground or I'll shoot you in the bloody back!'
Albright kept walking.

Will pulled the trigger on one of the pistols and shot Albright
in the thigh. He went down with a strange animal-like shriek.
Donnybrook ran to attend him and a booing noise arose from
the small crowd.

They rode back to Cape Town and it wasn't until the next
afternoon that Will was arrested. Albright survived the gunshot
but the wound suppurated and a fever nearly did away with
him. Popular sentiment was against Will from the start and the
verdict of the rapidly constituted court martial was a foregone
conclusion. He had no connections of any kind and, but for
the DSO, he would have been reduced to the ranks and sent to
a penal station on some godforsaken rock thousands of miles
from anywhere.

As it was he was simply lectured by the Judge Advocate, cash-
iered without pay or remittances and quietly drummed out of
the army. He was blackballed in every club and pub in town and
formally told to quit Cape Town. He found his way to Durban
and it was there, among the disaffected Boers and angry Dutch
immigrants, that he saw the pamphlets offering loans and passage
to the German regions of Africa and elsewhere.

Will met with the Reich agent who told him that fortunes were
still being made among the rubber plantations of the German
colonies in the Pacific.

Will said that he didn't care where he went, he just wanted
to go.

And so it was that on a bitingly cold Southern Hemisphere
winter day Will boarded the third-class gangway of the massive
SS Kronprinz Wilhelm bound for the port of Herbertshöhe in far-off
Deutsch Neu Guinea.

3
Captain Kessler's Request

Will had built his house far enough out of Herbertshöhe so that he or his servant girl could see trouble coming from a very long way off. Hauptman Kessler's appearance on the road shortly after three o'clock was not, then, a surprise. Kessler was riding Brunhilde, his great grey mare that somehow had weathered every attack by mosquito, black fly and dengue fever.

'Get the kettle on, love,' Will told Siwa and watched her as she scuttled wordlessly inside to light the range. 'And put some clothes on too, you know how easily scandalized these Germans are,' he added through the window – or rather through the space where a window might someday be.

The horse came slowly along what the authorities had optimistically called Wilhelm II Strasse and when it reached the foot of the hill Kessler nudged it into a canter. It was a sin to even make a horse trot in this heat, but Brunhilde was as strong as any Yorkshire Dray and she had outlasted equine arrivals from Arabia, Europe and Australia who had died by the score along this coast, some only a few hours after disembarkation.

Will tied the cotton sarong about his waist and went inside, admiring the feel of the newly laid floor on his bare feet. It was so much better than the shabeen-like pounded earth he'd put up with here for the first year; if he had known that Lee and Sons took credit he would have had it in ages ago, certainly before the rainy season.

Will hastily tidied the room, sat in the window seat and stared thoughtfully at the one piece of art in his house, a reproduction of Alphonse de Neuville's *Defence of Rorke's Drift* that he'd won from Tommy Hanson at piquet the previous Saturday. He hated the picture, not least because it reminded him of South Africa, and only took it because Hanson had nothing else in his house worth a damn. He got up, walked into the kitchen, removed the cork from one of the storage jars and carefully inspected the good black tea. No mould or weevils and it smelt like tea.

'Could you make enough for both of us, Siwa? Although I suspect Klaus will prefer something a bit stronger,' Will said.

'Whisky?' Siwa asked, reaching for the bottle of Johnnie Walker.

'Christ no, he'll drink the whole thing. Get the *arak*.'

'I will hide the whisky bottle,' she said. It had been the missionaries on Ulu who had taught her to speak English and (rather less usefully) to sing hymns in Welsh. Apparently she'd even showed promise in the reading and writing department, or so Pastor Jones claimed in his reference note.

'Yes,' Will said, admiring her long black hair and those slim athletic legs that she had soon freed from the thick cotton baptismal dresses the Methodists had kept her in. 'And put something on or Klaus will think you are a fallen woman,' he added.

'If I am it is you that has made me so,' she said.

Will smiled. He had never been one for servants and relations between himself and Siwa had quickly devolved – or evolved if you preferred – into a scandalous equality.

'If you came off with that kind of talk in a German household they would have you whipped,' Will said.

'And that would be the last thing that they would do in this life,' Siwa replied, her dark brown eyes flashing.

'I believe you,' he said, crossed the floor and took another peep through the window. Brunhilde was giddily trotting up the muddy track, swishing her tail to and fro. She obviously remembered this house. He opened a jar of New Zealand porridge oats, grabbed a handful, softened them in his left palm with a pour from the water jug and walked out onto the veranda. He opened a copy of Tennyson and pretended to read it until the horse drew up.

'*Guten Tag*, Herr Prior,' Kessler said, halting the mare in front of the bungalow and tipping his hat.

'Oh, good morning captain,' Will replied, appearing to be startled from his deep contemplation of a poem with the unlikely name of 'Tit Honies'.

'I see that you are reading,' Kessler said, his odd pale eyes already bleary and red, and his moustache twitching uncomfortably.

'Nothing escapes you, Klaus,' Will replied with a grin.

Kessler returned the smile and both men looked at one another for a moment before their gaze sought sanctuary elsewhere. The dense tropical jungle began ten feet behind Will's little bungalow, so naturally they discovered the sea, a brilliant cold-looking blue with a thin distant line of cloud above what the English called New Ireland and the Germans had renamed Neu Mecklenberg.

'It is a fine day,' Kessler said, attempting to cover the silence.

It had rained for eight hours solid during the night, mosquitoes were in swarm, the heat and humidity were almost unbearable – if this was a fine day Will thought that he would like to see a bad one.

'It certainly beats the alternative,' Will said cheerfully.

Kessler's left eyebrow arched, compressing the German's livid, archetypal duelling scar.

'That lime pit in Simpsonhafen where you chuck your dead priests,' Will explained.

'We do seem to have a lot of those,' Kessler agreed.

Kessler's boots eased themselves in and out of the stirrups and Will knew that it was up to him to ask Kessler inside. A line of damp had made a sickle across the young German's blue uniform and his rear collar button had popped off. But Will, for some perverse reason, did not tell Kessler to get off the horse. Siwa was standing in the living room, glaring at him with her arms folded. Up-country, she seemed to be hinting, wars had been started for less than this. Will wondered, not for the first time, if he had perhaps gone a little mad out here.

'A good book?' Kessler asked again, attempting to resurrect their small talk and this time it hit the mark, for Will could not risk a conversation about Tennyson.

'Listen, Kessler, old chap, I'm just having a pot of tea, why don't you come inside and join me,' he said in a free and easy manner that didn't, in fact, come that easily. Will was dour Yorkshire on both sides of the family. Dour Yorkshire all the way back to the Garden of Eden – which, his learned old Aunt Bet claimed, was located just south of Harrogate.

Kessler's back stiffened. 'Yes. Tea. And if it is possible, I would like to talk with you for some of your time?' Kessler asked.

Hauptman Kessler dismounted and Will shook his right hand. Kessler's chubby cheeks were glistening with sweat and it was with obvious relief that he took off his hat.

Will gave Brunhilde the oats concealed in his left fist. Brunhilde whinnied affectionately and ate.

'She remembers you,' Kessler said and Will did not hide his pleasure. He liked to think of himself as someone who cared much more about the approbation of horses than of people, although this was far from the truth. Will admired the animals, yes, but he seldom rode and he was certainly not of the horse-and-hounds set. Brunhilde was a gentle old mare though, who would surely carry him home drunk from Herbertshöhe or safely at a gallop through the cannibal-infested mountains. He gave her a pat on her bristly forehead and as she munched the last of the oats, Siwa led her into the shade.

'After you, Klaus,' Will said to Kessler and pointed inside.

'Thank you, Herr Prior,' Kessler replied and his boots squeaked on the deck as they entered the house. They'd been shined to a dazzling mirror finish by one of his groom's native boot boys – in the Bismarck Archipelago even the servants had servants.

'Have a seat,' Will said and Kessler sat in the wicker chair with its back to the window.

'No, no, no, over here,' Will said, showing him to the comfortable wooden lounger he had bought from a catalogue in Singapore. It swung on springs and apparently was very good for the circulation. It also afforded a vista of the bold Lieutenant Chard battling the Zulus.

'How do you take your tea?' Will asked.

'Which ever way you are taking it,' Kessler replied cautiously.

'You wouldn't want something a little stronger, would you now?' Will wondered.

'You have schnapps?'

'Siwa, lass, some of our finest *arak* for the gentleman,' Will said.

'Wait a moment!' she yelled from somewhere outside.

Kessler's eyebrows raised and Will gave him what he thought of as a Music Hall comedian's stage wink. Kessler who had never been to a Music Hall in his life wondered if Will was in the first stages of the river blindness which was all too common among plantation men.

Siwa came inside and they heard her fussing in the kitchen. She poured a liberal mug of *arak* for both of them and brought it in on a rattan tray that she carried on her head.

'Thank you, Siwa,' Will said as she knelt before them.

Of course, she hadn't bothered to put the sarong on at all and Kessler discreetly looked away. 'To your health,' Kessler said and knocked back the 120-proof *arak* with the ease of a practised colonial dipsomaniac.

'Another?' Will asked.

Kessler shook his head. 'I am on duty, so to speak.'

'It'll have to be the tea then,' Will said. 'I'll be mother.'

He poured two English teas: strong with goats' milk and sweetened with cane sugar. The florid German hid his disgust when the first sip of the foul brew touched his now pink lips; but, ever the diplomat, he smiled.

'Your, uh, Siwa makes a very good tea,' he added after another couple of polite sips.

'Aye she is a find is that lass. She speaks English too, not pidgin mind, real English.'

'A product of the Welsh Mission, no doubt.'

'Yes.'

'And how are your plantations coming along?'

'About as well as everyone else's,' Will replied.

Kessler nodded. He knew what that meant. The imported Indian rubber trees were dying, blight had destroyed the most recent banana crop and all of the experimental tea plantations in the hills were in the process of failing. If Will had invested his own money in this godforsaken land he would soon have been ruined and if it had been the bank's money then one day Will Prior would no doubt have ceased to exist, another faceless European on the overcrowded packet to Hong Kong or Sydney or Singapore.

'It is a poor season,' Kessler said, politely taking another sip of the vile, lukewarm liquid. He raised his eyes to the ceiling and his face seemed to communicate the notion that it was an unlucky collision of misfortunes that had brought him and Will, these cups and this tea, to this place at this time.

Will was reflecting on the fact that Kessler already looked ancient and wasn't near his thirtieth birthday. He was a middle-sized young man who had been shrunk by the tropics. Literally. He had lost maybe an inch in the last year and his skin had assumed the same colour as the leather furniture in the yacht club. This brandy casking had not, however, had a corresponding impact on Kessler's personality, and fortunately Will had not heard of any incidents of the kind German officers committed when they began to go really crazy.

'You should give us a subsidy to live out there. That's what the Japanese government do in their colonies. You Germans just let us all wither on the vine . . . '

Kessler put down his china tea cup and took snuff from his tin box. He offered it to Will, who, remembering his manners, offered Kessler a cheroot from a rough cedar cigar box. Both men refused the other's tobacco, sniffing and lighting their own in turn.

When he had sneezed and dabbed his nose with a silk kerchief Kessler observed sadly: 'But, my dear Herr Prior, the Imperial government already is giving us a subsidy. A surprisingly large one.'

'Here in Neu Pommern?'

'Of course. Every colony is a tremendous drain on the Fatherland. This is not to mention, also, the money that we spend on the coaling stations for the Kaiserliche . . . '

Kessler's voice trailed off, worried, perhaps, that this was becoming dangerously indiscreet.

'Well, you need to do more. When the papers in Berlin get wind of this disaster that you call a colony they'll kick up a fuss.'

Hauptman Kessler shook his head. 'You are mistaken, Herr Prior. This is not England. Public opinion is of no importance. Certainly not over questions of money. For the Reich it is a question of prestige. As long as a little nation like the Dutch are in the Indies, we will be in the Indies, as long as the Belgians are in Africa we will be in Africa,' he said.

'You're probably right, Klaus. I know little of politics.'

'And you, Will? You are not working *too* hard?'

'No. That fella Brown looks after my acres along with those of Mrs Herring and Lieutenant Ransom.'

'So you have time for the finer things. Botanizing perhaps? It is an undiscovered country in the mountains.'

Indeed it was, up beyond the tea and coffee plantations where even the brave boys of the Deutsches Heer feared to tread.

Will stroked his moustache. Reflecting upon it, he had no idea how he spent his days. The time passed certainly, but how and in what manner he was not sure.

Kessler sat a little straighter in the chair. 'Shall I tell you why I have come to see you today, Herr Prior?'

'Yes, please,' Will said, attempting to conceal his nerves. For this could be the interview he had been dreading. If Kaufman was calling in the loan and sending Klaus here to do the dirty work . . . New floor or no, he'd have to flee. He looked at Siwa through the window and wondered if she would hop the packet with him, or maybe she'd prefer to go back to singing 'Bread of Heaven' in four-part harmony at the mission school. He shuddered at the prospect.

'Herr Prior, it is a delicate business . . . ' Kessler began and coughed.

I knew it, Will groaned inwardly. *He's either going to demand the notes of credit or ask me to do the decent thing and blow me bloody brains out. Fat chance of either.*

Kessler attempted a smile and then said in a low tone: 'Herr Prior, Will, if I may, you are not, how shall I put it, still honour-bound in allegiance to the English Empire?'

'You want me for a spy!'

'No.'

'What then?'

Kessler leaned even further forward so that now he was nearly off the chair. His voice had sunk to a whisper: 'What I will tell you must remain between us, Herr Prior. Do you understand? Only myself, Governor Hahl and Herr Doctor Bremmer know the truth of it.'

'I'm listening,' Will said, intrigued.

'There has been another incident among the Cocovores,' Kessler said. He gave Will a knowing look.

'The Cocovores . . .. that's out near Fiji is it?' Will asked, dubiously, geography not his strong suit.

'No!' Kessler said.

'Where are they then?'

'Not where. Who. The Cocovores are not a group of islands. They are a group of men . . . No, no, let us not get into that, yet. First, I should tell you that Polizeimeister Beyer has been taken ill.'

'I'm sorry to hear that. What ails him?'

'Officially cholera,' Kessler said with a sigh.

'And unofficially?'

'Syphilitic brain disease. Rather an advanced case, I'm afraid. He had been dosing himself with mercury sulphate, but . . . '

'Oh dear. I hadn't seen him around for a month or so. I had no idea. No hope I suppose?'

Captain Kessler shook his head. 'And as you may be aware, Unteroffizier Fischer has gone with Munt to the Court in Apia.'

Karl Munt had murdered his wife, cutting off her head and putting it on a spike in front of his house. This after High Mass as the Catholic congregation had been letting out. The Governor's wife and her servants had seen it, which meant that there was no possibility of hushing it up, so, Munt, the only European dentist for a thousand miles, had been arrested. It was a big loss to the colony.

'Fischer's in Apia, Beyer's off his rocker, who does that leave?'

'The native *Polizeitruppe*.'

'That bunch of tripes? They'd turn tail at the first sign of a Ju Ju Man from the jungle.'

Kessler took a piece of paper from his trouser pocket. A by-now very damp piece of paper. 'Herr Prior, I am come on a mission of some import. I do not know how to ask you this without it appearing as an insult.'

'I am as hooked as a Humber trout, I assure you.'

'When you came here a little over two years ago you were made to provide a number of referees and affidavits.'

'Ah, about that, listen those references, now, some of them were rather elderly gentlemen so if you've had trouble—' Will began.

Kessler had taken a pair of gold-rimmed glasses from a case and placed them on the end of his nose like an apothecary. He unfolded the piece of paper and read: 'From March 1899 until May 1903 you were a member of the British Army's Military Foot Police, attaining the rank of First Lieutenant.'

'That's right.'

'As a military policeman did you look into ordinary crimes?'

'That was part of our duties, yes.'

'Did you ever investigate a murder?'

In the military foot police, Will reflected, a murder was one drunken private bashing another drunken private over the head and then crying about it until the MFPs came to arrest him.

'I've looked into the occasional murder. What's all this about?'

Kessler nodded. Yes, Will Prior would do very nicely. He was an ex-military policeman and had undertaken murder cases. He was not a fool and neither was he so scrupulous that he would run to the Fathers or the newspapers if he found scandalous goings-on. He was therefore the only man in the entire colony who could investigate the suspected murder of Max Lutzow on Kabakon Island.

Kessler stood. 'You are to get dressed. We must see Governor Hahl immediately.'

Will smiled and shook his head. 'I am not getting dressed for the Governor on this or any other fine Sunday afternoon.'

'No?'

'My dear Klaus, Sunday is a day for contemplation and relaxation, even in a German colony.'

Kessler shook his head. 'Twenty guineas says you will come.'

Will's eyes widened. 'Twenty English guineas?'

'Do you accept?'

'If you put it like that, yes, I accept.'

'Then attend to your toilet, Herr Prior,' Kessler said, already assuming the mantle of command.

'Siwa!' Will yelled. She appeared in the doorway, arms folded and frowning. 'Where's me kit, lass? I have to go out.'

She nodded and went into the back room.

'And one more thing, Will,' Kessler said.

'Yes?'

'It is Tuesday.'

4

The Immortal in the Morgue

I t was fortunate that Siwa had had Will's shirts, flannel trousers and Norfolk jacket washed and steam-ironed by Lee and Sons, otherwise he would have had nothing to wear but his cricket whites. While Kessler waited on the veranda, Will got into his trousers, pulled on his Liverpool Rubber Company plimsolls and buttoned his collarless shirt. He did not possess a tie or cravat, but with the cleaned and ironed jacket he felt that he looked presentable enough. Captain Kessler thought otherwise. 'Do you even possess a button collar?'

'Why would I in this bloody heat?'

'What do you wear at the club or the bar of the hotel?'

'This,' Will said.

Kessler sighed. 'If you are unable to change your toilet, at the very least you must shave,' Kessler said with a trace of exasperation.

Will made a face. 'Siwa! Shave!' he yelled. Siwa had obviously anticipated this exigency for she appeared a moment later with a bowl of water. Will adjourned to the porch and sat in a wicker chair. She lathered him and began shaving him with a Gillette safety razor. Pinching his long angular nose she ran the razor over his throat, cheeks and prominent chin, cleaning the razor in the water between strokes. 'What do you think of my new shaving device?' Will asked.

'You must not speak!' Siwa scolded, easing the blade over his carotid artery.

'Show him the razor,' Will said to Siwa who, ignoring him, stroked the blade over his Adam's apple.

'The whiskers?' she asked hopefully. It was obviously a point of contention, for Will did not even need to reply before she moved onto his cheeks. When Siwa had completed her shave, she bathed Will's face with a towel dipped in hot water. Will got up from the chair and as if completing an imagined conversation he added: 'My moustache is quite the thing, actually, in the civilized world. Swoons from the young ladies left and right.'

He grabbed a straw boater and slapped it on his head at a rakish thirty-degree angle. 'How do I look?' he asked. He knew in fact that he looked good. He had his mother's green eyes, cheek bones and soft oval face, and his father's dark red hair and whiskers.

'Will you be returning for dinner?' Siwa asked.

Will looked at Kessler. 'I expect not,' Kessler said apologetically.

Siwa's brow furrowed again. She took Will's sleeve. 'You will be cross with yourself if they find it necessary to bring you home in a wheelbarrow,' she whispered.

'Christ! Have *some* faith in me, eh lass?' he said, and with a sad little shake of her head she retired indoors.

Kessler retrieved Brunhilde from under the overhang and all three walked down the hill towards Herbertshöhe. The sleepy little settlement of perhaps three dozen houses was quiet. The warehouses of the Forsayth Company were inactive, the telegraph shack closed and the German New Guinea Company office empty. There were no Europeans on the muddy street and save for a few miserable natives chewing and spitting betel juice, not another living soul. The natives were naked, emaciated, their mouths stained purple. Most of them were infected with ringworm and they scratched incessantly when they were not spitting or coughing. The constant writhing and betel-chewing of the New Guineans was what had finally put an end to Kessler's church-going at the French Mission. 'You should do something for those poor devils,' Will said, giving them a wide berth.

'What can we do?' Kessler asked. There was no cure for ringworm and the only palliative was opium.

They walked a little further along Hanover Strasse. 'Quiet today,' Will remarked. It was always quiet, except for when a Forsayth boat was at the jetty or the monthly steamer entered the bay. For European companionship only the hotel or the yacht club could be relied upon, but Will increasingly avoided both those places – too many of the people propping up the bar reminded him of himself, or, how he would be a year or two down the line. Kessler tapped his watch. 'Do you have the hour, Will?' he asked without much hope.

'Not I,' Will said, with a guilty recollection that his grandfather's Great Western repeater had bought a case of brandy.

Since Will had been in town last, several people had boarded up their homes for the rainy season or gone bust or taken ship to Samoa or Australia. The Chinese general store he didn't patronize had closed and if a Chinaman couldn't make it here, nobody could. Even Governor Hahl usually avoided Herbertshöhe, out surveying his islands, or off on some jaunt up-country, where, if there was any justice, he'd be killed and eaten like several prominent Europeans before him.

Brunhilde's cheerless clip-clop became a doleful commentary on the white man's need to venture to Earth's more forlorn places. Herbertshöhe was undoubtedly a dreary place and it would have been duller still but for the local grandee 'Queen' Emma Forsayth who still managed to dragoon interesting people from anywhere within a hundred leagues. It was a sign of the esteem with which Emma held Will that he had only been invited to her house once in his entire time here.

Kessler stepped over a woolly haired Melanesian who was lying dead drunk at the side of the road while Will pickcd a purple berry off a tree.

'The undertaker's business is brisk enough without such insanity,' Kessler said, shaking the berry out of Will's hand.

'Wild grape,' Will protested.

A line of fruit bats half a mile long flew along the waterfront and banked left for the jungle. The sky was full of trailing figbirds and imperial pigeons and above them goshawks and grey teal.

Both men felt their hearts sinking. The sun was four fingers above nearby New Ireland now and night would be here in an hour or less. It had clouded over but the dwindling day had lost none of its fug: it was breezeless and heavy, a day for steamers and canoes, but not praus. Everything was caught in that oh-so-familiar torpor of coastal New Guinea, a torpor that sucked European men into early graves and that seemed even to affect the lizards, rodents and the flocks of cheerless parrots and lorikeets sitting patiently on the telegraph wires, waiting for some inebriated soldier to shoot them.

Will felt oppressed, but this was always his emotion at sundown when he was without the benefit of *arak* or Siwa. He swatted a blood-bloated horsefly from Brunhilde's neck while Kessler considered how much to tell Will before they encountered Doctor Bremmer and Governor Hahl.

'Will . . . '

'Yes?'

'The first thing I must emphasize is discretion. Scandal is a poison that could spread from Herbertshöhe to the whole colony.'

'And of course back to Berlin,' Will said.

Kessler nodded. 'I will tell you the brute facts. No doubt Doctor Bremmer will explain everything in more biological detail.'

'Go on then.'

'Two days ago an Australian man called Clark brought his skiff in from Kabakon with the body of a German national and instructions to give him a Christian burial. He had died of malaria.'

'Clark?'

'An Australian pilot, he carries messages and small cargoes between here and Ulu and throughout the islands. He is dependable and more reliable than the canoes.'

'Never met an Australian yet who was on the level. Who was the dead man?'

'His name was Lutzow, Max Lutzow, a music critic and journalist, well known in some circles.'

'Never heard of him.'

'Neither had I before he came here, but apparently he wrote for the *Süddeutsche Zeitung*. He was also a concert pianist at one time.'

'I take it Doctor Bremmer was not convinced by the malaria explanation?'

'Lutzow did not die of malaria.'

'So who killed him? Clark?'

'Not Clark. Nearly three months ago Lutzow joined a community which has been established on Frau Forsayth's island of Kabakon.'

Will was intrigued. 'What do you mean by *community*?'

'Their leader is a man called August Engelhardt. A 'charismatic'. He also is a journalist and pamphleteer. They call themselves the *Sonnenorden*. Sun worshippers. They believe that nudity and the eating of coconuts will give them immortality.'

'Coconuts?'

'The fruit that grows closest to the sun. Engelhardt believes that worshipping the sun and eating only coconuts purifies the body of "the foul pollutants and excesses of modern twentieth-century life". Free from these toxins apparently humans can live an unlimited lifespan in Paradise.'

'I assume Kabakon has a healthy supply of coconuts?'

'I would imagine so, for they are forbidden to consume anything else! They call themselves Cocovores, as the coconut is considered to be the only pure food.'

They had reached the low fence around the Governor's mansion. They tied Brunhilde to a rail, smartened themselves up and walked to the swing gate. A native sentry was standing to attention under a small bamboo awning. He was a New Guinean wearing a police uniform of thick khaki with a gleaming white pith helmet low over his face. He had on a bandolier, but carried no firearm.

Kessler saluted him and marched onto the gleaming sandalwood veranda.

'How many of these Cocovores are there?' Will asked.

'We do not know exactly, twelve or thirteen perhaps. Originally twenty or so.'

'Are there women there as well as men?'

'Lately they have been trying to recruit women but I do not think they have met with much success.'

'The idea is that they go around naked all of the time?'

'Yes, at least that is what they say on their advertisements.'

'Naked women on a tropical island. Where do I sign the pledge?'

Kessler approached the door of the Governor's mansion, which was made of heavy pine and had been shipped in from some old pile in Saxony. It wasn't particularly ornate or beautiful, just heavy. The rest of the house was bamboo.

The window shutters were open and the servants had seen their approach, but Kessler rapped the large gleaming brass wolf's head knocker anyway.

Will picked up on something Kessler had said. 'What do you mean 'originally twenty'?' he asked.

'I'm sorry?'

'You said "originally" there were twenty.'

'Several left almost immediately, a few more arrived, several more left. Kabakon was not the Paradise which many had been led to believe it would be, but perhaps more significantly Lutzow was not the first of the Cocovores to die,' Kessler whispered, while the servants bustled around inside.

'No?'

'Two died in the hospital here. Another on the island. All, apparently, of malaria. The man who died on Kabakon was, presumably, buried on the island itself. No one thought anything about it; there was nothing strange about these deaths and Governor Hahl signed the death certificates as a matter of course.'

The Governor's door opened and a nervous little chap informed them that the Governor was not at home. Kessler didn't believe it. 'Don't be an idiot, Bohm. He will be "at home" to me. He has asked to see me.'

Little Bohm looked genuinely put out. He was a secretary and wasn't used to dealing with guests at the door, but the steward was dead, the footman was in an isolation room of the hospital with an unknown fever and the deputy footman had run off into the jungle to find the 'Silver River' – as likely a place as the 'City of Gold'.

'Hauptman Kessler, sir, he is not at home. He is not physically in the house. He is at Queen Emma's with Doctor Parkinson and an English lady. He has asked me to tell you to join him there,' Bohm said in a stage whisper.

'I see,' Kessler said, taken aback. 'Well, we shall go over there. Thank you, Bohm, carry on.'

On the way back down the steps Kessler shook his head in annoyance.

'What's the matter?' Will asked.

'I wished to keep Frau Forsayth out of this. I hope Governor Hahl has not told her of our suspicions.'

They unhitched Brunhilde and headed back towards the centre of the settlement. They walked back through the dusty, empty town, filled only with mosquitoes and dragonflies.

'I will leave off Brunhilde if you do not mind,' Kessler said.

'With the sun going down it's the only sensible course of action,' Will agreed with a slight shudder. On other parts of the globe the twilight hour was a delight, but in New Guinea the feeling was markedly different. The day belonged to man, but the night belonged to the things that crept and crawled and flew from tree to tree in the dense, ancient, primordial jungle.

They walked along the little coast road for fifty metres until they came to Kessler's house: a large, ugly bungalow on stilts overlooking the bay.

'Gerhard!' Kessler called out.

A native boy – clearly not Gerhard – ran from the darkness, took Brunhilde by the reins and led her to a stable block with Ross mosquito screens over the shutters: perhaps the real reason for Brunhilde's longevity.

'If you will just excuse me for one moment, Will,' Kessler said, going inside.

Will nodded. The sun had set over Cape Stevens and the sky had rapidly turned the curious purple-black colour that it assumed in the rainy season. Herbertshöhe had almost no street lighting and since the local ants would devour any candles they came across, the few internal house lights were kerosene or whale-blubber lanterns. With this light and the rich star-field it was just bright enough to read on most nights, if one was so inclined. But why read when you could watch Siwa dance the Ramayana or go with her, watching for snakes, into the jungle behind the house until you came to the waterfall that brought river-water clear and cold from some unknown place in the highlands.

Kessler had been inside for five minutes.

'What's going on in there?' Will asked.

'Oh, I am sorry, Will,' Kessler said from somewhere. 'This is taking . . . I should have asked you . . . Braun, can you escort Herr Prior inside and get him a glass of schnapps?'

The door opened and a blond youth in a shining uniform ushered Will inside the bungalow. The youths were always blond, winsome, pale. This one so pale he was probably already on the coffin-maker's list.

'What the hell are you doing, Kessler?' Will shouted, declining the schnapps with a shake of the head.

'I will not be a moment, Will. Make yourself at home.'

It was a dreary house: a few old-fashioned pieces of furniture, some dull native drawings and several genuinely disturbing local Duk Duk masks. Kessler did, however, possess an extensive library and a rather impressive gramophone machine. Will took a volume off one of the shelves and found that it was in Greek. He put it back again.

'Do you like those things?' Will asked, pointing at the masks.

The blond youth shrugged.

Duk Duk was one of the better-organized local religions, their witchdoctors forcing the natives who worked in the plantations to pay them a regular spiritual tax out of their meagre wages. And if they didn't: hexes, curses, spells, the whole shooting match.

'May I have a go on this gramophone machine?' Will asked.

'Do not let him touch it, Braun!' Kessler shrieked, and a moment later appeared in full evening dress of black dinner jacket, white shirt, butterfly collar, gold cufflinks and black bow tie.

'Oh really, Klaus, is this necessary?' Will asked.

'Have you dined at Frau Forsayth's before?'

'I had luncheon,' Will sniffed.

'She is quite strict with her gentlemen callers, we Germans certainly, although she may pardon you; she has a soft spot for Englishmen.'

'I hadn't noticed.'

They walked outside just in time to see Doctor Bremmer hurrying along the track to Gunantambu.

'Herr Doctor Bremmer!' Kessler yelled.

Bremmer jumped. '*Gott in Himmel* you frightened me,' he said.

Much to Will's chagrin he saw that Doctor Bremmer was also in full evening dress. The men greeted one another and Kessler asked Bremmer if he too had been summoned to Frau Forsayth's.

'I received a note from the Governor, not one hour ago. I assume this is not about the unfortunate business of . . . ' Bremmer's voice trailed off. He was a tall, slim, restrained man who had come here from German Kamerun and before that Hamburg. Bremmer was clearly a Jew but his religion was only likely to become a problem when the time came to bury the poor sod, after he had succumbed to the new diseases he was exposed to daily in the fever wards.

'I fear *it is* about the unfortunate Herr Lutzow,' Kessler said.

'Indeed?' Doctor Bremmer asked, raising an eyebrow.

'I have asked Herr Prior to help us investigate these, uh, peculiar circumstances and he has agreed to offer his services.'

Bremmer turned to Will and bowed.

'Come, let us go, gentlemen,' Kessler said.

The way to Gunantambu, Queen Emma's palatial residence, led past the telegraph office and along the coast. It was too dark for Will to see the conspiratorial gleam in Doctor Bremmer's eyes but he realized that it had to be there, for as they walked by the new hospital the young man stopped to light a cigarette and then wondered casually: 'If you are with us Herr Prior, would you perhaps care to see the victim?'

'Surely you've buried the bugger by now?' Will said, astounded.

'On the contrary.'

'What did you do? Put him in a brandy cask like Nelson?'

'Something like that,' Kessler said.

They entered the hospital through the back door to avoid poor Beyer in the mad room and the fever patients in the main wing. The hospital had no nurses at this time but there were several New Guinean attendants sleeping on the floor of the dispensary.

Bremmer took them through the fever ward and a supply room.

'This way,' he said, and led them down an unlit stairwell to a basement Will had never noticed before.

'Where are we going?' Will asked.

But the Germans were determined to preserve the mystery and did not answer. At the bottom of the stairs they reached a door and here Bremmer lit a match to see where the lock was. He inserted an iron key and turned it.

When the door opened Will felt a strange blast of chilly air. He followed both men inside and when Bremmer lit an oil lamp it became clear how for two days they'd kept the body from becoming a rotten piece of meat.

In the centre of the small concrete room, Max Lutzow was lying on a massive slab of ice, partially covered by a thin grey blanket. The room itself was at or around thirty degrees Fahrenheit – a temperature Will had not experienced for years.

He examined the clear white ice and touched it. 'You have installed an ice manufacturing machine at the hospital?' Will asked incredulously.

Kessler laughed. 'We could not afford such a machine.'

'Then how?' Will wondered.

'Queen Emma gave the ice to us,' Doctor Bremmer said.

'Oh, I see,' Will said. And now of course it made sense, for Queen Emma was famous for her champagne parties. He looked at Kessler and shook his head. 'A man dies on one of Queen Emma's islands and instead of burying him like a Christian you ask her for blocks of ice from her machine, and you have the temerity to think that you can keep her out of it? You're losing your touch, Klaus, even my curiosity would be piqued and I don't give a whistle for much.'

'Do you wish to take a look at him?' Kessler asked.

Will nodded. Lutzow was a large, rotund man, balding with melancholy black whiskers. His skin was yellow and shrivelled, his delicate thin fingers blue-ish green. He had lost weight in the last few months for the skin was loose about his abdomen and neck. His feet were curiously rough and scarred, probably from spending a considerable amount of time shoeless.

'So you were going to live forever, were you?' Will asked Lutzow. He turned to the doctor. 'What makes you think he was murdered?'

'You do not?' Doctor Bremmer asked.

'At first glance it looks like a classic case of the yellow jack to me.'

'I took the liberty of performing an autopsy,' Doctor Bremmer said and bowed again to Hauptman Kessler. It did not take a genius to deduce that Bremmer had done the autopsy at Kessler's express order.

'Oh?' Will said, looking suspiciously at Kessler, whose face had become a mask.

'Yes.' Doctor Bremmer lifted the blanket to reveal a long autopsy scar running from Lutzow's neck to his abdomen. He had been sewn up with neat and careful cross-stitching which impressed Will no end. Bremmer was no hack.

'What did you find after this autopsy of yours?'

Bremmer shook his head. 'We need to examine the damaged tissue and without a microscope nothing can be said definitively.'

'Nevertheless. Tell him what you have found,' Kessler insisted.

'His lungs contained seawater,' Bremmer said.

'Well, he was brought here by boat, wasn't he?' Will said.

'In a boat, not towed by a boat,' Bremmer said.

'He was drowned?'

'I believe that he was.'

Kessler looked at Will expectantly.

'So they lied about the malaria. Did Clark notice anything untoward when he picked up the body?'

'Nothing that he communicated to the navy personnel.'

'Funny that *he* wasn't afraid to touch a fever-ridden corpse?'

'Clark has had malaria, yellow jack, dengue fever, black fly fever and the sleeping sickness – it did not trouble him to touch the body,' Kessler said.

Will lifted one of the dead man's eyelids and stared into the lifeless jelly of his iris. 'He's a big fellow isn't he? You would have thought he would have put up a bit of a fight if someone was trying to drown him.'

'Perhaps he was outnumbered?'

'No sign of a struggle at all, though. No bruises on his arms, no rope burn around the neck or wrists,' Will said, and let the eyelid fall. 'What was Clark doing on Kabakon?'

'He was bringing the post,' Kessler said. 'He found the settlement in the midst of a commotion. Apparently, Lutzow's body had recently been discovered and it was suggested to Clark that he convey it to Herbertshöhe for a Christian burial.'

'Who suggested it?'

'I do not know.'

'Hmmm, chances are that if Clark hadn't been there on Kabakon that particular day, they would have just buried him with the others,' Will said.

'We certainly would not have been able to examine the body then,' Doctor Bremmer said.

'No,' Will agreed. He picked up Lutzow's hand and examined under the fingernails. 'Have you washed the corpse?' he asked Bremmer.

'I have not.'

'And you found no signs of a struggle?' Will asked.

'Nothing,' Bremmer said and coughed. 'Of course I am not an expert in this kind of doctoring,' he added, looking at the slowly melting ice draining into a cut in the floor.

'Can you help me to turn him over?' Will said to the others. Neither man moved. 'Come on lads, he's not going to bite us.'

'We are dressed for dinner,' Kessler protested.

Will raised his eyebrows and Kessler and Bremmer reluctantly helped Will turn Lutzow, who was, naturally, completely rigid.

Will examined Lutzow's back and shoulders and sighed.

'Yes?' Kessler asked.

'Are you sure you haven't let the undertaker see him at all?' Will asked Bremmer.

The young doctor shook his head. 'No. No one has been in this room except for His Excellency Governor Hahl, Hauptman Kessler and myself.'

Will nodded and stroked his moustache.

'What do you make of that?' Will asked, pointing at a pair of semicircular bruises on Lutzow's shoulders.

'Mosquito bites?'

'Could be,' Will said, shaking his head.

'Or?' Kessler demanded.

'Let's get out of here, I'm going to catch my death,' Will said.

They put the blanket back on the body and left the room. Bremmer locked the cellar door and they climbed the stairs to the main floor of the hospital. It took all three of them a few seconds to cope with the transition from thirty degrees Fahrenheit to around eighty. Once they'd recovered, they resumed their walk to Queen Emma's along the coastal track.

Doctor Bremmer offered Will a cigarette and he accepted. A skinny, naked Kanak boy asked them in pidgin for tobacco and Will passed the cigarette on. They continued past the large buildings of the Forsayth Company where Doctor Parkinson (Frau Forsayth's chargé d'affaires) stored coffee, cotton and rubber from Queen Emma's extensive plantations – so extensive, in fact, that they nearly doubled the amount of land owned and cultivated by the German New Guinea Company.

The trail now took a sharp right turn and became a narrow palm-tree-lined boulevard that had recently been lit by small electric lamps on stubby iron poles – the only such piece of street lighting in all of New Guinea and possibly in this part of the hemisphere. This path up to Gunantambu was swept and drained too, which was just as well because by now Will's 'waterproof' Liverpool Rubber Company plimsolls were completely soaked.

'Shall I tell you what I think?' Will asked.

'Please do,' Kessler said.

'It could well be murder. They may have drowned him but they didn't need to force the poor fella that hard. They'd given him enough opium to knock out the Derby winner. This explains the yellowing in the eyes and face, the swelling in the tongue . . . '

'Go on,' Kessler said.

'So it could be that they rendered him pliable with the opium, took him to the nearest rock pool and drowned him. Those bruises on his shoulders might be where they held him down.'

'More than one of them?' Kessler asked.

'I believe so. There is still the chance that it was an accident or a possible suicide. He ingests the opium and wanders to the sea for a little night swimming or self-murder, but I think not.'

'Because of this bruising?' Doctor Bremmer asked.

'That for one, but also the fact that he wasn't in the water for any length of time. Gradually the skin on the palms and soles of a body becomes white and wrinkled in water and after seven or eight hours can be peeled back. Saw an instance like that in Gibraltar once. Suicide. But it's not the case with Herr Lutzow is it?'

'No,' Bremmer said.

'And another thing,' Will continued. 'His body had no shark bites. Corpses that have spent any time in these waters tend to attract the attention of the tiger sharks do they not, Klaus?'

'Yes,' the German assented.

'But what motive could there be for murder?' Bremmer asked.

'We must endeavour to discover it,' Kessler said.

5

Queen Emma's Soirée

They were met at the ornate portico of Queen Emma's house, Gunantambu, by Evans, the saturnine, starchy, Australian maître d'hôtel. 'Come along gents, the lady of the house is hungry and wants her dinner. You are all very late!' he said in a counterfeit English butler's accent.

'I do not think we are late. As a matter of—' Kessler began, taking out his watch.

'Come on gents, no time for that, go right in,' Evans said.

Kessler and Doctor Bremmer walked into the dining room, but Will, who was in the rear, found his wrist grabbed and held firmly in Evans's surprisingly undainty paw.

'What do you think you're doing?' Will said.

'I know you,' Evans said in his native, rather intimidating, Sydney Cove diphthongs. 'I'll be keeping an eye on the silver, mate, so don't even think of trying anything.'

Will shook his wrist free and attempted to make his moustache bristle in the way the German military men did so well, 'My dear fellow, you must have mistaken me for someone else entirely.'

'I don't think so, Mr Will Prior, you just make sure the number of knives and forks at your place is the same as when you got here.'

'I've never suffered such impertinence in my life,' Will was going to say, but he was weary of the fight and instead nodded meekly and walked on, thankful that Evans hadn't commented on his plimsolls, which were squeaking now like poisoned rats in a granary.

'Finally!' Queen Emma said when he at last entered the dining room.

'I do beg your pardon,' Will said, his cheeks crimson.

'Sit, sit and we can begin,' Queen Emma ordered with a grin that was both indulgent and a little impatient.

The table was set for seven and the room was much as Will remembered it. Open on the north side to catch the sea breeze, with sliding American-style screen doors keeping out the insects. A lethal-looking chandelier hung from the high-beamed pine ceiling. European oil paintings from three different centuries hung on the walls. The floor was a scrubbed and polished teak, but Queen Emma was a flamboyant eater and the table and chair legs were covered with ant traps.

The only innovation since Will's luncheon – when there had been twenty people in here and a servant behind every chair – was the cooling device: a large mechanically operated fan blowing over a gigantic slab of ice from Emma's ice-making machine. With the breeze and the ice, the room was a pleasant seventy degrees Fahrenheit.

Emma herself was unchanged. Easily fifteen stone and tanned from her yacht, but still extraordinarily beautiful. She was dressed in a purple sarong with bare arms and shoulders and a décolletage that took a frightening plunge. Her eyes were dark and intelligent, her cheeks ruddy and her famous laugh – which Will could hear sometimes all the way from his house – was evidently intact. The daughter of a Samoan princess and an American trader, she had been schooled in Australia and taught business by both her father and her first husband, the Scottish entrepreneur James Forsayth. Emma was the richest woman in German New Guinea and one of the richest women in the South Pacific. She had built her empire on copra, rubber and a few coal seams, originally in Samoa and now mostly in New Britain and New Ireland. The Germans had let her be when they had annexed the place, which was wise because she was the only one who seemed able to turn a profit in these parts – no matter what was happening in the world economy.

Apart from the fidgety Doctor Bremmer and rather tense Captain Kessler, the other guests at the table were Doctor Parkinson, Governor Hahl and a mysterious lady whom Will had never seen before. She was obviously European and a bluestocking, not quite of Emma's size, but getting there. She was no beauty, although her cheeks were red and her eyes were clear, green and sharp. She had curly brown hair crammed under a rumpled pink hat that might have been in fashion twenty years ago. *A half a crown, she's the sausage-eating sister of Governor Hahl,* Will said to himself.

Hahl himself was a languid little man, with a waxed face, waxed moustache and a tight coiffure resembling that of the tin soldiers Will had played with as a boy.

The famous Doctor Parkinson, Queen Emma's plantation manager and aide-de-camp was tall, clean-shaven, blue of eye and Danish. He had to be pushing fifty-five, which was positively ancient in the fever latitudes. He, more than anyone else, was responsible for Queen Emma's wealth. He had a knack for wise investments, buying failing plantations and turning them into profitable endeavours. He was an eccentric who liked to watch birds, botanize and paint still lives, but he was probably the most intelligent personage in the colony – whatever that honour was worth.

Will sat in the only remaining chair as chilled French champagne was served to the party. All the men but he were in full evening dress.

As was the custom at Gunantambu, Kaiser Wilhelm's health

was drunk, followed by the health of King Edward and then a final toast to the memory of the monarch who connected them both – King Edward's mother, Kaiser Wilhelm's grandmother, Queen Victoria.

Everyone stood, toasted, drank and found their seats again.

'Lovely stuff!' Queen Emma said in her own peculiar accent: not quite Polynesian, American or Australian.

'Indeed,' Governor Hahl agreed.

'Evans!' Emma yelled and the butler came scurrying into the room.

'Yes madam?' he enquired, his eyebrows arching upwards in a way that skirted the boundary of outright mutiny.

'You forgot to announce the three gentlemen.'

'I did what?'

'You didn't announce the gentlemen. Now nobody knows anybody, do they? Miss Pullen-Burry can't be expected to talk to strangers, can she?' Queen Emma said and poured herself another full glass of the deliciously cool champagne.

Evans bowed. 'Of course, madam. Doctor Bremmer, Hauptman Kessler and Mr William Prior, allow me to intro- duce our esteemed hostess, Mrs Forsayth, Miss Pullen-Burry, His Excellency Governor Hahl, and Doctor Parkinson,' Evans said quickly, and then strode out of the room looking miffed.

'Thank you, Evans,' Queen Emma said. 'Tana, make sure everyone's glasses are filled.'

A young native man entered, bowed, barked a few orders in pidgin and for the rest of the dinner Will's crystal glass was kept brimming with chilled champagne by silent Kanak servants. The members of the string quartet on the dais were also Kanaks and it had to be admitted that they played well, although without much enthusiasm. Will knocked back his first glass of champagne and started on the second.

Will had been seated at the end of the table next to the mysterious Miss Pullen-Burry (*Miss*, not Fräulein, he noted). He was opposite Doctor Bremmer and at a diagonal to Klaus. Queen Emma sat at the head of the table with Doctor Parkinson to her left and Governor Hahl on her right. Whether this seating arrangement was intentional or not, Will couldn't help but feel that he was in the seat of least honour. How he had annoyed Evans, he had no clue; he certainly had not stolen silverware the last time he had been here – at least he didn't think he had.

The dishes came thick and fast and if you hadn't finished by the time Queen Emma was done that was just your tough cheese as your plate got whisked away quicker than a bang in a Cheapside brothel.

There were times too when Will wasn't exactly sure what he *was* eating. Stuffed quail he recognized, as he did the yellowbelly gudgeon, wild pig, New Zealand lamb, sweet potatoes, bull shark, stuffed parrot, durian, Polynesian long-finned eel and corned beef, but there were dishes – lizards perhaps and sea snails – that left him clueless.

He'd always had a good appetite, though, and he consumed everything with gusto. Miss Pullen-Burry had attempted to keep her end up too, but she had twice dry-retched during the durian course, heroically managing not to throw up into her handkerchief.

Will had little option but to eat and especially drink as he found himself the odd one out in the various English and German conversations taking place at table. Miss Pullen-Burry and Governor Hahl conversed with Queen Emma, which disconnected both of them from any discourse with him, and Doctor Bremmer and Klaus appeared to be captivated by Doctor Parkinson's tales of butterfly-collecting in obscure habitats in the highlands.

On the one occasion Doctor Bremmer managed to catch Will's eye, the conversation turned to matters medical.

'You have not had the malaria, Herr Prior?'

'No.'

'You use the bark?'

'I usually sleep under a Ross net.'

Queen Emma seized upon this. 'I myself need no net! I have never had a moment's illness in my entire life!'

'We are not all blessed, alas, with the sturdiness of your constitution, Frau Forsayth,' Doctor Parkinson said. 'However, I think it is prudent for all white men and white ladies in particular to sleep under these nets.'

Queen Emma was sceptical. 'What is your opinion, Doctor Bremmer?'

'I insist that the patients in the hospital do so. I myself got the malaria in Africa, but I am quite recovered. My worry here has been . . . ' he began and chose not to elaborate – evidently something to do with his bowels.

'If you can get through your first year here you will live to be a hundred!' Emma declared.

Doctor Bremmer nodded sadly and Will noticed that he had only been picking at his dinner. Poor chap probably wouldn't see Christmas.

There was a fizzing noise and the mechanical fan blowing upon the block of ice suddenly stopped.

'Evans!' Queen Emma screamed.

'What is it now?' an acerbic voice demanded from an unseen room.

'The fan is broken again!' Queen Emma yelled.

'Hold on to your bloomers, I'll be there in a jiffy!' Evans yelled back.

'Emma, we are quite cool,' Doctor Parkinson said, but Emma patted him on the hand affectionately.

'This will only take a few seconds,' she insisted.

Evans appeared with two Kanak boys and a thin piece of rope. They speedily disassembled the mechanical fan, attached the piece of rope to one of the bits of machinery and began tugging it back and forth. The blades of the fan began to turn again, although not as quickly as before.

'Happy?' Evans said to Queen Emma and left the room without waiting for a response.

'He really is quite disgraceful,' Queen Emma said, with a grin to Governor Hahl, who didn't appear to get the joke.

The talk resumed until a course of black sea urchins appeared and Queen Emma silenced everyone with a hand slap on the table. 'This is our penultimate dish, one of my favourites; please do enjoy. I must make use of the powder room.' As she got up from the table the men rose and she waved them down again. 'Eat, eat,' she commanded.

With Queen Emma temporarily *hors de combat* and the men speaking of the game-bird shooting possibilities in the hills, Miss Pullen-Burry finally turned to Will.

'She is a remarkable woman, is she not?' Miss Pullen-Burry asked.

'Quite.'

'The esteemed Doctor Parkinson tells me that she is the oldest European woman in the archipelago.'

'I don't see where European comes into it. She's from the American Samoa and she grew up in Australia.'

Miss Pullen-Burry ignored this. 'Doctor Parkinson estimates that her estates are worth 250, 000 pounds.'

'Is that so?' Will said a little icily. In Leeds one did not discuss money matters at table.

Miss Pullen-Burry looked at her plate and Will examined her. Unlike Queen Emma, she wore no rings. Her gaze was steady and her conversation in both English and German lacked the web of metaphors which was the depressing signature of the bluestocking. Either she had not been out from Dover long enough to cultivate that poisonous mix of fatalism and melancholia which characterized the English abroad or she had been absent from Britain so long that she had come out the other end as something entirely new. She certainly sensed that she had made a faux pas, for immediately she smiled and changed the subject. 'I see from his uniform that your friend Hauptman Kessler is a Bavarian.'

It was clever of her, Will thought, to see that Klaus, of all the people here, was his particular friend. Kessler perked up on the other side of the table. 'This is quite correct Miss Pullen-Burry. I am proud to serve in the army of His Majesty the King of Bavaria.'

'I am unable to tell the difference between a Bavarian, a Prussian or an Alsatian,' Will muttered.

'For a man in your profession you have remarkably poor powers of observation, Herr Prior,' Klaus said jovially.

'Certainly I am no match for that denizen of Baker Street whose adventures are to be found in the *Strand* magazine,' Will replied.

Doctor Bremmer asked Klaus a question and the conversation on the far side of the table resumed.

Will and Miss Pullen-Burry sat in stony silence for several moments.

'If I may be so bold, which profession is that, sir?' Miss Pullen-Burry finally asked Will.

'Hauptman Kessler refers to the fact that I was a military police officer.'

'Indeed? That must have been most interesting.'

'You would be surprised at how thoroughly dull it was, ma'am.'

'Oh dear. However, I did notice that you used the past tense to describe your vocation.'

'I left the service shortly after the South African war. I am a simple farmer now.'

Again the conversation died. And after a minute's silence, again it was Miss Pullen-Burry who revived it. 'Governor Hahl tells me that there are a dozen languages on New Ireland. A hundred here in New Britain.'

'I know little of languages, ma'am. I learned German with difficulty and I have forgotten my French,' Will said.

Will finished yet another glass of champagne and wondered how many that was. Almost certainly too many.

'It is no doubt in God's plan that these local tongues will die and German will become the lingua franca of this portion of the Pacific,' Miss Pullen-Burry was saying.

'If I may be so bold, madam, why have you come to this portion of the world?' Will asked.

'I seek new experiences. I am a writer, Mr Prior.'

'A lady novelist?' Will said, appalled.

'I am a writer of impressions and places.'

Oh Christ, Will thought and drank more of the chilled champagne.

'I have been meaning to ask you about that. Have you published any of these impressions, Miss Pullen-Burry?' Governor Hahl asked from the end of the table.

Will wondered how old Miss Pullen-Burry was. Thirty? Fifty? It was impossible to tell with that type. She was probably a virgin. That kept a certain youthful aspect to one's appearance.

'I have published two books and I am working on a third. Hence my visit to Queen Emma's residence and my sojourn in German New Guinea.'

Will nodded and Klaus, who had begun to pay closer attention, asked: 'And what have you learned about our colony so far? Enough to make a book?'

'I have learned much from Herr Doctor Parkinson. I have learned that December is the rainy month when the north-west monsoon begins. I have learned that the price of copra is twenty-three pounds a ton, but it can go as low as thirteen pounds a ton. I have learned that six thousand nuts make one ton of copra and that each tree produces sixty nuts a year and that once they mature all one must do is keep the roots clean. I have learned that the Kanak boys who scale the trees and collect the nuts earn six shillings a week. I have also learned that many Kanaks are kidnapped to sugar estates in Queensland while the Royal Navy turns a blind eye. A disgraceful practice known as blackbirding!'

It was one of those curious moments when the other conversations at the table had ceased and in a far wing of the house they could hear Queen Emma singing to herself and grunting from what was obviously the seat of ease. Emma's song was surprisingly mournful and beautiful, perhaps a lament for her lost girlhood when she too had been sent to Australia.

'Your information is incorrect, madam. Blackbirding no longer flourishes in New Guinea. The Kaiserliche Marine has seen to that,' Kessler said with a nervous glance at Governor Hahl.

'I'm afraid I must correct you Hauptman Kessler, blackbirding is still a menace. Even along this coast. Some of my best workers have been taken west of Simpsonhafen. The Australian pirates run to the protection of the Royal Navy and the Kaiserliche Marine does little to stop them,' Doctor Parkinson said dispassionately.

'Doctor Parkinson is unaware of the new squadron on its way from Samoa under Admiral Graf von Spee. I can assure Miss Pullen-Burry that the Kaiserliche Marine and His Imperial Majesty's government are doing everything in our power to stop this most disgraceful enterprise,' Governor Hahl said reassuringly.

'I am glad to hear it,' Miss Pullen-Burry said. 'If the civilized races do not act in concert then our poor example will be copied by the less fortunate denizens of this world.'

'How long have you been in Herbertshöhe, Miss Pullen-Burry?' Doctor Bremmer asked.

'I have been here a week and I shall stay until the end of the month. I plan also to venture to New Ireland and perhaps into the interior of New Britain,' Miss Pullen-Burry replied with a smile.

Will was not so disguised in drink that he failed to notice Kessler give Governor Hahl a look of concern.

'You plan to venture into the interior?' Doctor Bremmer asked, surprised.

'You do not approve, sir?' Miss Pullen-Burry asked.

'We have few German females in our colonies, but the high-lands are no place for a gentlewoman. I mean no offence, madam, but even if the natives can be restrained from their bellicosity, they are . . . one hardly knows how to say it . . . '

'Yes?' Miss Pullen-Burry asked.

'They wear no clothes and they copulate without shame. You would be exposed to affront,' Kessler said.

'Hauptman Kessler, in these days of militant feminism one most not be overly gallant. The striving for women's votes con-tinues, not just in England but across the civilized world! In New Zealand women have been enfranchised and the heavens have not poured out their wrath. Indeed I often think how the angels must weep to see how things are managed nowadays in happy Christian Europe,' Miss Pullen-Burry said.

'Would you have had women serve in the late war, Miss Pullen-Burry?' Will asked.

The dessert course was being brought in now. It was ice-cream – a treat Will hadn't tasted since London.

'Perhaps the late war would have not have taken place had

women been allowed to give their views on the relations between the Boer farmer and the English one.'

'Surely you are not of Mrs Pankhurst and her ilk?' Governor Hahl asked, taken aback.

'You are amazed that women revolt at the idea of being chattels, sir? Mr Campbell-Bannerman would do well to recruit sound women to his cause. But I expect nothing from a government that winks at the seditious gospel of Kier Hardyism and is careless of how it imperils the lives of our fellow subjects and threatens our supremacy in India.'

Will shook his head. She was an odd mix of high-Tory spinster and bluestocking suffragette. No, perhaps not so odd. Her face was pink with annoyance and Will was wondering if he could somehow set her off in an apoplectic fit when Queen Emma came back into the dining room. The gentlemen rose.

Queen Emma sat and with a wave dismissed the remaining servants save for the men operating the fan. She let the cool air from the melting ice waft over her for a moment. 'Of course you know that Kabakon and the other islands in the Duke of York group are famous as haunts of the Night Witches,' she said to Miss Pullen-Burry, presumably continuing a conversation from earlier in the day.

'I did not know that,' Miss Pullen-Burry replied.

'Oh yes, sometimes from the veranda one can see them flying all the way from New Ireland to here. They are in search of weak souls that they may influence to do ill. They do not come near Gunantambu. They know that my soul is not weak. I do not listen to their entreaties or their promises. In any case I keep a Langan, a high priest of the Duk Duk, in my house at all times; his spells frighten the Night Witches and vex them most cruelly.'

'Very wise, I'm sure,' Miss Pullen-Burry said.

'I am telling you this so that you will have all the information before you make a decision whether to go or not, my dear friend Bessie,' Queen Emma said.

Miss Pullen-Burry nodded. 'I am resolved, Mrs Forsayth, I still wish to go.'

Queen Emma laughed. 'Then go you shall! Such spirit is only to be found in an English lady. Even Governor Hahl's formidable wife would dare not truck with the Night Witches.'

Governor Hahl smiled but did not nod. He would like to see the entity who could make his Brigida afraid. An entire regiment of Night Witches would be sorely tested by her frosty expression.

'Shall we get down to business?' Queen Emma asked and looked at Doctor Parkinson.

'Business, yes,' Parkinson said with pursed lips.

Governor Hahl looked at Kessler, who coughed and muttered. 'I think we should adjourn to another room, Frau Forsayth, not all of us have been—'

'Miss Pullen-Burry is my guest,' Queen Emma exclaimed regally. 'And she has become my good friend in these last few days. She knows all the details of the case. Everything Governor Hahl has told me, I have told her. I have informed her of Doctor Bremmer's opinion concerning the late Herr Lutzow and I have told her what Doctor Parkinson knows about the *Sonnenorden*. It has excited her interest and she has agreed, on my behalf, to accompany the expedition to Kabakon.'

Kessler was on his feet. 'Frau Forsayth I really must object! This is a matter of extreme delicacy. What Governor Hahl evidently has told you was said in the strictest confidence!'

'You forget yourself, sir,' Queen Emma said in a voice of chilly authority.

'Sit down, Kessler,' Governor Hahl muttered.

Kessler looked at Hahl and then at Will. He seemed surprised to find himself standing there with everyone staring at him. Will waved him down with a discreet hand gesture and he slumped back into his chair.

'My apologies, madam,' Kessler said.

'I think what my colleague was trying to say, Frau Forsayth, is that the situation on Kabakon is uncertain. We have it in mind to send only Herr Prior, who was a distinguished officer in the British Army's military police; he will be accompanied by my representative Hauptman Kessler,' Governor Hahl said.

Queen Emma gave Doctor Parkinson a sideways glance. The phlegmatic Dane coughed, turned to Governor Hahl and smiled a little assassin's smile. 'Your Excellency, I do not wish to bore you with legal niceties; however, Kabakon is Frau Forsayth's island and if she wishes to have a representative there for the course of these investigations, then with all due respect, we really must insist upon it.'

'I am afraid that is quite impossible,' Kessler said, already seeing events spiral away from him before they had even left Herbertshöhe.

The port arrived and with it cigars. Much to Will's amazement, both Queen Emma and Miss Pullen-Burry cut and lit two cigars and began smoking them. When the servants had gone, Kessler continued where he had left off.

'Under no circumstances can the, uh, charming Miss Pullen-Burry accompany myself and Herr Prior to Kabakon. It is no place for a lady and this investigation is not the work of a lady, even one as spirited as Miss Pullen-Burry,' he said.

Will gave him a nod of encouragement.

'Miss Pullen-Burry will go and that is an end to it,' Queen Emma said. 'She goes in lieu of Doctor Parkinson who is otherwise engaged in a long-planned expedition to photograph birds for his book. Ha! Is there anyone at this table not writing a book?'

Will would like to have said that he wasn't writing a book about his tedious existence anytime soon, but Kessler was busy objecting again.

'We must nip this foolishness in the bud, Frau Forsayth. Only Herr Prior and myself will be travelling to Kabakon.'

Miss Pullen-Burry and Queen Emma said nothing.

Doctor Parkinson shook his head and, looking directly at Governor Hahl, he said softly: 'I'm afraid we must insist.'

The port arrived next to Will and he poured himself a generous measure. He passed the bottle to Doctor Bremmer and gave him a fatalistic look. In Queen Emma's house there always seemed to be some kind of ferment going on. One did not go to the South Seas to seek ferment. One came here to slip slowly into oblivion. Even poor old Jim of the *Patna* had had ferment thrust upon him.

Governor Hahl ignored Doctor Parkinson and turned directly to Queen Emma and Miss Pullen-Burry. He took Emma's hand in his. 'Ladies, these matters cannot become known outside of these islands. You must see that it would be entirely inappropriate for a female writer to visit the *Sonnenorden*, even if there has been no wrongdoing. My duty is first and foremost to protect the good name and reputation of the Reich and our Imperial Majesty from whom all honour flows in the Empire.'

Queen Emma smiled like a lioness in Regents Park. 'I had hoped that we would not find it necessary to raise the legal niceties,' she said.

'The legal niceties? There are no legal niceties,' Hauptman Kessler muttered.

'Kabakon and the other islands in the Duke of York group were bought by the late Mr Forsayth under treaty from the temporary German administration in Samoa. Under the terms of this treaty no German colonial officer can enter Mrs Forsayth's domains without her express permission, or unless acting under a direct decree by the Governor of Samoa,' Doctor Parkinson said.

Governor Hahl looked at Kessler who had no clue if this was true or not.

'I can show you the documents if you wish,' Queen Emma said.

'Do you deny us permission to go to Kabakon?' Governor Hahl asked.

Queen Emma laughed. 'Surely it will not come to that. I no more wish to deny you permission to go to Kabakon, than you would wish to overrule me, by telegraphing Governor Solf.'

Governor Hahl's smile evaporated. He certainly did not wish to involve Governor Solf of Samoa in these events. The one thing Governor Hahl feared more than Brigida's frosty expression was Solf's duplicitous wife Catherine and her boundless capacity for making mischief.

Governor Hahl stared for a moment into the purple blackness of the port. 'Emma, what is it that you want?' he asked at last.

She gave his hand a gentle squeeze.

'I wish to have a witness to what has happened on my island of Kabakon. Herr Doctor Parkinson who normally acts as my factotum has made himself unavailable,' she said.

'What about Evans?' Kessler asked.

'That dog! I would not trust him to bury me.'

Governor Hahl looked at Miss Pullen-Burry and slowly his face creaked into a tiny grimace, like the dry smile of a tortoise. 'This must not become the subject of a book, Miss Pullen-Burry. You must give me your word that nothing that happens on Kabakon will ever appear in print anywhere.'

'Oh, my word of honour,' Miss Pullen-Burry said.

'You must go at your own risk, we cannot accept responsibility for any injury which may befall you on this trip,' Governor Hahl insisted.

'I am quite capable, Governor Hahl. However if an accident does befall me, I assure you that it is my responsibility alone.'

'We may want something in writing,' Kessler said sourly.

'I would not object to that,' Miss Pullen-Burry said.

'It is settled then. Captain Kessler and Bessie shall go to Kabakon together,' Queen Emma said.

They had forgotten him, but Will said nothing. Policemen, even military policemen, even ex-military policemen, were doomed to be outsiders.

'Good! Let us celebrate. We can do better than champagne,' Queen Emma replied, and out came a bottle of cognac laid down in the previous century. Will drank two glasses of the heady stuff.

The normal discourse resumed, but Will took no part in it. He began to nod in his chair.

'We will commence at dawn!' someone said at last, startling him from a doze.

'My bungalow is not far,' Will attempted but the words did not come out quite right.

He had eaten and drunk far too much and in the end two Kanaks had to push him home in a wheelbarrow just as Siwa had predicted.

Will tried to kiss her, but she brushed him off. It was obvious that she was extremely angry with him. She had the Kanaks lay him on his bed and dismissed them with half a pfennig each.

Will groaned and tried to sit up.

'Be still,' Siwa said and stripped him of his clothes.

'I'm going to be sick,' he said.

She brought a chamber pot.

'I have told you before: you cannot drink so much!' she said. She knelt beside him and stroked his back. 'You are not used to such rich food and wine,' she said more gently.

'Perhaps I have made a fool of myself.'

She cleaned him and took him to the bed, but although the pillow was soft underneath him the room was turning like a carousel. The insects, tree kangaroos and other marsupials had commenced their night calls. Vesper bats flitted across the moon.

'Kabakon is a dangerous place,' Siwa whispered, apparently already aware of the 'secret' plan to go to the island.

'Don't tell me *you're* frightened of the Night Witches too?'

'I will ask Kot to protect you,' she said after a long pause.

'Do that. Yes. That'll help,' he said and thus comforted, the room eventually stopped spinning and with Siwa's cool hand on his forehead he finally fell asleep.

6

Doctor Parkinson's Request

A wafer of light drifted through the shutters and a hand on his shoulder shook him.

'Siwa,' he groaned, but it wasn't her. It was a man.

Will sat up and stared at Doctor Parkinson, dressed to the nines in a white suit, bright green tie and a pith helmet.

'Mr Prior, are you awake?' Doctor Parkinson asked in a low whisper.

'I am now,' Will said.

'Do not stir, sir, Hauptman Kessler will not be coming for you for another hour or so.'

'Well then why in the name of—' Will began, but as Doctor Parkinson's lips formed their customary purse the thought that Will was going to articulate died in his thorax. He sat on the edge of the bed and threw the sheet over Siwa's naked back. 'I'm listening.'

'Mr Prior, I believe there is something you can help me with.'

'Yes?'

'When you return from Kabakon, Mrs Forsayth and I would appreciate it very much if you would find yourself able to share your impressions with us,' Doctor Parkinson said amicably.

Will looked into the Dane's languid, grey face. 'You want me to report to you, not Governor Hahl?'

'Of course you will report to Governor Hahl, but we would be delighted if you were able to share your candid observations with us *ab ovo usque ad mala,* so to speak.'

Will rubbed his chin. 'Don't you trust Hauptman Kessler to give you the full story?'

'Of course,' Doctor Parkinson said. 'However, aside from the investigation into these macabre events there is a . . . there is a fiscal angle that interests Frau Forsayth.'

'What fiscal angle?'

'The Cocovores have taken a ninety-nine year lease on Kabakon Island. Under certain circumstances this lease may be legally terminated.'

Will nodded. 'And you want me to find out if the Cocovores have violated their terms of residency?'

Doctor Parkinson nodded.

'Does murder violate the terms of the lease?'

'I'm afraid not. I examined the document last night. There are only three clauses that interest us: piracy, the violation of a foreign power's sovereignty, and permanent damage to the island's material resources. Do you understand the nature of those exigencies?'

'And do you think they've been destroying the place, or indulging in piracy, or preparing for an invasion of Australia?'

Doctor Parkinson smiled. 'Our information about Kabakon has been contradictory and incomplete. That is why we would appreciate your assistance in this matter. Emma did not wish to trouble Miss Pullen-Burry with our concerns and enquiries, but I saw that an alert man of discretion such as yourself would be able to help us.'

'Anything for Queen Emma.'

'We shall, of course, compensate you for your trouble.'

'I will be happy to assist you.'

'Excellent, I see that we understand each other.'

'We do.'

Doctor Parkinson bowed. 'I must depart.'

'Yes. The trip to the highlands to photograph birds Emma spoke of. I hope you have a pleasant journey,' Will said.

Doctor Parkinson gave a bitter laugh. 'I am not going anywhere near the highlands or anywhere else for that matter. Life is precarious enough in Neu Pommern without additional adventures.'

'Indeed,' Will agreed.

'Goodbye Mr Prior.'

'Goodbye Doctor Parkinson.'

Parkinson exited through the kitchen door.

Will's face found the down pillow and Siwa's soft neck and the next time he was shaken awake it was by a bevy of excitable Kanak boys chewing betel.

'You go, now!' one boy said.

'You very late!' another one claimed.

Before he could respond Siwa had jumped out of the bed, found a machete and chased them from the hut.

'It's all right my dear,' Will replied and wearily slid his legs out of the impossibly comfortable bed.

'Come on, Will!' Kessler shouted from somewhere outside.

'Hold your horses, chum. I am just going to brush me teeth,' Will muttered.

Siwa came back in with the machete while Will mixed the tooth powder.

'Forget such foolishness!' Kessler yelled impatiently. He had never 'brushed his teeth' in his life and at nearly thirty he wasn't going to start now.

Will brushed his teeth, had a quick nip from his hip flask, dressed and ordered the Kanak boys to bring his seabag.

Tears were running down Siwa's cheeks. She was holding a wooden idol in her hands, no doubt entreating Lord Kot to protect Will on his sea voyage and to save him from the clutches of the demons on the Island of the Night Witches.

Will smiled at her. 'Remember that I'm a soldier, my dear. I can look after myself,' he insisted.

She did not reply but kissed him sternly on the cheek.

Will marched outside and shook Kessler warmly by the hand. The German was dressed in a loose shirt, bright blue jacket and canvas trousers. Will had never seen Klaus so informally clothed before. He seemed relaxed, excited.

'I see that the prospect of travel agrees with you, Klaus.'

'Getting away from here would make any man agreeable,' Kessler agreed happily.

7
Kabakon

They left in a rabble of green butterflies, the water beryl, the sky a golden hair on a fuchsia cloth. The skiff *Delfin* caught the wind and the pilot, a German naval rating Will hadn't seen before, asked them to move themselves to the lee side of the craft.

They complied without complaint even as the spray frothed over the gunwales onto the little vessel's deck.

'Isn't this delightful?' Miss Pullen-Burry said.

Will was in no mood for conversation and it was up to Kessler to give her a civil response. Will's mind was elsewhere. It was the first time he had seen Herbertshöhe from the water and the harbour and wharves made it look an ugly sort of place. Squalid. Untidy. Un-German. He had arrived at night and hadn't noticed this. He shuddered at the recollection of that ghastly first week in the hotel when his letters of introduction had gotten him nowhere. If he hadn't charmed Parkinson into believing that he came from the agriculturally savvy Yorkshire gentry, things could have become unpleasant.

The *Delfin* moved quickly and within a few minutes all that could be seen of the town were the Forsayth warehouses on the shore. After another quarter of an hour the entire settlement was indistinguishable from jungle. No road, no telegraph office, no plantations, nothing: just the brown, primeval forest.

Will found this comforting. Undoubtedly, after the Germans and the other Europeans had left this stretch of coast, New Britain or Neu Pommern or whatever you wanted to call it would return to its natural condition: a state of war with all the works of civilized man. And perhaps the menacing volcanoes behind Simpsonhafen would put an end to the European folly sooner than everyone was expecting.

The air trembled as the sun began its merciless ascent in the eastern sky. The pilot passed Will a mug of something under a lid and Will initially refused it, assuming it to be the hair of the dog. But then he caught a whiff of coffee and drank.

The butterflies must have been at the end of some difficult migration for they were dropping by the thousand, exhausted, into the Bismarck Sea; only a lucky few landed on the teak deck of the *Delfin*, rested, and moved on.

Will let his half boots dangle into the tips of the waves. The breeze was freshening from New Ireland and the Kriegsmarine pilot nudged the tiller a point closer to the wind. White braids of foam fell away from the stern.

It was a beautiful morning yet Will was feeling hipped and he didn't really understand why this was so. He was getting paid in English guineas and if he could successfully solve the case his social standing in Herbertshöhe would rise. Perhaps if Polizeimeister Beyer were to take a turn for the worse . . .

His mood, however, was one of pervasive despondency.

It was probably the residue of a dream about South Africa. His nightmares were always about Africa and presumably the bad dreams he couldn't remember were about Africa too. And maybe too he was anxious about being without Siwa for the next few days. He would miss her touch, her voice and that way she could bend her wrist backwards almost onto her forearm. Her cooking, her laugh, her *body*. If only she were here: her little half frown would be so reassuring, but then again, perhaps it was just as well – he *had* grown awfully dependent on her . . .

They had cleared the bay now and Will looked south into the Solomon Sea. Old Freddie Clinker, two plantations over, and a keen fisherman, claimed that you could see nine-thousand-foot-high Mount Balbi in Bougainville from around about here, but even squinting and holding his hand above his eyes, all Will could see was the southern part of New Ireland and beyond that only the vast blue emptiness. The day was as fair a day for viewing as there could be, but there was not even a trace of a mountain.

Will should have known it was a likely story.

Miss Pullen-Burry prodded Will on the arm. 'Are you distressed, Mr Prior? Cold? I have a blanket in my valise.'

'No, thank you. Quite the reverse, ma'am.'

Indeed, the temperature was probably up into the seventies on Fahrenheit's scale. Warmer than he had been expecting on the open sea. To prove the point he took off his waistcoat and set it behind him. Now he was clad only in shirt, canvas trousers and riding boots.

Miss Pullen-Burry was dressed for a wake in some sort of black crinoline number, reminiscent of the late Queen. A worried-looking Kessler was wearing a long sou'wester and the pilot, as befitted a navy man, was shoeless and shirtless.

Will's stomach grumbled. Somehow, in all the preparations, breakfast had been forgotten about.

'Don't you find the sea air bracing, Mr Prior?' Miss Pullen-Burry asked him.

Not especially, no, he wanted to reply, but even ten thousand miles from Greenwich, the social niceties prevented this reply.

'Charming, I'm sure,' he said.

'You grew up by the sea, I believe,' Miss Pullen-Burry persisted.

Who had told her that? And what else had people been saying about him?

'No ma'am. Leeds. In Yorkshire.'

'Oh, indeed? My cousins, the Leigh-Browns, have a little place near Ripon. Do you know the Leigh-Browns?'

'No, ma'am,' he said after a significant pause which he hoped would communicate his desire to terminate this conversation.

'Oh, you would adore the Leigh-Browns. Not at all what you would think from the size of their estate. Don't give themselves airs. My cousin Emily rides with the Badsworth Hunt. Always the head of the chase. They say that she could have been a jockey. Thin as a willow and twice as strong. Worth three thousand a year and risks her neck with the best of them. Beautiful too, a regular Venus, don't ya know? You would adore Emily, all men do, such a joy,' Miss Pullen-Burry said.

'Indeed.'

'Oh yes. I shall mention your name in one of my letters. Do you get back to Yorkshire often, Mr Prior?'

'Never.'

'Such a shame, one must always keep in touch with one's homeland. I was in Jamaica several years ago and I met a few families who had never been home at all! I put them in my book. Received the most obliging letters. Can you imagine never getting home at all?'

'Perhaps they were home.'

Miss Pullen-Burry looked baffled. 'I do not follow you, sir.'

'Perhaps they considered Jamaica to be their home.'

Miss Pullen-Burry laughed. 'Jamaica? No, no. It is not like Australia or America, Mr Prior. A mere veneer of civilization. It is much more like the situation here in New Guinea. I shall explain it all in my book.'

Kessler coughed significantly. 'No books about this, Miss Pullen-Burry, with all due respect, last night we made it clear that—' Kessler began but she interrupted him with a slap of her hand on the deck.

'Oh don't fret, Hauptman Kessler. I shan't mention anything about this little . . . whatever this is. If you are worried, I shall send the entire manuscript to Governor Hahl for his approval. No, no, my book will be about the German colonies in the Pacific in general: Samoa, New Guinea, New Britain. I shall endeavour to enlighten my English readership, such as it is, about the feats of our cousins in these foreign climes.'

Will nodded at Kessler and gave him an *I told you so* look, which the German ignored.

'For we *are* cousins are we not?' Miss Pullen-Burry went on. 'We have so much in common. Germany and England are natural allies. Not England and France. My book will attempt to sow the seeds of amity between the two nations.'

'Ah, I would very much like to read *that* book,' Kessler said.

'Whale!' the pilot said suddenly, pointing to starboard.

All heads turned and after a moment they saw a spout of white water and a dark head fifty or sixty yards from the boat. 'How wonderful!' Miss Pullen-Burry exclaimed, reaching into a hidden pocket in her dress, producing a notebook and pencil, and sketching the brute with surprising dexterity. Her draughtsmanship was the first thing Will had admired about Miss Pullen-Burry since he had met her.

'It may not be so wonderful if the creature sinks us!' Kessler said nervously and turning to the pilot added, 'Can you keep the monster away from us?'

The pilot ignored him and kept on precisely the same course for Kabakon Island. No Bavarian *army* officer was going to tell him how to run his ship. The whale kept in a parallel course and then disappeared from view, possibly because of the large number of small grey sharks that were now following the *Delfin*.

'Oh, shall thou draweth Leviathan with a hook!' Miss Pullen-Burry, exclaimed in raptures.

'Or in your case with a pencil,' Will added.

Miss Pullen-Burry smiled at him and wrote down the remark.

Well that's my place in history assured, Will thought. He reached into the scuppers, pulled out one of the dead butterflies, shook off the excess seawater, and placed it on her notebook. 'Butterflies and whales. You could be a regular Mr Wallace, Miss Pullen-Burry.'

'Lovely!' she said, delighted and began drawing the butterfly too until Klaus showed her how to press and preserve it intact between her notebook's pages.

Kabakon now occupied more than half of the horizon. It looked flat, dull, small and brown. It certainly wasn't Will's idea of Paradise. Why the *Sonnenorden* couldn't have bought the much larger landmass of New Ireland itself was beyond him. You could get thousands of people on New Ireland. You could make it into a little nation if you wanted.

They were steering for a bay on the south shore whose crescent shape became more pronounced with every passing minute. Everyone was nervous now.

When he was about a kilometre out, the pilot tapped Will on the shoulder and pointed at the tiller. Will nodded and took the polished wooden steering rod, while the pilot examined a chart, presumably checking for reefs. There were none, but seeing that Will was enjoying himself, the pilot got up and took in the main and let Will steer the *Delfin* into the half-moon-shaped cove.

'Keep going?' Will asked.

'*Ja, ja,*' the pilot said and Will took them all the way through the surf, the pilot only grabbing the tiller again as the *Delfin*'s keel shuddered up onto the beach.

'Careful, Miss Pullen-Burry!' Kessler shouted as the *Delfin* skidded up the volcanic black sand and began to lean over alarmingly. Kessler seized Miss Pullen-Burry's arm and held her steadfastly.

'I am perfectly all right, Hauptman Kessler,' Miss Pullen-Burry replied, somewhat put out by this overt gallantry.

Will hadn't had such a thrilling experience in a long time and he grinned broadly as the young pilot dropped the mainsail and its boom onto the deck and nodded at Will as if to say 'well done'.

The pilot then took a rather feeble-looking anchor and threw it up the beach. 'Ladies and gentlemen, would you kindly disembark?' he said.

Will grabbed his seabag and stepped off onto the sand.

Kabakon looked even worse close up than it had from the water. Mosquitoes in swarm, huge red assassin crabs, a few scraggly looking coconut and banana trees. No one was on the beach. There were no footprints, no sign of civilization or smoke from fires deeper among the palms. Perhaps a more impressive settlement lay beyond the shoreline with Polynesian girls, rum, cornucopias, but it seemed most unlikely.

Behind him Miss Pullen-Burry refused Kessler's hand and climbed off the boat by herself. The pilot unceremoniously dumped her trunk and Gladstone bag next to her. Kessler was last off the *Delfin*, carrying a little leather valise and his own enormous steamer trunk.

'Well, we made it across,' Will said to Kessler.

'You were sceptical?' Kessler asked.

'The Kaiserliche Marine isn't the Royal Navy, is it?' Will said, but Kessler knew this was a rather feeble attempt to get a rise out of him.

'I must put off immediately if I am going to make this tide,' the pilot said to Kessler, giving him a curious sort of half-salute, perhaps in acknowledgment that terra firma was the dominion of the German Army.

'The tide? Oh, yes, by all means,' Kessler said. 'But make sure you are back tomorrow.'

The pilot nodded, gathered his anchor, placed it on the deck and began pushing the boat back into the surf.

'Ah, a real desert island at last! "Now would I give a thousand furlongs of sea for an acre of barren ground,"' Miss Pullen-Burry said, waxing poetic.

Will ignored her and took Kessler by the arm. 'Hold on a minute, chum. Don't let Captain Slocum over there leave us. Make him wait here.'

'He must catch his tide.'

'Have you ever been around sailors? They're always talking about tides and currents. It's a load of rubbish. Make him wait for us. You're in charge, aren't you?'

'What is the matter, Will?' Kessler asked kindly.

'We don't know what we're dealing with here on Kabakon. We might need to beat a hasty retreat.'

Kessler stroked his moustache and waved to the young pilot who was back on board the *Delfin* now. 'This time tomorrow, my good fellow!' Kessler shouted.

The pilot nodded, hoisted the mainsail and began tacking the *Delfin* away from the shore.

'Well now you've done it. We're stuck here for at least a day,' Will said.

Kessler ignored him and went to help Miss Pullen-Burry with her trunk.

'Thank you, Hauptman Kessler,' Miss Pullen-Burry said, taking one handle, while he took the other. They began carrying it across the black sand towards the coconut palms.

Will caught them up and took Miss Pullen-Burry's side of the trunk. She thanked him with a whispered 'bless you' and took a moment to catch her breath.

'Look around you, Klaus, where is everyone?' Will said. 'How do we know they're not all dead of some terrible plague?'

'A plague? Nonsense! We would have heard,' Kessler said.

Will looked out to sea. The *Delfin* was three hundred yards from the beach now and there was no hope of calling it back.

They carried Miss Pullen-Burry's trunk to the shade of the palm trees and then went back for Kessler's and Will's gear. Will slung his bag over his shoulder and took one of the handles of Kessler's trunk.

'Christ! What have you got in here? One of Mr Wells's cylinders?' Will asked.

'A few changes of clothing, a small supply of food.'

'Clothing? I don't think you fully appreciate the Cocovore charter.'

'A German officer does not remove his clothing in front of civilians. And there is Miss Pullen-Burry to be considered.'

When they returned from this second luggage foray, Miss Pullen-Burry was rather surprisingly talking in German to a very thin, tanned, blond young man who in fact was completely naked.

'Good morning!' he said, smiling happily at them.

'Good morning,' Kessler said and introduced himself and Will.

'Heinrich von Cadolzburg at your service,' the young man replied with a little bow.

'Nice to meet you, Heinrich,' Will said.

'Everyone calls me Harry.'

'Harry then.'

Although the young man was handsome, his distinguishing feature was not his bright blue eyes, nor his unkempt beard, nor his skeletal ribcage. In fact all three of the newcomers found that they were staring at Harry's penis, which dangled down to an inch above his left kneecap. It looked a little like the albino stoat Sergeant Mulvenny had kept as a rat-catcher in South Africa, except that it seemed to have a bit more life than Mulvenny's stoat, which had disdained rats and lived exclusively on porter from the sergeants' mess.

A macaw screeched in the trees above them and, startled, Miss Pullen-Burry said: 'Herr von Cadolzburg, may we see, your, your, uh, settlement, your . . . camp?'

'Harry, please,' the young man insisted and then added, 'I suppose you've come to join us then, have you?'

Miss Pullen-Burry gave a non-committal shrug and before Will could say anything Kessler blundered in: 'On the instructions of Governor Hahl, we have come to investigate the death of the late Maximilian Lutzow.'

'Lutzow? Oh, yes, Lutzow,' Harry said sadly. 'Poor fellow, it is a shame. He could have become one of the pillars of our community.'

'Shall we go over to the *community*, I'm finding it rather close under the trees here and would enjoy sitting,' Miss Pullen-Burry said, and then, somewhat unsure of herself, added: 'If you have seats?'

'We have the finest furniture from Germany. Our houses too are German. They were prefabricated and shipped to us from Bremen. I think you will be amazed!' Harry said.

'I am sure we will be,' Miss Pullen-Burry replied.

'Is it far?' Kessler asked.

'No, not far, it is just through the trees, but leave your luggage, we shall have one of the Kanaks bring it,' Harry said.

'Ah, so you are not exclusively German, then?' Miss Pullen-Burry enquired.

'Nearly, there are only two of the little devils left, the rest have been sent back to New Ireland. They will keep eating fish, which August has strictly forbidden.'

'The famous Herr Engelhardt! We will get to meet him?' Miss Pullen-Burry asked.

'Of course!' Harry said cheerfully.

They walked along the track, with Will lagging a little further behind. He tugged Kessler's arm, so that he could admonish him. 'Why did you have to tell him that we'd come here to look into Lutzow's death?' Will whispered. 'We could have drawn him out a little first.'

Kessler resented the tug at his shirt and gave Will a black look. 'This is not some English colony where the population has been browbeaten into silence by generations of oppression by the Red Coats – these are free Germans; they will tell us everything we need to know with open hearts.'

Will nodded. 'Open hearts, eh? We'll see about that.'

Kessler increased his pace to catch up with Miss Pullen-Burry and Harry, and after a minute's persecution by fat black flies Will reluctantly increased his pace too. When he got back to the triad they were quoting poetry at one another, something the Germans down the club did too, insufferable bastards.

'*Die Luft ist kühl und es dunkelt. Und ruhig fließt der Rhein. Der Gipfel des Berges funkelt, Im Abendsonnenschein*,' Harry said, which got a little round of applause from Miss Pullen-Burry.

'Sorry to interrupt, er, Harry. Can I ask, how many Cocovores – I believe that is the correct word – of you are there?' Will asked.

Harry shook his head sadly. 'I am ashamed to say that there are less than a dozen of us left. Poor Max. August thinks as many as a hundred could live on this island.'

'A hundred here?' Will said sceptically.

'Oh yes, it is quite possible, Herr Prior, and it will happen sooner or later. Our pamphlets have been taken up all over Germany. Perhaps next year August will return for a series of lectures. And when we grow in numbers we will populate Kabakon and the other nearby islands.'

'Maybe the whole of German New Guinea,' Will said sardonically.

'Yes!' the handsome young man replied enthusiastically.

They had gone about three hundred metres from the beach now and were at the end of the little track through the coconut plantations.

'Welcome to the Augustburg!' Harry announced.

'Delightful,' Miss Pullen-Burry exclaimed.

Will looked at Klaus with mild astonishment. The settlement was a good bit more elaborate than he had been expecting. Not exactly a Polynesian fantasy, but this was no Crusoe shack with a couple of goats tied up nearby in a pen. There were a dozen large dwellings in a near circle around a central piazza. The buildings were nothing like those of the Kanak, or even the crudely built plantation houses over in Herbertshöhe. Some of them bore a peculiar similarity to Swiss chalets and all were thick-timbered with sturdy roofs made from corrugated iron which had been painted a brilliant red. A well had been dug on the far side of the central plaza and a banqueting table, obviously of German manufacture, had been placed under the shade of a coconut palm for communal meals. There was a round gazebo with comfortable-looking armchairs in it and a privy house on the edge of the trees. The oddest thing, however, was definitely the twenty-foot-tall totem poll fashioned from a single trunk and depicting a dozen fantastically carved heads in various states of agony.

'A veritable other Eden,' Miss Pullen-Burry exclaimed.

'Charming,' Kessler murmured.

'How do you like it, Mr Prior?' Harry asked in English.

'It's impressive, but what in the name of Christ is that thing in the middle there?'

'I suspect that our Lord Jesus Christ is not what the *Sonnenorden* had in mind, Mr Prior,' Miss Pullen-Burry said.

'That is a Malagan. You have heard of these things?' Harry asked.

Will nudged Kessler as Miss Pullen-Burry began sketching it in her book.

'Purely for my own memories,' she assured Klaus in a whisper.

'The Malagan is a conduit between this world and the world of the spirit.'

'Is it like the Duk Duk religion I encountered in Herbertshöhe?' Miss Pullen-Burry asked.

'A little but there are no fraudulent priests or so-called witch doctors,' Harry explained.

'Where did you get it?' Miss Pullen-Burry asked.

'August got it from a chieftain on New Ireland whom he helped in a small matter of a rebellion.'

They helped a chieftain on New Ireland deal with a rebellion? Will thought and wondered if this could be considered an act of piracy. He would certainly mention it to Doctor Parkinson when they returned to Herbertshöhe.

'Each Malagan is different,' Harry was saying. 'This one represents the gods of the sun and moon and the southern stars.'

'Where the spirits of the ancestors are said to reside?' Miss Pullen-Burry asked.

'Very good!' Harry replied, impressed. 'In many ways the cosmology of the locals here is similar to that of our pagan ancestors in Germany. August believes that a common religion once covered the globe from the Americas to the Australias, a polytheistic religion of many gods that was superior to the Abrahamic faith foisted upon us by the Christians, the Jews and the so-called Prophet Mohammed.'

Harry folded his arms to allow this profound insight to sink in. 'Come, I will show you everything,' he said, leading them into the central plaza.

Miss Pullen-Burry followed, but Will seized Kessler's arm. 'Could be a trap, Klaus. Get us in the middle, run out of the huts and chop us to bits with machetes and axes. Sacrifices for their gods, just like poor Lutzow,' Will hissed theatrically.

'Please stop grabbing my arm,' Kessler said, unable to tell if the Englishman was joking or not. He marched ahead and Will followed the others to the piazza area, which had been covered by pounded gravel and smooth river stones.

'Where is everyone else, Harry?' Miss Pullen-Burry asked.

'Oh they are all off bathing and sunning at Sol Island on the north shore,' Harry said.

'Why didn't you go with them?' Harry wondered.

'Someone had to stay and keep an eye on the Kanaks. Who knows what mischief they might get up to?'

'Ah, yes, about our luggage . . . ' Miss Pullen-Burry began.

'Thank you for reminding me,' Harry said.

Harry went to a nearby hut and two natives went scurrying out the back of it in the direction of the beach.

'Your things will be here shortly,' Harry said.

'When are Herr Engelhardt and the others expected to return?' Kessler asked.

'Probably this evening. When the sun has gone down. We often sunbathe from morning until night.'

'This evening?' Kessler asked, put out. That would be an entire day lost.

'Perhaps we should go over there?' Will suggested.

'Yes,' Kessler agreed.

'You will have to swim it,' Harry said.

'Swim?'

'They've taken our only vessel: a rather splendid outrigger canoe.'

'I cannot swim,' Kessler said.

'You can't swim?' Will asked, surprised.

'No.'

Will looked at the German officer with affection. 'Do you not find, Klaus, that that makes your journeys in small boats rather more exciting than is absolutely necessary? I understand the attraction of adding a certain frisson to our life in these islands, but surely swimming is a prerequisite.'

'I would say not,' Kessler replied stiffly.

Will rubbed his moustache. 'Maybe you're right, better to drown than be eaten by the sharks, I suppose.'

It was almost eleven now and Miss Pullen-Burry was swaying a little in the heat.

'Come, sir, a glass of water for the lady and that seat that we were promised,' Kessler insisted.

Harry bowed and led them to his own dwelling, which was just off the trail near the outhouse. It was a square hut made of heavy wood, utterly unlike the circular huts of the locals or the rude plantation dwellings of Herbertshöhe. A hammock had been hung from the roof beams, although there was also a German, antiquated-looking, four-poster bed, a commodious, if somewhat strange thing to see in these climes. There was a dresser, a washbasin – with a drain leading outside – and an ornate writing table with chairs. Harry showed Miss Pullen-Burry to a leather padded sedan.

He took a crystal goblet from a cupboard, poured her a glass of water from a covered pitcher and climbed into the hammock.

Kessler sat on the other chair and Will made do with sitting on the bed.

'*We* are all swimmers here on Kabakon. We take as our model Goethe, who swam every day of his life,' Harry said.

'And yet Shelley did not swim,' Miss Pullen-Burry replied, after she had taken a sip of the water.

'Oh?' Harry said, running his hand through his blond, almost white hair.

'Lord Byron writes that when Shelley was cast into the sea on his final voyage, he resigned himself immediately to the watery element. He neither cried out nor showed alarm but sank with equanimity.'

Harry looked upset, as if it was the latest news, and bad news at that. 'Lord Byron, himself, however, was a famous swimmer, was he not, Miss Pullen-Burry?' Harry said, recovering a little.

'Indeed. He swam the Hellespont and the length of the Grand Canal in Venice. He thought his poems were nothing compared to his feats of swimming,' she replied. 'He had plans to swim the English Channel and may well have done it before Captain Webb,' Miss Pullen-Burry said.

She took another drink. 'This water is delicious.'

'We have our own spring. It is very deep. It is water from the very beginnings of the Earth, laid down before the corruption of our present times – its properties are quite incredible. You will see,' Harry said.

The ensuing conversation ranged over various health-giving waters, boats, Goethe, Shelley, Byron and swimming, before the two Kanaks appeared with the trunks.

Harry didn't seem to know what to do with them so Kessler suggested that Miss Pullen-Burry be given a hut temporarily to prepare her toilet.

'And we will need a place too if we're going to be staying here tonight,' Will suggested.

Harry sprang out of the hammock, oblivious to the fact that somehow his penis had become erect during this reverie about accommodation and the history of swimming. 'I do not know where you should go,' Harry said and stroked his beard.

'The lady must go somewhere,' Kessler insisted.

After some humming and ha-ing, during which Harry's erection subsided, he suggested that Miss Pullen-Burry might share Helena's hut, while Will and Kessler could take Lutzow's old place.

'Helena?' Miss Pullen-Burry wondered. 'You mean there are women here?'

'Oh yes.'

'How many?' Kessler enquired.

'Three. Helena: the Countess Höhenzollern, her companion Fraulein Herzen, and Fraulein Schwab,' Harry said to the astonished newcomers.

'Three women!' Kessler said, shocked.

'Anna has her own hut and Fraulein Herzen and Helena are together, but there is ample room in the dwelling of the Countess, so perhaps she would not be put out by the additional company. I will show you the way,' Harry said. He directed the two Kanak bearers first to the Countess's large hut, which it turned out had three chambers, two camp beds, a double bed and a private commode.

'Remarkable!' Miss Pullen-Burry said and she would have been even more amazed had she not spent the previous week at Emma Forsayth's palatial home.

Harry then led the men to Lutzow's former dwelling, which had no bed or furniture save a solitary and rather rickety-looking chair and table and a hammock hanging from the ceiling. 'We stripped the place after Max died but when August returns, he will get something for you, I imagine,' Harry said.

'This is perfectly adequate. I have brought my own bed; Will can take the hammock,' Kessler said.

'Oh? Then I will leave you to it, gentlemen. You know where the well is, but I shall have some utensils brought in. If you will pardon me, I have writing to catch up with,' Harry said.

'One moment. I would like to ask you some questions about the circumstances surrounding Lutzow's death,' Will said.

Harry shrugged. 'The person to talk to is Anna – Fraulein Schwab.'

'Why is that?'

'She was with him when he died. She comforted him as he breathed his last.'

'Miss Schwab was there when Lutzow died?'

'Oh yes. She held his hand. She was very upset, as you can imagine.'

'And Miss Schwab is where, now?'

'Sol Island with the others.'

'And how did she say that Lutzow died?' Will asked.

Harry seem puzzled. 'Malaria! He died of the malaria.'

'Malaria? Are you sure?'

'Yes! Doctor Bethman diagnosed it. He was quite positive and August has seen many cases, of course. We knew immediately.'

'So you're saying that Lutzow died of malarial fever and that he held this Miss Schwab's hand as he died?' Will checked.

'Yes. Anna was quite distraught. Will that be all? I have my correspondence . . . '

'That will be all . . . *for now*,' Will said.

Harry bowed and departed.

'An agreeable young man,' Kessler said.

'You think so? He seems a little unhinged to me. I wouldn't be surprised if he killed Lutzow and all the others or if he tried to cut our throats as soon as we fall asleep. It'll be up to you to save us, Klaus; that hammock has death trap written all over it.'

Kessler was in no mood for 'English humour'.

'He insists that malaria killed Lutzow.'

'He's lying.'

'I found him quite sincere.'

'How do you explain the water in Lutzow's lungs?'

'I do not know.'

Will stripped down to his trousers, sat on the chair, put his boots on Kessler's trunk and lit a cigar. Kessler sat on the top of his trunk and loosened the top button of his trousers.

'Well, I suppose we'll find out who's lying and who's not when the others get back,' Will said, blowing out a ring of cigar smoke just as the heavens opened and a hard, piercing tropical rain began to fall.

8

Fraulein Herzen

Kessler set up his camp bed, a clever Deutsches Heer wooden fold-out affair, with its feet embedded in paraffin wax laced with arsenic to keep out the ants and above it a mesh net on a wood frame for the mosquitoes.

'I like your cot,' Will said, with a trace of jealousy.

'I will take the hammock if you wish.'

'No, no. You keep it, Klaus.'

There were dinging sounds on the roof and when Will pushed open the shutter and looked through the window he saw hail all over the courtyard. He hadn't seen hail in the tropics before; he didn't know that such a phenomenon was even possible.

Kessler lay down on the bed and took a pinch of snuff. He was comfortable but far from happy. Reports on the Cocovores had been sketchy from the beginning and he had never seriously thought that a few eccentrics on an island would ever give him anything to worry about. He already had enough on his plate. As the senior military officer in Herbertshöhe, Kessler not only had to answer to Governor Hahl, but was also responsible for a monthly intelligence report to Abteilung IIIb of the Imperial Intelligence Service in Berlin.

Kessler had gotten the bulk of his information about August Engelhardt through the impressive cable which had been laid all the way to Deutsch Ostafrika and from there to Europe. Berlin felt that Engelhardt and his cohorts were harmless crackpots and this had been backed up by Kessler's only local source of intelligence – Frau Forsayth. But she had completely failed to mention that there were three women among the Cocovores and at least two members of the German aristocracy (one of whom, apparently, was a Höhenzollern!) Berlin would certainly not enjoy hearing that and Kessler shuddered at the prospect of having to fill them in.

Kessler undid the top two buttons of his shirt and sat on the edge of his bed. 'I want to ask you something, Will,' he said.

'Ask away,' Will said, eyes wide with expectation.

Kessler wondered for a moment if he could confide his concerns to the Englishman. He considered it and shook his head sadly. 'Do you play chess?' he asked.

'I don't play as such, but I know how to play if that's what you're asking,' Will replied suspiciously.

'Excellent. Then we shall eat and have a game until the others return.'

Kessler had brought schnapps, sausage and pickles and, forgetting about poor Miss Pullen-Burry, the men ate and drank and played chess until dusk.

Miss Pullen-Burry was quite happy to be forgotten about. Before even making herself at home in her new accommodation, she had busied herself with putting pen to paper in her journal. If she was not permitted to write about Kabakon she could at least polish the notes she had made on her experiences over the last few days.

Nothing is more dismal than Herbertshöhe in its present stage. There are malarial swamps in close proximity to the wharf and the place is fever-ridden. The Germans refresh themselves with lager beer, the refugium peccatorum *of these parts, for the tropical afternoons inflict one with indescribable thirst. Mrs Forsayth's hospitality and generosity of course are boundless but I am not prepossessed in favour of the miscellaneous, miserable specimens of humanity she brings to me for my instruction. This morning one shy youth was brought forward as the picture of a desirable bridegroom. His teeth, which were blackened, betokened that he was desirous of entering the married state. Another one of Queen Emma's 'pets' is a repulsive dwarf who entertains the good lady with stories he has picked up from the German sailors at the . . .*

Miss Pullen-Burry put down her pen and stared through the open door at a perfectly naked young woman who had appeared in the camp.

She was about twenty-two, or perhaps younger still, slender, with long black hair and very pale skin covered with mosquito bites. She was emaciated and before her sojourn here would have been considered pretty. She stood for a moment in the rain before calling out Harry's name.

Harry came from his hut, as did Will, Kessler and, porting an umbrella, Miss Pullen-Burry herself.

Introductions were made. This was Fraulein Ilse Herzen from Kiel, Helena's maid, Harry explained.

'Secretary and travelling companion to the Countess,' Fraulein Herzen corrected him in a strong Hamburg accent.

'I beg your pardon,' Harry muttered.

Both men and Miss Pullen-Burry said it was a pleasure to make her acquaintance and she replied that the pleasure was mutual.

'I have been to Hamburg, a most engaging city,' Kessler said.

'You may keep it. An ugly place full of sailors whose primary interest is rape, an act they are usually too intoxicated to perform.'

Will laughed at that.

'You, *Englishman*, have you come to join our community?' she asked him.

'No,' Kessler answered for them. 'We have come to investigate the death of Max Lutzow under orders from the Governor of New Guinea.'

'Poor Max. Dead from the malaria they said, although I think . . . ' she said and her voice trailed away as she looked at Harry.

'What do you think?' Kessler probed.

'Well, if you must know, I think, his death was unnatural,' she said.

'What do you mean?' Will asked, trying to avoid staring at her breasts. He hadn't seen a European pair of breasts since . . . well, since Cape Town. These were small, pert Plattdeutsch breasts, with brown nipples, but European nevertheless, and Will found himself intrigued. Intrigued by the whole package, in fact. Fraulein Herzen was thin and wan but, apart from the mosquito bites, really quite lovely.

'He did not believe in our project. Bethman says that he mocked the island gods and the Malagan. Bethman says that he could not do that and expect to live,' she said, her eyes widening.

'My dear what can you be implying? Do you believe that the gods killed him?' Miss Pullen-Burry asked.

Fraulein Herzen examined the English lady for a moment. 'Perhaps. Who can say?' she answered brusquely.

Harry seemed embarrassed by this. 'I think malaria is a more likely explanation, Ilse.'

'Where is everyone else?' Kessler asked.

'August sent me to tell you that he and the others are staying on Sol Island tonight so that they can greet the dawn tomorrow.' She gave a little laugh. 'I do not think they were expecting such a turn in the weather!'

'I suppose not,' Harry said.

'They will be soaked and cold,' Fraulein Herzen added gleefully.

'And the sun will rise if they ask it to or not!' Will said.

Everyone stood there in the rain for a moment, not saying anything, in that way that Englishmen and Germans did so well.

'It was a pleasure to meet you my dear, but perhaps I shall turn in,' Miss Pullen-Burry announced.

'I shall too,' Fraulein Herzen said.

'May I escort you to your hut?' Will asked, offering the young lady his arm. 'The ground is quite treacherous.'

'I am quite used to it, thank you sir.'

Will nodded. 'It was very nice to meet you Fraulein Herzen.' He walked back to Lutzow's hut and wondered if Siwa had packed the bottle of Johnnie Walker. He had just found it in his sea bag when Kessler appeared with bananas and coconuts.

'From Harry,' Kessler explained.

'They eat bananas too, then, do they?' Will asked.

'Apparently Engelhardt discovered that bananas also grow at the tops of trees.'

'You Germans, your brilliance knows no bounds.'

They made a small meal and shared the Johnnie Walker and schnapps. They played chess until Kessler's constant victories became tedious and the German began discreetly trying to show Will ways to win, ways that Will seldom understood. By eight o'clock both men were exhausted and the worse for drink. It was pitch black and still raining and the light from the spirit lamp was a depressing yellow.

'I think I'll turn in,' Will said.

He coated the hammock's ties with Kessler's paraffin arsenic and climbed into the awkward thing. He draped a mosquito net over himself as best as he could and was soon asleep. Kessler had planned to make notes in his journal but he was too tired and followed Will to bed.

Miss Pullen-Burry could not sleep despite being offered the Countess's modern spring-framed bed. The girl was sleeping in a similar bed in another part of the hut.

Miss Pullen-Burry clawed her way through the folds of mosquito netting.

'My goodness it is close,' she said to herself. She took a drink from the carafe of well water and carefully replaced the pewter lid.

She tiptoed to the hut entrance and peered outside. The rain had stopped, the moon was out and it was warm. Her body was drenched with perspiration. In this dell on Kabakon, she reflected, it was so much more humid than Queen Emma's well-ventilated and airy guest room in Herbertshöhe. The jungle beyond was full of the usual noise that she had grown used to in New Britain. The moon was shining on the Malagan totem and nothing seemed to stir in the compound.

She had, however, the curious sensation of being watched.

No doubt she *was* being watched. Tree kangaroos, birds . . .

She took off her long nightgown, went back to bed, and lay naked under a cotton sheet.

She thought back to nights like this on her travels in India and Java and Ceylon. She was far from the temperate climes of England and, despite the heat, this suited her very well. Sometimes three thousand leagues didn't seem far enough from her cold, disappointed mother and her cold, stupid father, and from the girls at school who condemned her for not being beautiful or funny or good at games. It was interesting that Will had picked up on the falsity of her remarks about the Jamaicans never going home to England at all; perhaps he was more perspicacious than it first appeared. Perhaps . . .

After a while sleep did come but it was an anxious, apprehensive, unrestful sleep. She woke just after five when the wind brought in the sound of distant singing in German. She got out of bed and went to the hut door to listen.

It could only be August Engelhardt and the other disciples of the *Sonnenorden* on nearby Sol Island, imploring the local star to rise in the eastern sky in the manner which it had been doing for the better part of the last several million years.

She caught a few snatches of song before the wind changed and the singing died away. 'I must write that down,' she said to herself.

She sat at the Countess's mahogany writing table, but instead of committing the Cocovores' song to the damp paper of her journal she found herself instead sketching the sleeping German girl whose soft eyebrows were knitted and whose thoughts and dreams seemed to be as bothered as her own.

9

Morning in the Augustburg

Will awoke to the smell of coffee.

He opened his eyes to see Kessler bent over the spirit stove cooking the beans Turkish fashion.

'Is there enough for two?' he asked.

'Of course!' Kessler said. 'How do you like it?'

'I like it with milk and sugar, but I suspect that that is going to be impossible.'

'What a fellow you are,' Kessler said and winked at him, his duelling scars squashing his face into a gnomish grin – not the most pleasant thing to see first thing in the morning.

Will threw the mosquito net off his face and linked his fingers behind his head.

'This thing's awful. How did *you* sleep?' Will asked.

'Badly.'

'Bad dreams?'

'Well . . . '

'Remember what Queen Emma said. That'll be those Night Witches. This is their way station from New Britain to New Ireland.'

Kessler looked at him severely. 'I wonder that you joke of such things.'

'Who says I'm joking?'

'What do you want to eat with your coffee?' Kessler asked.

'What have you got?'

'Sausage, tongue, salted ham and tinned kidneys.'

'Any toast?'

'You are lucky to get anything decent on this island.'

'I'll just have a bit of sausage then, and thanks, Klaus.'

'You are welcome.'

Will swung himself out of the hammock and scratched at his neck. Of course he *had* been bitten right through the net, either by ants or midges or mosquitoes who had found a way through the defences.

He borrowed Klaus's mirror and looked at the bites. 'Well, that's me dead more than likely,' he said with mock doom.

Kessler looked at him. 'Surely you got at least a touch of malaria in Africa?'

'No. I was . . . fortunate,' Will said, his face falling suddenly into such a look of black depression that it surprised the German. Kessler examined him out of the corner of his eye: this Englishman was even more mercurial than most of his kind.

'Come, have coffee,' Kessler said.

Will could see that Klaus was proud of the little breakfast he had prepared. 'It looks good,' he said.

Kessler grinned. He hadn't cooked for himself in years and for a brief moment it brought back memories of his bachelor years or that one glorious summer when he had gone mountaineering with his father and uncle in the Tyrol.

Will opened the window shutters to let in the sunlight and gazed into the piazza. A large brown possum looked up at him. He shooed it with a 'fuck off', a phrase that every man, marsupial or Johnnie Foreigner understood.

'Any sign of Engelhardt and the others?' Kessler asked. 'I think I heard them singing before the dawn.'

'Singing? No, the place is still deserted,' Will said, and returned to the table. He sipped at the cup of coffee that Kessler had put in front of him. Miraculously, it did have milk and sugar in it and it tasted good. Maybe not quite up there with the careful brew that Siwa prepared each morning, but not bad.

'How did you do that?' Will asked. 'The milk, I mean.'

Kessler smiled and said nothing.

'You didn't smuggle a goat in that trunk of yours, did you?'

'It is a secret of the *Reichs Heer*,' Kessler said.

'A secret, eh?' Will said distractedly. On the other side of the 'Augustburg' Fraulein Herzen had made an appearance in the doorway of her hut. She was carrying a chamber pot out into the jungle. In the fresh light of morning Will saw that his initial judgement had not been in error: she really was a beauty. Long-limbed, pale, bright of eye, everything the poets were always going on about.

'Pssst, Klaus, over there! By God, she's a Venus,' Will said, opening the hut door to get a better look.

Fraulein Herzen dumped her chamber pot in the jungle and walked back to her hut on tip toes.

'What legs, Klaus!'

Kessler shook his head, 'One does not take advantage of a lady's distress,' Kessler said with a sniff.

'Are you serious? There are three *Sonnenorden* lassies here and they're all going to be naked all the time. Where are you going to look, Klaus? At your boots? You might as well get used to it now.'

'I do not think it will be necessary to bring the ladies into this investigation.'

'You don't, do you? Dear oh dear. You are fortunate that you brought me into this. You really are lost on the moors, chum. Did you never read Dumas? *Il y a une femme dans toutes les affaires*, or words to that effect.'

Kessler did not reply, focused as he was on sawing Will a piece of sausage. He gave him a hearty chunk and tossed it onto Will's plate.

There was a knock at the door. 'May I come in, gentlemen?' It was Miss Pullen-Burry.

'We are not decent!' Kessler yelled, rapidly buttoning his trousers.

Miss Pullen-Burry waited until Klaus gave the all-clear before entering with a bundle of newspapers. She was wearing only a thin silk Japanese-style nightgown which did little to hide her modesty.

'What do you have there?' Will asked.

'I only wanted to give you some copies of *The Times*. Frau Forsayth kindly placed half a dozen numbers in my trunk. Fresh from England.'

'That's very good of you, Miss Pullen-Burry,' Will said.

'What is the news from England?' Kessler asked, picking up one of the neatly bundled papers.

'Mr Campbell-Bannerman promises France our aid in the next European war,' Miss Pullen-Burry said with disapproval.

'Henry Campbell-Bannerman. You English have such extraordinary names,' Kessler said.

Will picked up one of the copies of *The Times*, but the paper was almost incomprehensible to him. He'd been thinking in German and speaking German for so long now that English seemed an odd, imprecise, clipped tongue. He put down the paper and bit into the sausage, which was smoky, fatty, rich and delicious. And it went very well with the coffee.

'Please join us, Miss Pullen-Burry,' Klaus said. 'We have coffee.'

'Coffee? Well, perhaps, one cup.'

She sat at the writing desk and Kessler brought her a cup of coffee and a sausage.

'Just the coffee will be fine, Hauptman Kessler, I am going to attempt the "vegetarian" way of life for our time here on Kabakon.'

'I admire your enthusiasm,' Kessler said, taking back the sausage.

'One must always strive to seek new experiences,' Miss Pullen-Burry said, drinking the coffee. 'Don't you agree Mr Prior?'

'A quiet life is what I seek,' Will said.

'Herr Prior was in the South African war,' Kessler added by way of explanation.

'Indeed? A sad business. Englishmen and Dutchmen quarrelling so very far from home.'

'Quite.'

Miss Pullen-Burry sipped her coffee. 'I once travelled to the land of the Mormons who drink neither alcohol nor tea nor coffee in their own 'Augustburg' in Salt Lake City. Salt Lake City is a gloomily resonant name is it not?' she asked.

'Where is that exactly?' Kessler asked.

'Utah. A thousand miles from the nearest city. Heterodox religion flourishes in extreme places. Deserts, mountains, islands. That is why August Engelhardt and his followers have come here, I'll be bound. Germany has become too civilized for such people. Company promotes understanding, but solitude is the school of genius, as Gibbon says.'

Neither man replied and Miss Pullen-Burry had the impression that she was becoming tiresome to the gentlemen. She knew that European men were not used to a woman holding forth on such topics. A young, beautiful lady could be forgiven, but not a plain, middle-aged spinster such as herself.

'Well, I shall leave you gentlemen to your toilet,' Miss Pullen-Burry said, 'I believe the rest of the *Sonnenorden* are on their way and I must do my best to look presentable. Thank you very much for the coffee, Hauptman Kessler.'

'You are very welcome Miss Pullen-Burry.'

Will bowed from a recumbent position and Miss Pullen-Burry returned his bow and slipped outside.

Kessler picked up the pile of newspapers. 'May I read one of your papers, Will?' Klaus asked, holding up the paper.

'Be my guest. Why don't you read to us while we eat?'

Kessler avoided the most controversial topics, but read aloud births, deaths and the court circular. A Canadian called Tommy Burns was the new heavyweight boxing champion of the world. The King had been ill. The –

'Hold on Klaus! Here they come,' Will said, pointing through the window that faced the jungle.

'Where?' Klaus asked, looking outside.

'Over there in the trees,' Will whispered.

Both of them stared through the window as first one and then all of the *Sonnenorden* marched through the forest and entered the piazza. There were nine or ten of them, and two, indeed, were female.

The men were naked, thin, bearded, tanned, covered in insect bites and scars from old insect bites. The two women also, of course, were naked, but they were both carrying parasols to protect themselves from the full glare of the sun, and to Will's eye, they didn't seem quite so thin or badly bitten. Relative newcomers to the island maybe, or not fully paid-up members of the vegetarian covenant.

'I wonder which of them is the Countess Höhenzollern?' Kessler thought out loud.

As soon as the Germans were within the circle of dwellings, they knelt down in front of the totem pole – the Malagan – and began bowing like Mohammedans. 'Christ, what are they up to? This is a rum show . . . '

The Malagan sufficiently worshipped, the *Sonnenorden* began dispersing to their tents.

'What do you make of that, Klaus?' Will asked. 'Klaus?'

But Kessler had stopped watching the ceremony and was pulling on his full dress uniform.

As well as the Deutsches Heer bed Kessler had also brought a clever portable hanging stand to keep his kit wrinkle free, both his dress uniform and his slightly less formal Captain's garb. The dress uniform was dark blue with gold lace piping and a couple of medal ribbons.

Will watched Kessler struggle into his boots. 'Do you need a hand?'

'How do they manage with only two servants in this wretched community? How am I supposed to put my . . . '

'Do you want me to help you?'

'Stop talking and get dressed. You English are always talking!'

Will dressed himself in a loose white cotton shirt and canvas trousers. He slipped on his wet plimsolls and with that was ready to go. Kessler was still fiddling with his brass buttons.

Will helped him with the top two and Kessler quickly strapped on an ornamental cavalry sabre which was heavy and blunt and would not be useful, Will thought, when the *Sonnenorden* really did come to assassinate them.

'Could you hold this up for me?' Kessler asked, giving Will his small hand mirror.

Will did so while Kessler checked the symmetry of his jacket. He was puffy and red and the whole effect had the air of a touring company of Gilbert and Sullivan.

'I wouldn't go out like that,' Will said.

'Why not?'

Will was going to say that he looked ridiculous, but he immediately reconsidered as poor Klaus was the easily offended type. 'Your boots could do with a wipe. Allow me,' he said. He grabbed a chamois from the top of Kessler's trunk and gave the boots a quick going over. 'Perfect. Now you could greet the Queen of Sheba without any reservations.'

Kessler nodded, oddly moved. 'Thank you, Will,' he said. 'Now, come, let us introduce ourselves.'

Will grabbed his straw boater, which had something living perched on the brim.

'Gentlemen! The *Sonnenorden* are here!' Miss Pullen-Burry said, appearing in the doorway.

'So we see,' Will said.

'Ma'am,' Kessler said, hurrying past her into the piazza.

'He looks very smart today,' Miss Pullen-Burry remarked to Will.

'Dress uniform,' Will said, attempting to shake what was a small lizard from his hat.

'Typical of his type don't you find? The Germans in Herbertshöhe and indeed elsewhere are very keen on uniform. I have remarked on this before. The bakers have a uniform, fishermen have a uniform, grooms have a uniform. In England few tradesmen wear the same thing, but Germans are different; they like to belong to things and take pride in this belonging. I suppose that's why the sight of a dozen naked Germans seems so particularly shocking.'

'Sorry, what?' Will said, finally getting the persistent little reptile out of his hat band.

'Nothing,' Miss Pullen-Burry said. 'Come, we mustn't be late for the introductions.'

Will nodded, touched his thin moustache and marched out into the piazza with Miss Pullen-Burry in pursuit.

10

The Sonnenorden

T hunder rumbled in from the Bismarck Sea and it began to drizzle. Parrots and macaws screeched in the coconut trees. *'Guten morgen!'* Kessler shouted heartily and waved.

All of the *Sonnenorden* turned. None of them seemed surprised to see the three strangers, which meant that Harry tipped them off, Will surmised.

A gaunt, long-haired blond man came striding across the pounded shingle with his hand held out. He had a curiously angled, intelligent face and a bright gleam in his eyes.

'Good day to you both, gentlemen, madam. I am August Engelhardt. Welcome to our humble island,' he announced in an elegant, slightly old-fashioned German.

'Captain Klaus Kessler of the King's Bavarian Guards,' Kessler said. The two men shook hands. 'Allow me to introduce Miss Pullen-Burry, a traveller from England and guest of Emma Forsayth.'

'Charmed,' Engelhardt said with a little bow.

'Likewise,' Miss Pullen-Burry replied.

'And Mr William Prior, from England,' Kessler added.

Will and Engelhardt shook hands. Will couldn't help but notice that apart from a touch of sunburn, Engelhardt's penis was of normal appearance and about four inches long. Harry was an exception then, even among the immortals. A sunburn on the John Thomas couldn't be any fun. Will gave Engelhardt a sympathetic wince.

'It is a pleasure to meet you,' Engelhardt said.

'Likewise,' Will answered.

'And how can I assist you, gentlemen?' Engelhardt asked eagerly. *Yes*, Will thought, *not, where have you come from? Or have you come to join us?* It bespoke foreknowledge. A tip-off from Harry or Miss Herzen.

Kessler looked at Will, unsure how to proceed.

'Captain Kessler and myself have been asked by Governor Hahl to look into the death of Max Lutzow. Miss Pullen-Burry is here as Emma Forsayth's representative,' Will said.

'Oh? But Max died of malarial sickness.'

'Nevertheless, the Governor has asked us to look into his death. Perhaps you could introduce us to your comrades?' Will suggested.

Engelhardt laughed. 'How rude of me! Of course, come this way Miss Pullen-Burry, gentlemen.'

Engelhardt stood between the two new arrivals and the rest of the *Sonnenorden*. The women, Will noticed, were doing that languid right-handed fly-swatting gesture so common in Herbertshöhe, but most of the men were letting the flies and mosquitoes land on them with resigned equanimity.

'May I present, Helena, the Countess Höhenzollern,' Engelhardt said, 'Although here, of course, there are no titles.'

The Countess came forward and bowed. She was the smaller of the two women. About forty or perhaps forty-five. A red-head with long burgundy locks, pale skin, lovely round hips and sea-green, dark, intelligent eyes. She was attractive with small breasts, and pert red lips, high cheekbones. The Countess had mosquito welts on her back and legs, but her face had avoided the insects' wrath. She was tanned, of course, as they all were.

Will, Miss Pullen-Burry and Kessler were formally introduced and both men made their bow instead of shaking hands. Kessler said that it was an honour for him to meet someone from such a distinguished family. The Countess rather insolently gave no response.

'And may I also present, Fraulein Anna Schwab from Hesse,' Engelhardt said. This young woman was dark-haired, pretty, thin as a rail, with tiny breasts. She was aged around twenty-five and had gorgeous indigo eyes, a few mosquito scars and a lightly tanned oval face.

'Charmed,' Kessler said curtly.

'Delighted to meet you, miss. I haven't seen a young lady with such a, uh, delightful, complexion since I left England,' Will said and got back a contemptuous curl of the lip, not at all what he'd been expecting.

The men were presented next. First up was a tall blue-eyed man who looked unsettlingly like the late General Gordon. He was called August Bethman and said that he came from Berlin. He had an air of professional sincerity about him and they weren't surprised to discover that he had been a doctor before coming here. Will noted the big dick, big muscles and big moustache and Kessler made a note of his Prussian Junker accent. Bethman squeezed Miss Pullen-Burry's hand so hard that she actually winced.

Next was a broad-shouldered, handsome fellow called Jürgen Schreckengost, who turned out to be a German–American from Pennsylvania. Jürgen chose to speak English to Will, but his accent was so thick that Will could understand only every other word. Jürgen's penis was unremarkable but his ball sack hung alarmingly low on his thigh. Jürgen, Will reckoned, was not the guy who shinnied up the trees to get the coconuts.

Wilhelm Bradtke came next, the oldest of the Cocovores, an emaciated, wild-eyed type who was probably in his late forties or early fifties. He had the air of a man who talks your ear off in a railway carriage about his scheme for getting rid of the poor or tunnelling under the Channel. His face was an inverted triangle with his beard the lower apex. He was carrying a box in his hand which Will later discovered was a camera. Bradtke was from Posen and had an accent Will could barely follow. He was an agitated sort and his cock, Will saw, was about the size of an acorn.

The next man was a Russian called Misha Denfer. He was also broad and strong: apparently thriving on the vegetarian regimen. He was a good-looking fellow with red hair and a magnificent russet beard. He gave the two men a suspicious look, bowed very deeply to Miss Pullen-Burry and grunted a response to Miss Pullen-Burry's harmless pleasantries.

Next was a brown-haired, slender chap with kind, bovine, green eyes and an agreeable smile. His name was Christian Weber and he had been some sort of pastor and director of music at a church in Charlottenberg near Berlin. He spoke fast and Will just about got his story: apparently he had been with the Lutheran missionaries in New Britain for a while and had been on his way to some suicidal mission station in the jungle when he had run into Engelhardt in Herbertshöhe and decided that his destiny lay not in a Kanak cooking-pot but rather among the naked Cocovores in Kabakon.

Will had gotten bored with the cock-spotting game now and didn't even look near Christian's privates. Rather absurdly, Engelhardt presented Harry again to the three newcomers and each of them gave their bow.

'And you have met Fraulein Herzen?' Engelhardt asked Klaus.

'Yes. We were fortunate to see her yesterday,' Kessler said.

'So you have encountered all of our little society?' Engelhardt said with a grin.

'Indeed.'

'May I ask you all some preliminary questions about Herr Lutzow's death?' Will said.

'Poor Lutzow. A cruel case. He had only been with us ten weeks,' Engelhardt said sadly.

'A fine musician!' Christian Weber added sadly.

'And the particulars of his demise?' Will asked.

'Perhaps we could talk at breakfast? We are all very hungry after our night's exertions,' said the other August, Bethman, in his stern doctor's voice.

'Of course, you must pardon us,' Kessler said.

'You will join us in our meal?' Engelhardt asked.

'We would be delighted,' Kessler replied, answering for all of them.

'If you don't mind, I would like to take a walk, my daily constitutional before breakfast, dontcha know,' Miss Pullen-Burry said.

No one minded.

Will retreated to the shade of a coconut tree and watched while a long table was brought into the centre of the piazza. He sat and considered the morning's events. These people he supposed were his 'list of suspects', just like in a Wilkie Collins story, and again he thought about how different this case was from even a capital crime in the army.

He examined the *Sonnenorden*. A motley crew, if ever there was one. Engelhardt didn't seem like a killer, but he was deceptive and the man who deceives has begun his slide down the slippery slope into moral squalor.

And what in the name of God where they all doing here?

Immortality? Who could believe in such stuff?

He sighed and looked up between the branches of the coconut

palm at a surprising number of pygmy parrots and a pair of sulphur-crested cockatoos. Beyond them, the sky had thinned away to a mica greyness that was like wet newspaper.

The *Sonnenorden* had completed their breakfast preparations. Benches had been laid down on either side of the table and the black servants (or slaves, he supposed) were wiping up the fresh bird shit from the wood.

Fraulein Herzen appeared from her hut looking just as lovely as the previous evening. She avoided contact with the others and sat at the table by herself until Anna joined her.

A black servant brought a mound of coconut meat from a storage jar and set it in the middle of the table in a large wooden bowl. Schreckengost and Harry went off to a little shed and came back with two bunches of bananas.

A flagon of liquid was placed down next and a dozen Bavarian-style covered drinking vessels were produced. Ingenious, Will thought; the covers would be useful in keeping out the mosquitoes now beginning to swarm.

'Englishman, please, you must join us for breakfast,' Engelhardt said, waving to Will.

'All right then,' Will said, sitting himself down next to Fraulein Herzen. Kessler sat next to Will and the rest of the *Sonnenorden* arranged themselves randomly about the table. There was, surprisingly, no grace or any other ceremony. Everyone just began tucking into the fruit.

'We had been told that you only eat coconuts,' Klaus said to Engelhardt, while munching on a banana.

'That indeed was our original plan,' Bethman said a little icily. 'But there are bananas in abundance and they share many of the same health-giving properties as the coconut.'

Engelhardt laughed. 'Our ways must seem so strange to you, Hauptman Kessler.'

Kessler shook his head. 'Doubtless it was the coconut that Eve offered Adam in the Garden of Eden.'

Engelhardt shook his head vociferously. 'No, it is nothing to do with that. We believe that the fruit at the tops of trees, closest to Apollo, the sun God, is that which is most wholesome. Bananas, as you can see, also grow near the tops of trees.'

'Yes.'

With a not entirely steady hand, Bradtke, the old geezer, took Will's photograph with the machine he had been carrying. 'A camera?' Will enquired.

'An Eastman-Kodak box camera. The very latest model,' Bradtke said proudly.

'No doubt your photographs will be used to illustrate a book or pamphlet about life on Kabakon,' Will said.

'For the many books to be written about this bold experiment in living!'

'To long life!' Engelhardt said and the *Sonnenorden* en masse removed the lids and drank from their mugs. Will lifted his mug and was surprised to find that it contained neither water nor coconut milk but *arak*, into which a rather large amount of opium had evidently been dissolved: in other words it was home-made laudanum.

Will had had laudanum many times before this and he had seen its abuse among his father's patients. Burned and injured men were often prescribed laudanum. Without question it saved their lives, but unless the doctor was careful he'd have an opium fiend on his hands . . . And here these characters were drinking it for breakfast.

'Heady stuff,' Will said to Klaus.

'Yes,' Kessler agreed enthusiastically.

Will took another sip. There was no question that this was more potent than any tincture he'd tried before. Unless he was

ADRIAN McKINTY

very mistaken it was dissolved in a ninety or one hundred proof doubled-distilled *arak*, to which a little coconut milk had been added. But it was the opium which packed the wallop: several mugs of this mixture would knock an elephant on its arse.

Will watched the others drain theirs as if they were tars splicing the main brace in the navy. Except tars never looked quite so fetching as did Fraulein Herzen, Anna Schwab and the Countess.

As they drank, a second bowl of coconut meat was passed around the table. Will ate a piece of the dense, chewy meat and caught Klaus's eye.

Klaus nodded at him and Will cleared his throat. 'If I may ask about the circumstances of Herr Lutzow's death . . . ' Will began.

'Your trip has been a waste of time. There are no *circumstances*. He died of the malarial sickness,' the Countess said.

'So we have been informed. But malaria has a latency period, does it not? It is never *that* sudden. No one thought of getting Herr Lutzow to the hospital in Herbertshöhe?' Will asked.

'His final descent was rapid and he was in such pain; the torment of a sea crossing was quite unnecessary,' Engelhardt added.

'Our own sweet Anna was with him, right to the end,' the Countess said.

'So I understand,' Will said, turning to Fraulein Schwab.

Miss Schwab nodded solemnly. 'I held his hand while he was dying, until the last faltering beat of his heart. So sad. So very sad. It was a tragedy.'

'Ach, the man was a fool!' August Bethman muttered.

'Why must you speak so, Bethman?' Fraulein Herzen cried, tearing up a little.

'My dear, are you all right?' Kessler asked.

'You must pardon me, gentlemen,' Fraulein Herzen sniffed, and excused herself from the table.

Will and Kessler stood but none of the other men did.

110

'We have upset the lady,' Kessler said. 'This is a painful subject.'

'Yes you *have* upset her. She is very young. Too young to have come here. I should have seen that before I engaged her,' the Countess said bitterly.

Miss Schwab nodded. 'Far too young. I should never have recommended her.'

Will was not to be deterred by the interruption. 'Fraulein Schwab, so you were with Herr Lutzow until the very end?'

'I was trained as a nurse. I thought that I might be able to comfort him. And I did try my best,' Anna Schwab said.

'I am sure you did,' Engelhardt said kindly.

'His face! You should have seen his face. So pale! His hand was weak, I could not feel a pulse. If only he had been here longer . . . '

'Longer?' Will said, *so more mosquitoes could have bitten him?*

'Longer,' Bethman insisted.

Will examined Engelhardt and looked at Klaus.

'We know little of your ways, sir, but as I understand it, immortality is the central part of your credo,' Kessler began. 'Does not Lutzow's unfortunate death—'

'No, it does not! The island and our diet cannot be expected to effect an overnight transformation. Lutzow was only here for ten weeks. Apart from Christian, the rest of us have been here considerably longer,' Engelhardt said brusquely.

'You clearly do not understand, Herr Kessler! The island takes a while to work its magic,' Fraulein Schwab said, to murmurs of agreement from around the table.

'The rest of you, then, are immune to the malaria and the other diseases of mortal men?' Will asked.

'You may mock us, Herr Prior, but while you indulge your bellicose passions, we will live our lives in reading and contemplation and stay here quietly and safely and sit out the twentieth century at our ease,' Bethman said.

'Bellicose passions?' Kessler asked.

'War is coming! Everyone knows it. Civilization will be annihilated!' the Countess said with a touch more glee than regret.

'England and Germany will fight to control the oceans. The ensuing apocalypse will embroil the whole world. They will all be destroyed, but we will be safe on this island,' Bradtke went on.

'I am sure wiser councils will prevail. There has been no general war in Europe for a long time,' Kessler asserted.

'If I could bring you back to Lutzow—' Will attempted.

'You are wrong, Hauptman Kessler! Armageddon is on the march. You know it is the truth. Man craves bloodletting. It is his nature and the next such war will be the *Götterdämmerung*. The end of everything. But we will stay here and we will grow strong and a hundred years from now, when the survivors of your civilization are scrambling around in the ashes, we will come forth and lead the world to a new tomorrow,' Engelhardt said.

'A hundred years?' Kessler asked.

'The limits on the lifespan of man in the book of the Jews have no meaning for us here,' the Countess said sourly. 'The so-called Holy Bible has poisoned mankind, robbed us of our true birthright. Here we are far from such nonsense. I have already outlived my mother and dear papa and sister, who the doctors say were killed by the cancer, but who were really killed by the blights and poisons of the modern world!'

There was an awkward silence for a minute or so during which Denfer and Schreckengost finished their food, nodded to Engelhardt and went off into the plantations. A few seconds later they could be heard barking orders at the Kanak servants who were also out there doing God knows what.

'I too must go,' the Countess said, and excused herself. She was followed by Anna Schwab and August Bethman.

Harry and Bradtke began talking about photography and after a time they, too, departed.

Engelhardt cleared his throat. 'I have a fondness for the English. English ladies in particular. I wonder where Miss Pullen-Burry has got to?'

'Yes, where indeed?' Kessler wondered, a flicker of concern drifting over his composed soldierly face.

The Pilot

W here Miss Pullen-Burry had got to was the beach, where she had encountered the young German pilot who had sailed them across the sea yesterday. The pilot was correcting Miss Pullen-Burry's impression that the Kaiserliche Marine was a relatively novel development in German maritime history. 'You are mistaken, madam: although the Imperial Navy is young, the Hansa tradition of seafaring is old.'

'Is that so?'

'Oh yes, Frau Burry, it goes back hundreds of years. Long before even Frederick the Great and the first Empire.'

Miss Pullen-Burry wrote this information in her notebook. 'I see. And whereabouts in the present Reich do you hail from, sir?'

'I am from Kiel.'

'Kiel. A delightful city, I'm sure.'

'It is a good place for fishing, perhaps,' he conceded. 'But it was not big enough for me. I wished to see the world!'

'I share your sentiments, sir. I grew up in the English provinces. You would not know Cumberland . . . it is celebrated among the poets but I found it a rather dreary locale, at least compared to the South Seas, or the Americas.'

'I wish to travel to the Americas one day.'

'May I ask your name, sir?'

'Of course. I am Karl Goldman,' the young man said impatiently.

'Karl,' Miss Pullen-Burry said, writing it in her book.

'Some of the other men call me "Kat", Karl said, and he *was* slender and had a certain feline grace.

'My mother was a Dane from Bornholm, another race of seafarers,' Karl offered.

Miss Pullen-Burry scribbled furiously. The young man paced back and forth. 'Do you have any cigarettes?' he asked.

Miss Pullen-Burry shook her head. Karl looked at the sun and waning tide and shook his head. 'I must go. I have other duties in Simpsonhafen. You will tell Hauptman Kessler to consult the tide charts and be here for the turn tomorrow. I will not have my time wasted like this and you can be sure that I will inform Oberleutnant Hoffman.'

'I am most dreadfully sorry. I imagine Captain Kessler forgot his appointment. If you can spare a few more minutes, we could go over to the settlement and talk to him.'

'No. He has missed his chance! I will be here tomorrow and I will wait for him on the beach: if he does not come by the turn of the tide, I will leave. I do not command a steam launch, madam.'

'Indeed not.'

The young man glared at her for a second or two as if the guilt was collective. He clicked his shoeless heels together and then went to gather up the anchor lying on the black sand.

'Once again, I am most dreadfully sorry for your inconvenience,' Miss Pullen-Burry said.

'Yes,' Karl said huffily. 'If this were an operation of the Kaiserliche Marine, I can assure you that it would not have happened.'

Karl looked at the clouds and examined the water seeping between his toes. 'You see the white water forming on the reef?'

'I do.'

'That is why I must go. This bay is navigable only at the flood. Of course an army officer – and Bavarian – would not understand such things.'

'I will attempt to explain it to him.'

Karl waited another minute and finally bowed to Miss Pullen-Burry. 'Already the draft is perilous. *Au revoir*,' he said and pushed the *Delfin* back into the surf. When it was afloat, he nimbly climbed on board and hoisted the main sail. 'Is there any message for Governor Hahl?' Karl asked, as he tacked the little sloop.

Miss Pullen-Burry considered for a moment. 'Arrived safely. Everything going smoothly,' she said. Karl nodded, waved to her and sailed the *Delfin* out of the crescent-shaped bay.

'What an intense young man,' Miss Pullen-Burry said to herself and made a lightning pencil-sketch of his frowning features in her book. She put the pencil between the pages and closed the book with a sturdy rubber band. With a last look at the *Delfin*'s diminishing sail she turned and walked back through the plantations to the Augustburg.

She found only Will, Klaus and Engelhardt sitting at the communal breakfast table.

Will saw her first, coming across the piazza. He nudged Kessler and both men stared at her for a moment.

Apart from a sun hat, Miss Pullen-Burry was quite naked.

'This is how it starts, Klaus,' Will murmured in English. 'The veneer of civilization is paper thin. That's something you learn, in extremis.' And bringing his thumb and forefinger close together he hissed, 'Civilization and anarchy, just this far apart.'

'We, *you and I*, must be on our guard,' Kessler agreed.

'I'll watch your back, chum, and you watch mine,' Will said. 'Of course.'

Miss Pullen-Burry marched over the smooth river stones,

smiling. 'Good morning, gentlemen!' she said. 'Or is it afternoon, now? The day has quite flown.'

The men said good morning. She sat at the table and immediately fell into conversation with Engelhardt, showing him her drawings of yesterday's whale and Queen Emma's house and other interesting vistas from her travels. She ate some of the pounded coconut and declared it 'quite delicious'.

After a little small talk about travelling, different foods and customs of disparate regions, Engelhardt explained to the newcomers that everyone in the camp usually took a siesta or attended to reading or meditation from noon until four o'clock.

'After a couple of pints of this joy-juice, I'm surprised anyone can walk to their huts,' Will said in a low voice.

'I too must go, I wish you every success with your "investigation" and if there is anything at all I can do to be of assistance, please let me know,' Engelhardt said, and excused himself.

'And I myself must take a short rest,' Kessler said, struggling to his feet. He was still in his dress uniform and Will noticed that the poor chap's face was redder than ever. 'However, before I go, may I enquire, Miss Pullen-Burry, where you have been and what wonders you have seen?' he asked.

'I saw many birds. Parrots and those big white ones. And great grey sharks near the reef. And I talked to your pilot at the beach. A penetrating young man called Karl. He was most upset that you, apparently, had forgotten him.'

'He is still there, I take it,' Kessler said.

'No. He said he had to sail back to Simpsonhafen,' Miss Pullen-Burry said.

'My God!' Klaus cried, aghast. 'Why did he leave?'

'His tide. Do not distress yourself Hauptman Kessler; he said that he would return at the same time tomorrow,' Miss Pullen-Burry said.

'Tomorrow! Yes, of course. Thank you, Miss Pullen-Burry.'

'My pleasure.'

'We must not forget him tomorrow! He is our only lifeline to the wider world . . . I have never missed an appointment,' Kessler said, still reeling from the horror of it.

'We won't tell anyone, Klaus,' Will said kindly.

'Gentlemen, I will leave you. I must see if I have inconvenienced the Countess with my trunk,' Miss Pullen-Burry said. Will and Kessler stood there as she walked across the piazza to the Countess Höhenzollern's hut.

'A naked Englishwoman! A naked German noblewoman! To think that I have lived to see such things,' Kessler groaned. 'And to miss an appointment . . . Perhaps this island is an ill-omened place.'

Will shook his head. 'We made certain mistakes today, Klaus,' he said.

'About the boat, yes.'

'No, not the boat. I think it was a mistake asking about Lutzow over breakfast with everyone there. I should have conducted separate interviews and compared their accounts before they had time to agree or concoct a common story. I'm afraid that was a grievous error on my part, old man.'

Kessler smiled and patted Will on the back. 'Never fret yourself, my dear fellow,' he said. 'You can conduct separate interviews tomorrow and compare the stories then.'

'Tomorrow, yes, but today would have been better.' Will yawned. 'Oh dear. That tincture was strong stuff. Maybe a short nap wouldn't be a bad idea after all.'

12

The Pendulum of Desire

Will awoke in darkness, drenched with sweat and with creatures biting at him through the mosquito net. 'For Christ's sake!' he said, swatting at his face. The lattice vibrated but Will's blow did little to disturb any of the local arthropods who were using it alternately as feeding station, battleground and place of reproduction.

'Get out of here!' Will cried, trying to scoot away at least the flying cockroaches, but there was only a limited amount he could do from inside the net. Black thumb-sized hissing beetles had in any case broken through his defensive perimeter and were crawling up his leg. Despite many seasons in the tropics, he had not become accustomed to the evening fauna, and as he tumbled out of the hammock his pathetic cry was abbreviated by the close proximity of the hard German floor. He got to his feet and did a little dance to get the insects off him.

'You could help me,' Will said, but when he looked over at the Deutsches Heer bed Kessler was not in it. Will grabbed his plimsolls and began killing the cockroaches who were frantically running for cover, but it was a mug's game and after three executions he stopped, found the chair and sat.

He looked through the window. It was raining hard and

pitch black. Where had the day gone? Surely he had only lain down for a minute.

He found his watch on the table, but he couldn't read it. The hands had been covered with a luminous paint that in theory allowed you to see them at night, but it was so dark here on Kabakon that they were utterly confounded.

Will reached into his sea bag and found a packet of matches. It took three strikes in the humid air for the match to ignite, but when it finally did he held it close to his wrist.

The time was a few minutes before seven, which meant that he had slept for nearly five hours! How he was supposed to fall asleep again that night was beyond him. He hadn't even brought a novel and he knew that to be with one's own thoughts was a recipe for disaster.

He looked in the seabag just in case Siwa had shoved in a few creature comforts, but there was nothing apart from shirts, the Johnnie Walker and a tin of cigarillos.

He thought for a minute, got up, and started rummaging through Kessler's sea chest, which the trusting idiot had left unlocked.

Clothes, a pistol, a container for an electrical device whose function Will could not guess at and a few dense texts on what appeared to be military history and tactics. A backgammon set, a jug of the cheapest rotgut *arak*. Nothing of interest until he found a small lockbox: a metal and teak affair with a tiny brass keyhole. The sort of thing where a lady might keep her billets-doux.

'No key, though,' Will muttered.

He looked across at Kessler's uniform strung from his foldable clothes stand.

'If I know Klaus Kessler,' Will said to himself.

Of course he shouldn't, but he found that he couldn't help himself . . .

He took a quick look outside to check on the wandering German, but Klaus was either away for a walk or stuck in the privy with opium constipation. Will went through Kessler's uniform jacket and trousers until he discovered a key chain. The smallest key on the chain opened the box. Will lifted the lid. The first thing he found was Kessler's commission in Abteilung IIIb of the Imperial Intelligence Service, which had been signed by General von Bülow. *Aha!* Will thought. Underneath the commission were his promotion certificates: fascinating stuff – Kessler had an intelligence rank of major, a full rank above his official grade in the Bavarian Army.

Under the commission and the promotion certificates there were several letters wrapped in black ribbon that were from someone called Hans. When Will opened one of them he was surprised to find that it *was* a billet doux. He read it, first with a sense of amazement, then a dim recognition of what his unconscious already knew, then a sort of dissipated melancholy. When he had realized the full extent of his trespass he put the letters carefully back in the box and placed everything in the trunk. He returned the key chain, lit a cigarillo, sat down and began blowing smoke at the mosquitoes.

Will had known a few poofters in the army. Not a terrible set on the whole, no worse than any of the other bastards you had to deal with in this life, although, he thought, you wouldn't want to rely on one in a pinch.

You wouldn't want to rely on a chap who goes through another chap's belongings as soon as his head was turned, Will reflected sadly.

He resumed staring out of the window into the blackness, but there was nothing there to distract the mind. Rain through the trees and a thunder so distant it could only be coming from Ulu or perhaps New Ireland.

Will closed his eyes and listened to the drumming on the roof. New Guinea was rain. His childhood in Yorkshire was all rain.

Will opened the cigarette box and counted his cigarillos. Just sixteen of them. Could that get him through the next day or so? He lit the oil lamp and sat there in its putrid light. His head ached from the laudanum. He rubbed his temples and carefully stubbed out the smouldering cigarillo and put it back in the tin.

'I cannot believe I did not even bring a pack of cards,' he said.

He tried to think about Lutzow and the case but his mind would not work in that direction. He had another hunt through his own seabag for anything of interest and this time he found his scissors.

'Yes,' he said and trimmed the edges of his moustache in the dresser mirror. He was paler than he'd been in a long time and there was a greenish tinge to his cheeks. He snipped at the edges of the moustache, until it became a little more disciplined. He cleaned his nails with one of the scissor points and then made them make clickety noises for a while. He tried whistling along to the clickety noises, but finally he bored of this ensemble and lit another cigarillo. What would man do without tobacco? 'It would be the rope and a chair for all of us and no mistake,' he said.

He had read Hazlitt once in his father's library and that old file had said that his favourite recreation was to be left alone with his own thoughts somewhere in the country. 'He would have loved this hell hole,' he muttered.

Just then, Will noticed one of the ladies sitting by herself on the far side of the piazza, under the little gazebo. Will couldn't tell which of the ladies it was, but even Miss Pullen-Burry would be tea and biscuits at the palace compared to this.

Will sprang out of his chair, pulled on his trousers, his plimsolls and finally his good linen shirt that Siwa had packed for him.

It was still pissing down, so he found his straw boater on a peg, removed the now-to-be-expected lizard, shoved it on his head and ran outside.

The rain was falling in large, cold drops that drenched him immediately. He slipped in a puddle in front of the gazebo and almost went arse over tit but recovered himself and walked up the steps where he found Fraulein Schwab sitting in front of a chess board, starkers of course, but with a shawl about her shoulders.

The gazebo had obviously been made in Germany and shipped out here in sections like the huts, for it was carved from heavy pine and covered with a thick resin to protect it from the insects and the climate. It was richly ornamented with gargoyles, oak-leaf patterns and odd occult symbols. Between one of the arches a plaque proclaimed in high Gothic: *'I have already told you that ye are Gods!' Psalm 82:6.*

'Good evening!' Will said, trying to catch his breath.

Anna Schwab barely looked up at him before resuming her concentration on the game. Perhaps she hadn't actually noticed him and Will wondered if she was still in a laudanum trance.

'Good evening Fraulein Schwab,' he said, slightly louder.

'I heard you coming. Your shoes make an extraordinary amount of noise.'

'Yes, the seals . . . I mean to write to the Liverpool Rubber . . . they're not supposed to—'

'And besides, Herr Prior, I was expecting you,' Fraulein Schwab interrupted.

'Do you mind if I sit?' Will asked, already somewhat irritated by her manner.

'If you must,' Fraulein Schwab said, in a tone that was only a degree removed from impertinence.

'Who are you playing?' Will asked.

'My sister.'

'Your sister is *here?*'

'She is in Baden Baden.'

'I see. I see . . . Er, you're black?'

'Obviously.'

Even Will could see that black was in serious trouble. White had taken black's queen, both bishops and a knight, for a few pawns and a knight. She felt his gaze on her face and she looked up at him.

'How long have you been thinking about your move?'

'Two weeks. And the packet is not due to leave until next week.'

'You've got a little time to get yourself out of the difficulty then, haven't you?' Will said.

Fraulein Schwab smiled. 'Yes,' she replied.

Will felt encouraged by this. 'So, if I may enquire, why were you expecting me?'

'You are a policeman. You have to come to Kabakon to spy on us. You are looking into Max's unfortunate death. I was with Max when he died; naturally you would wish to question me when I was alone.'

'You are mistaken on one point. I am an ex-policeman doing a favour for Governor Hahl in an unofficial capacity. I cannot compel you to answer my questions.'

Fraulein Schwab nodded. 'Nevertheless, I will answer whatever it is you wish to know.'

'All right. Who killed Max Lutzow?'

Fraulein Schwab pursed her pretty pink lips together. 'You should ask what killed him, not who.'

'What killed him?'

'A lack of faith.'

'A lack of faith?'

'Your hearing is excellent.'

'Perhaps you could explain what you mean,' Will said, starting to get quite annoyed now.

'Lutzow had doubts about our project here on Kabakon. He was weak. He was unable to renounce the world. He was unable to let go of his worldly attachments,' Fraulein Schwab said with a chilly sadness.

Even in German her accent was upper-crust and oddly intoxicating. And the delicacy of her features and the blue darkness of her eye would have marked her out as a beauty anywhere.

'So, you were with Lutzow until the end?' Will asked.

'Yes. I was. I held his hand. I knew, of course, that it was too late. He could not triumph over himself. The rot had set in.'

'This was on Saturday evening? Last Saturday?'

'Perhaps. We do not keep track of days here.'

'How long had he shown symptoms of malaria?'

'More or less since he arrived. All of us have had malaria. Most have conquered it as we have conquered all these weaknesses.'

'I take it that you do not believe that insects – mosquitoes – are the agents of malarial transmission?'

'Perhaps they are, but it is weakness in us if we succumb. Man is mightier than any insect that crawls upon the Earth or flits upon the air. On Kabakon we set ourselves the task of triumphing over the flesh.'

'When did you know that Herr Lutzow was not going to win the battle against the flesh?' Will asked a trifle sardonically.

'We had hopes until close to the very end.'

Was she lying? If so she was good at it. Not an ounce of doubt in her expression. No tremble of the lip, no side glance of the eye, no hand to the mouth, no redness of the cheek.

'So you were with Herr Lutzow when he actually died? When he breathed his last breath?'

'Yes, I was with Max as he breathed his last breath,' she insisted.

Her lovely eyebrows knitted together almost in a single dark line. 'Do you doubt my word, sir?'

'Not at all. Merely . . . I mean, how did you know that he was dead? Was there a death rattle, a moan?'

'I was holding Max's hand, talking to him, bathing his forehead with well water . . . and, as the evening progressed, his grip grew weaker and weaker. I felt the life-force ebb from him. After a time I noticed that his hand was quite cold. I rose and went for August and he came and examined Max. We held Helena's hand mirror over his mouth and we saw that there was no breath. Bethman had been a doctor in Germany so August summoned him and he came and attempted to take Max's pulse.'

'Was there a pulse?'

'There was no pulse. Max was dead.'

'And then what happened?'

Fraulein Schwab looked at him quizzically. 'What do you mean?'

'What did you do with the body?' Will asked.

'We did nothing.'

'You just left him in the bed?'

'Yes.'

'You must have had some plans to bury him?'

'We had not discussed it.'

'You hadn't discussed it? A man dies and you hadn't discussed what to do next?'

'We had not.'

'I don't believe that. A man dies and you just go on about your business?' Will asked.

'It was the middle of the night. Most of us were asleep and August did not think it worth waking everyone merely to break sad news.'

'So you decided to leave him in his bed.'

'All the actions we take here on Kabakon are unanimous. We could not have made any decision until the morning, when everyone would be awake.'

'Who did know that Max had died that night?'

'I do not see why that is important.'

'It is important to me. Who knew?'

'August knew and Bethman knew and the Countess knew. I think Harry was awake. Possibly some of the others, I do not know.'

'You told the others in the morning?'

'Yes.'

'And that's when you discussed what to do with the body?'

'We would have discussed it then, but of course Harry and Fraulein Herzen had met the Australian by then and we decided that it would perhaps be best that Max was buried in Simpson-hafen, where he would be more comfortable.'

'He wasn't comfortable on Kabakon?'

'No, as I say, Herr Prior, he did not fully embrace our project here.'

Will nodded. He leaned back in the gazebo seat, which he discovered was a kind of rocking chair. He was a little troubled. His critical faculties were not operating at full capacity because of two factors: the residual traces of the opium, and Fraulein Schwab's patrician good looks. Will had never been able to resist a pretty face, which was not a problem in the army, but here he needed to get over it.

He reflected upon her words. Her manner was business-like and direct and she did not seem like a fantasist, but what she was telling him did not chime with the physical evidence. Could Doctor Bremmer and Fraulein Schwab both somehow be correct? Perhaps the fault lay with Clark, the Australian pilot? Was it possible that the body fell off the boat as he was bringing it across the Bismarck Sea?

Could seawater enter a dead man's lungs? Will had no idea. Or maybe water had gotten into Max's lungs while they were manoeuvring him into Clark's vessel in the first place? How much seawater had Doctor Bremmer been talking about?

Now that he thought about it there were many possibilities. Those bruises, perhaps they *could* have been produced post mortem.

Will shook his head. No, it was not penetrating glances that were ruining his concentration and it wasn't the laudanum either: this was a genuine paradox.

'What are you thinking?' Fraulein Schwab asked.

'I have not distilled my thoughts into a form that is easy to communicate.'

'I would like to hear them, no matter how muddled.'

'It is often said to be otherwise, Fraulein Schwab, but men are less exigent than women. I need more time.'

'On Kabakon that is something which exists in abundance.'

'Who helped carry Lutzow to Clark's boat?' Will asked.

'I do not know. It was raining. Some of the bigger men, I assume,' she said, and looked away. Not, he saw, to disguise her guilt, but rather to conceal a yawn.

She was growing tired of him.

Will took his hat off and set it on the table. The rain had cooled the air to about sixty-five degrees. He almost felt cold. Thinking it made him shiver involuntarily. Could this whole trip have been a wild goose chase? Doctor Bremmer did not look like a fool, but the tropics did strange things to men; it turned competent men incompetent and incompetent men into hopeless dipsomaniacs.

He was about to ask another question when he saw Christian and Harry standing on the piazza performing some sort of ballet. Their hands and feet were moving together in listless gestures of the most extraordinary kind.

'What on Earth are they doing?' Will asked.

'*Tai chi chuan.*'

'What is that?'

'Some of us here practise it. Helena learned it from the Chinese traders. It is a form of exercise.'

'It does not look very efficacious.'

'They say it promotes longevity.'

'If you wish to join them, please be my guest.'

'I do not follow their particular school of thought. I believe that you must begin with the mind. The body is the slave of the mind, not the reverse.'

'You say Lutzow did not wholly embrace your philosophy. Would you mind explaining to an ingénue what that philosophy is?'

'Of course!' Fraulein Schwab said, her face lighting up. For the first time, she appeared more interested in the conversation than the chess board. 'You have read Schopenhauer, Herr Prior?' she asked, her beautiful white teeth gleaming in the darkness.

'Schopenhauer? Er, not as much as I would like. Remind me of the uh, the basics.'

'We are lambs in a field disporting ourselves under the eye of the butcher, Herr Prior. Time is continually pressing upon us, never letting us take a break but always coming after us like a taskmaster with a whip. If at any moment Time stays his hand, it is only when we are delivered over to the misery of boredom.'

'I see,' Will said, baffled.

'Each man desires to reach old age, where it is bad today and worse tomorrow, until finally we reach the worst of all: death. All of life is striving without release. There is no such thing as the satisfaction of desire. Desire may be satisfied for a short time but it will always immediately be replaced by another desire. There is no progress, there is no rest, the desire is endless and meaningless. When we are satisfied boredom arrives almost instantly until the satisfaction of desire itself becomes painful.'

'I think I see what you're on about,' Will said.

Fraulein Schwab nodded excitedly and her tongue darted between her lips like a small serpent. 'Life oscillates like a pendulum between desire and boredom. Whatever we achieve is just a drop of water in a sea of desire. The best we can hope for is to become aware of the striving, aware of the self, aware of consciousness itself.'

'That's very interesting. And where does God fit into all this?' he asked.

Fraulein Schwab snorted. 'God? Mr Darwin has removed our need for a God. And if there were such a being, surely it is evident by now he is indifferent to us and our fate, or as some believe, he actively hates us. One need only look at the suffering everywhere in this world to see the truth of that. I see no evidence of a benevolent deity in our universe. Only when man attains his apotheosis will that vacuum in our universe be filled.'

'But, it's not all misery is it? What about music and love and—'

'Speak not of love. Love! Love is an illusion foisted upon us by Nature to get us to reproduce. You speak of lust and sexual congress, not love.'

'Out here on Kabakon things are different, are they?' he asked.

'Things are very different here. Here, like the beasts of the field, we live in the present. We have no hypocrisy. Our goods are held in common.'

'And you are beyond the need for, uh, sexual congress?'

'When we have a desire we fulfil it, knowing that it means nothing. Why do you ask? Do you desire sexual congress with me?'

Even in the darkness Will blushed and could not manage a response.

'Well?'

'Madam, how can you speak so?'

Fraulein Schwab frowned. 'Of course. You have been here only one day. Your soul lies out there. Not here.'

'One does not, uh . . . With gentle ladies one does not—'

'I pity you, Mr Prior.'

'I beg your pardon.'

'Over there,' she said vaguely pointing towards the beach, 'you live within the hypocrisy of class and social distinction. You are imprisoned by your mores. Your life swings between hope and fear; here on Kabakon there is neither hope nor fear. We wake, we breathe, we bathe in the sun, we eat the fruit of the sun. We no longer strive, we are no longer driven by Time's whips. We live here and we are happy.'

'Frankly, you do not look that happy to me,' Will said, recovering himself.

'No? Do not take reserve for unhappiness, Mr Prior. I am content.'

'If you say so.'

'I do.'

'On Kabakon do you not also live by bizarre rules and mores? You bow down to a totem. You are vegetarians,' Will added.

'I bow because it pleases me to please Engelhardt. He believes that the Earth itself is a deity, the Earth is alive.'

'The vegetarianism?'

'Eating animals is morally indefensible. Here we eat only   '

'I know. Coconuts and bananas. And opium. Quite a bit of opium too, it seems.'

'The Sumerians called the opium poppy *Hul Gil*, the joy plant. They believed, as we do, that in its path we are led to another realm beyond this one. And what we take is Bayer heroin: opium perfected by German science.'

Fraulein Schwab leaned forward and by accident or design her arms were pushing her breasts together to form a décolletage. 'And you, Mr Prior, what do you believe?' she asked.

'I do eat meat. Deer and pig and fish and beef when I can get it.'

'But what do you *believe*?'

'What everyone else believes. I am no backwoodsman. I have read Mr Darwin, but I am not yet convinced by his arguments.'

Fraulein Schwab laughed as if this were the greatest joke in the world, but then her hand reached to her mouth in embarrassment when she saw that Will was serious.

'But my dear sir. Doctor Schopenhauer and Doctor Darwin have solved all of the philosophical problems of humanity. Doctor Darwin has removed a need for a first cause, Schopenhauer has shown us our modern dilemma!'

She smiled and put her hand on his. Will felt the electricity in her fingertips.

'You must read Schopenhauer again. Please, sir, allow me to give you my copy of *Die Entstehung der Arten*.'

'All right.'

'Follow me,' Anna said, and putting her shawl over her head she ran across the piazza to one of the huts.

Will followed Fraulein Schwab to her rather drab little bungalow, almost identical in every respect to the dwelling he shared with Klaus, but somehow bleaker because it was filled with furniture and pictures. There was a large German bed and next to it a smaller camp bed. No mosquito netting on either, Will noted. Under the window (which had glass) there was an armoire, a dressing table and on the opposite wall a frightening-looking tribal mask of the Duk Duk variety. A bookshelf ingeniously snaked around all four walls. Heavy German volumes of forbidding texts. A strange-looking chair and a Persian rug completed the set-up.

'How do you like my accommodation?' Fraulein Schwab asked, lighting an oil lamp.

She looked younger in here and Will realized that he'd been wrong about her age. She may have just turned twenty-two or twenty-three. A healthy diet and avoidance of the sun would return her to rude health if she would but allow it.

'Charming,' Will said.

'Sit in the "ergonomic" chair; it is very comfortable; it was designed by a Swedish professor of anatomy. And call me Anna if you wish,' she said.

Will sat in a hard, wooden, incredibly uncomfortable chair that was only a step above an Inquisitorial torture device. 'Will you tell me the truth about something, Mr Prior?' Fraulein Schwab said, sitting on the edge of the bed and smiling again.

He really liked her smile. Her whole face glowed when she smiled. 'May I ask you a question of an intimate nature?'

'If you please,' Will replied.

'Do you have syphilis?'

'Do I have . . . ?'

'Do you have the syphilis?'

'No. I do not have the syphilis.'

'I mean no moral censure. I ask only as a precaution. I do not wish to be lied to.'

'I do not have syphilis,' Will insisted.

'But when you visited low houses, you may have contracted the disease. And please do not tell me that you have never frequented such places. You were a military man.'

'In—in South Africa I used a method of contraception which science tells us is an effective prophylactic,' Will said, amazed by the turn in the conversation.

'You are free of all the social diseases?'

'I believe so.'

'We may indeed have intercourse, then,' Fraulein Schwab said. She was just about the most attractive female who had ever said or suggested such a thing to Will in any language. Anna Schwab was a magnificent specimen of womanhood. Long proportionate thighs, delicate breasts and a deeply intelligent, inquisitive face. Yet although they were east of Greenwich and south of the line, Will had grown up in the dark heart of Yorkshire and he still found himself shocked by the proposition. Fraulein Schwab was German, a nudist, a Cocovore, but undoubtedly a well-born lady. Will coughed.

'Why do you hesitate? Do you not desire me?'

'Madam, perhaps I misunderstand your, er, philosophy. I thought you said that the purpose of living on Kabakon was to free yourself of desire,' Will uttered lamely.

'Of course! Which means that desire is both meaningless and the most important thing in the world. On Kabakon we will live for a hundred years because we repress nothing, we say everything, we tell the truth. When we wish to act, we act.'

She pulled Will towards the bed and kissed him on the lips.

'Be warned, though, that for you the satisfaction of this desire will be both transitory and meaningless,' she whispered. 'But perhaps you are not able?'

Will kicked off his plimsolls and undid the braces holding up his canvas trousers. He pulled the shirt over his head and since he was wearing no undergarment, within a trice he was as naked as the wet September day in 1880 when he'd been born.

'You have no difficulty becoming aroused,' Anna said, with a cold, biological glint to her eye.

'Who would, looking at you my dear?' Will said, clambering onto the bed.

Fraulein Schwab waved her hand in the direction of the window. 'Most of the men on Kabakon,' she replied sadly.

'Malaria will do that to you,' Will said and kissed her on the mouth to silence her.

And yet, after a minute or so, she opened her eyes and looked at him. 'Is there anything the matter?' she asked.

'No!' Will said.

'Are you sure?'

'Well, I . . . '

She gently pushed him off. 'You have done this with a woman before now?' she asked.

'Of course!' Will said.

'Perhaps you prefer boys?' she suggested.

'I have a . . . There is a young person to whom I am greatly attached, she . . . this is . . . ' Will stuttered.

'There is no need to explain. Hand me that tin of Turkish cigarettes next to the bed,' she said.

He did as he was bid and she lit a cigarette and did not offer him one.

Fraulein Schwab shook her head. 'It was mere curiosity on my part. A passing foolishness. The character of the will is suffering. The only way we can escape suffering is to cease to strive.'

'Very true,' said Helena, the Countess Höhenzollern, coming into the hut with Miss Pullen-Burry. Both were naked but for clog-like shoes on their feet. Both were carrying large black umbrellas which they proceeded to shake just outside the hut door – a valuable two seconds that allowed Will to pull a sheet over his privates.

'Refusal to be driven onto the rocks of suffering by the relentless will is the source of our true escape,' Helena said, and then, seeing Will, she exclaimed, 'Good evening Herr Prior!'

'Good evening Countess, Miss Pullen-Burry,' Will said, with a steady voice.

'Good evening, Mr Prior,' Miss Pullen-Burry responded.

'Is he bothering you?' the Countess asked Fraulein Schwab.

'Not at all,' she exclaimed and then, laughing, added, 'I'm afraid that the heart was willing but the body incapable.'

Will clamped his teeth together, appalled.

Miss Pullen-Burry pretended a lack of understanding. 'You are feeling unwell Mr Prior; perhaps the diet does not agree with you?'

'I do very well madam. Ladies if you will excuse me, I must go, there has been a uhm . . . Fraulein Schwab and I were . . . If you will just step outside for one moment, please.'

Miss Pullen-Burry got up to go, but the Countess waved her down again.

'You are in *our* domain, Mr Prior, this is the Augustburg, the settlement of the *Sonnenorden*. We choose not to leave.'

Will's cheeks stayed the same colour, but they changed from the red of shame and embarrassment to that of outright anger.

'Madam, I am attempting to be discreet. I wish you to leave so that I may get dressed,' Will said with cold rage.

'Sir, as you can see, *we* are undressed. On Kabakon we practise naked cocovorism – that is our *raison d'être*.'

'Very well,' Will said aggressively, throwing back the sheet and grabbing his clothes from off the floor. He pulled on his trousers and slipped his feet partially into the plimsolls.

'Goodnight ladies,' he said, and slinging his shirt over his shoulder, he walked back across the piazza to his hut.

Inside, Kessler was dozing under his Deutsches Heer mosquito tent. He looked dry, composed and restful, without a care in the world.

'Klaus!' Will tried, but he got no answer. 'Klaus!'

Kessler moaned, but did not open his eyes.

Will went to the doorway and looked out – he could just make out the ladies talking in Fraulein Schwab's hut on the other side of the piazza. Laughing at him, no doubt. He closed the door, hunted for a towel, found one of Kessler's and dried himself.

He shook Kessler until the German awoke. 'Klaus!'

'What? Is it morning?' Kessler asked.

'No.'

'What is the matter?' Kessler asked. 'Is there a fire?'

'No. No fire.'

'What then?'

'I questioned Fraulein Schwab.'

Kessler looked at him and sat up. He climbed out of the mosquito net, grabbed his pen and notebook and sat on the edge of the bed. 'Tell me your report,' he said.

Will was relieved to see this side of Kessler. Wandering off and missing his appointment with the *Delfin* had made Will think that Klaus might have experienced some kind of psychic break, freed from his regimented life in Herbertshöhe.

'I don't have anything concrete to report, not yet, not as such. I don't think *she* killed him, anyway,' Will said.

'Who did?'

'I have no idea.'

Kessler put the pen and notebook away. 'In that case I am going back to bed.'

'Where did you go earlier?'

'I went for a walk.'

'In the rain?' Will said.

'I speak in euphemisms.'

'Bowel trouble, eh?'

'I do not wish to talk about it. Good night, Will.'

'I want to tell you something, Klaus,' Will said urgently.

'What?' Kessler asked, a flicker of concern around his green, saucer-like eyes.

'I don't like this place, there's something unwholesome about it.'

'There's something unwholesome about the entire South Pacific.'

'No, here, there's something wrong here. We should leave as quickly as we can.'

Kessler yawned. 'Of course, Will, as quickly as we can,' he agreed and yawned and went cheerfully back to sleep.

13

Leaving the Garden

The Night Witches came on ramshackle brooms on which perched crows, magpies, ravens and other more exotic creatures from the infernal aviary. Their robes were vermilion lianas weaved from their hair. Under their death hoods Will could see the white of a pure skull glinting in the light of the crescent moon. He was running naked on the beach, he had no weapon or hope of escape . . .

'Aaauhhh,' Will gasped and woke, staring into the dull face of one of the blacks who had helped carry their luggage from the beach on that first day.

'Aaauhhh!' he screamed again and the poor fellow jumped back. 'Sorry,' Will said. 'Bad dream. Duk Duk men. Night Witches . . . you know. Nonsense.'

The servant attempted to tell him something but his mouth was crammed full of betel and he was speaking in pidgin German. Will only got one word in three – apparently Harry wanted to see him.

'Run along now,' Will said and dismissed the man with a wave of his hand. 'I need something to drink. Is there any coffee?' he asked, but Klaus was not in the hut.

He lay for a while examining his fresh bites until Harry von Cadolzburg and Christian Weber came into the hut. Both, naturally, were quite naked, although Harry was wearing blue

tinted glasses which gave him either a comic or demonic air . . .
Will couldn't decide which.

'Good morning, Will,' Harry said.

'Good morning,' Will replied. 'To what do I owe this pleasure?'

'What do you have planned to do today?' Harry asked.

'I haven't planned anything,' Will said.

'We thought perhaps we could take you on a little tour of the
island and the plantations this morning. Would that suit you?'
Christian said brightly.

'Is the weather clement?'

'The rain has finally stopped,' Harry said in English, enun-
ciating each of his words as if they were individually wrapped
birthday presents.

Will looked dubiously through the window. The sky was grey
and a small cassowary wandering across the piazza looked wet
and depressed. 'Well, it's kind of you gents to offer, but I don't
know – I have not even breakfasted yet.'

'We will have some refreshment first, of course,' Christian
added.

Will yawned and swung out of the hammock. To his horror
the floor was alive with tiny scarlet crabs who had been washed
down from the plantations in last night's downpour. It must
have been a common occurrence, for Harry and Christian
apparently hadn't even noticed them. 'You couldn't possibly
pass me my shoes, could you, old chap?' Will asked, keeping
his feet an inch above the floor and examining his fresh harvest
of mosquito bites.

They gave him his plimsolls and tiptoeing through the crabs
he grabbed his kit bag and looked through it to see if Siwa had
packed his quinine pills. She had not.

'Where's Klaus?' Will asked.

'He went off somewhere, I think,' Harry said.

'What time is it?' Will asked, after another momentous yawn.

Christian and Harry looked at one another. They had no watches and no longer had much notion of the clock. 'Perhaps two hours after sun rise?' Christian offered.

Will poured the crabs, ants, cockroaches and spiders out of his trousers and pulled them on with some difficulty.

'Your clothes are not necessary here,' Harry said.

'Refreshment, you say?' Will asked, ignoring this remark. He grabbed a loose-fitting linen shirt to cover his torso.

'Come with us,' Christian said and Will allowed himself to be led outside to the long communal dining table. Christian brought him a flagon of well water and a bowl of what looked like pounded coconut meat.

'This is breakfast, is it?' Will asked, wondering if there was any sausage left in Kessler's trunk.

'Sometimes we take this, yes, we think you will like it,' Harry said.

Will ate the unctuous substance with mounting distaste. It had been flavoured with local spices and sweetened with molasses. There was a hint of raw spirit about it, too. After the third spoonful Will pushed back the bowl.

'Delicious,' he said. 'But I find that I am not really that hungry today.'

'It is good isn't it?' Harry said, finishing Will's bowl. 'The natives call it *chanak*. A kind of coconut porridge.'

'*They* eat it with sucking pig, fattened on the milk from a woman's breast,' Christian said.

'You don't have any of that sucking pig do you?' Will asked hopefully.

'Of course not!' Christian said delightedly, as if Will had cracked the most wonderful joke.

Will prodded the bowl with his finger. 'What's the smell?'

'It is fermented. We get it by the pot from Ulu,' Harry said. The natives chew on the coconut and spit it into a bowl and allow it to ferment for up to three weeks. August thought of adding molasses and 'heroin' to make it a breakfast treat,' Christian said.

'Ah yes, Miss Schwab spoke of heroin,' Will said.

'From Bayer. It is a kind of morphine, but without morphine's unfortunate addictive qualities. A remarkable medicine,' Christian went on.

Will frowned, wondering if the *Sonnenorden* were ever truly sober. 'I thought it was opium dissolved in *arak*. A sort of home-made laudanum.'

'Opium!' Christian said. 'Do you take us for Chinamen, sir?'

Will offered him a thin smile. The Chinamen he had come across actually worked for a living. No one around here apparently did much of anything. Except the blacks, of course.

'You were going to show me something,' Will said.

'Come, let us go before the heat of the day is truly upon us,' Harry said.

Will got up, stretched, and followed them into the plantations.

A dense layer of coconut trees surrounded the Augustburg but as they moved away from the settlement Will begin to see banana palms and a few rubber trees. It was a solid, mature plantation, at least twenty or thirty years old, and clearly established well before the *Sonnenorden* or even the Germans had come here.

'Impressive, no?' Christian said. 'The forest provides us all our needs.'

'And the Kanaks do all the work, eh?'

'The island does the work,' Harry said. 'All we must do is harvest the coconuts and bananas. These are strong trees resistant to fungi and the blight.'

Will nodded. His plantations weren't anywhere close to being this mature or developed. 'How did you find this place?' he asked.

'August found it,' Christian said.

'He was looking for somewhere with coconut plantations in the German Reich. Africa was his first thought, but then he and Willy discovered that plantations such as these could be bought in Deutsch New Guinea,' Harry said.

'They must be thirty years old. Lovely trees,' Will said, impressed. Harry led them up a small path through even taller, more elegant, palms.

'The eminent Doctor Parkinson suggested that we buy a portion of the Forsayth dominions in Neu Mecklenberg. Unfortunately, a planter was murdered there by the savages so August asked Doctor Parkinson to find us somewhere with few natives. The aboriginals here on Kabakon had all either died or emigrated or been taken to Queensland, and as the plantations were idle, Doctor Parkinson offered August a fair price for the entire island.'

I'll bet he did, the old goat, Will thought. *And if he could get them back for nothing because of a breach of contract . . .*

They had walked clean across Kabakon to a beach on the north shore. The day was clear and Will was impressed by the view of Ulu and Kerawara island and the long line of clouds above New Ireland in the distance. There were no boats on the water, although there was a large outrigger canoe sitting on the black volcanic sand.

'Your canoe?' Will asked.

Harry nodded. 'Like Cortez, August and Bradtke literally burned their boat when they came here, but the canoe was a gift from the Chieftain in Ulu and we have found it useful.'

'Those less competent in the art of swimming use it to go to Sol Island,' Christian said.

'It is a fine-looking craft,' Will said, with some admiration. It was a Polynesian ocean-going vessel, very different from the sad local dugouts you saw in New Guinea.

'Well I must say, you've got a nice spot, lads. I don't know if I'd want to "wait out the century" here, as you put it, but it's a nice place.'

'I was expecting much worse,' Christian sniffed. 'After having seen something of the highlands in New Britain . . . '

'You don't have any trouble then with the natives around here?' Will asked. 'New Ireland and Ulu are not that far off.'

'We have good relations with the Papuans,' Christian said.

'I suppose they're nervy about the Kaiserliche Marine gunboats, eh?' Will asked.

Harry and Christian shook their heads. 'The navy never comes here,' Harry said.

'How then?'

'August has reached an accommodation with the chieftain on Ulu. We pay him fifty marks after every new moon and he keeps the other natives away from us and provides us with servants and supplies when we need them. Of course the blacks are always running off,' Harry said.

'It's probably the beatings. Your New Guinean cannot abide a beating. They won't have it,' Will said.

'We never beat them!' Christian replied, shocked. 'It is nothing to do with beating. They are afraid. As the most southerly of the Duke of York islands, Kabakon is the stepping stone between New Britain and New Ireland; this is the place where the Night Witches launch themselves into the firmament,' Christian said.

Will said nothing and all three men walked along the black sand in silence for a time.

'So how long have you been here?' Will asked, to get the disturbing images from his dream out of his mind.

'Almost a year,' Harry said.

'Nearly three months,' Christian replied.

'Neither of you came out with Engelhardt?' Will asked.

'No. Bradtke, Engelhardt and Bethman were the original pathfinders,' Harry explained. 'When I arrived they were still living in tents and the huts were not yet completed.'

Harry then told Will the story of how they had put the prefabricated huts together with help from a Chinese work crew. Will was listening, but paying close attention to Christian. The man seemed ill at ease, nervous.

'The ladies could not possibly have come until the accommodation was finished,' Harry concluded.

'Ah, yes, the ladies. We were surprised to see ladies, here. Klaus was under the impression that you were an all-male order,' Will said.

Harry grinned. 'Perhaps that was August's initial intent and certainly he and Bradtke spoke often about the importance of transcending bodily desires. However, his, er, methods proved too radical for the rest of the us. And besides we needed the Countess's . . . '

'Money?' Will suggested.

'Support,' Harry agreed. 'August has no money. His father was a civil servant and Bradtke is even poorer. He was an engineer,' Harry said.

'Bethman?' Will asked, remembering the thin, aristocratic-looking man from yesterday.

'Bethman has money but his family will not release it; they have tangled him in legal snares,' Harry said.

'Because of his coming here?'

'I believe so.'

'So it's all down to the Countess Höhenzollern?'

'This project would have remained a purely Platonic notion had it not been for the interest of the Countess,' Harry said, pushing his blue glasses up his nose.

'And Engelhardt could not refuse her her retinue,' Will suggested.

'Indeed,' Christian said.

'But women were never . . . Ah, perhaps I should not say,' Harry began and trailed off, embarrassed.

'Yes?' Will enquired.

'Doubtless he will notice eventually,' Christian said.

'Doubtless I will,' Will insisted.

'Well . . . so committed were August and Bradtke to the idea of transcending our Earthly desires . . . '

'Yes?'

'They had themselves castrated in Hong Kong.'

'Good God!' Will exclaimed. 'Are you serious?'

'Quite serious.'

'But none of the other men . . . '

'No,' Harry said.

'Did you know about this before coming to Kabakon?'

'No. But August had written of this possibility in his pamphlets. It is a small price to pay for immortality.'

'If you say so.'

The path had led them back up the small incline between a strand of pristine rubber trees.

'And what, may I ask, brought you to the Indies, Mr Prior?' Harry asked, as Will was still digesting that wince-inducing piece of information.

'Me? Oh, I don't know. Adventure?'

'You were in the army?' Christian said. 'Is that not an adventurous line of work?'

'No. It is mostly routine. Quite dull.'

'You were in the wars?'

'I never saw a battle.'

The palms were swaying in the trade winds, moisture droplets skimming off the fronds and prismatically capturing the intense sunlight before evaporating. Will was captivated by this strange spectacle and forgot his mosquito bites and wet shoes and even the two men standing in front of him for a moment.

'Herr Prior?' Harry asked.

Will snapped out of it and looked into Harry's good, honest face. 'Fraulein Schwab, is she a trustworthy person?' Will asked.

'Of course! Why do you ask?'

'Fraulein Schwab says that she was with Lutzow until the moment he died. She says that she actually saw him die. And I am afraid to say that I do not believe her.'

'But why do you not believe her?' Harry asked.

At this stage of the investigation Will did not want to give them the information about the autopsy, but he knew he had to give them something. 'I do not wish to cast aspersions on a lady, but something about her way did not give me confidence that she was telling the truth.'

Harry and Christian exchanged a look and for a thrilling second Will wondered if they were about to set upon him with miraculously concealed blades or bunched-up fists.

'I do not think that Anna *was* with Max when he died,' Harry said, after a brief pause.

'Indeed not?' Will replied. 'How intriguing.'

'It is not what you are thinking,' Harry said.

Will smiled benevolently. 'What am I thinking?'

'It is nothing untoward,' Harry clarified.

Will looked at the young man and ran his finger along the line of his moustache. 'Why don't you tell me what you know?'

'I know only what Harry and the others have told me, I was asleep that night,' Christian protested.

'I, however, was awake,' Harry admitted. 'But why should I tell you anything?'

'My dear Herr von Cadolzburg, I know that you and your confederates have spent a considerable fortune buying this land

and building this little community but this is still Germany and the laws of Germany still apply here,' Will said, in a tone which he hoped conveyed the impression that he was attempting to navigate between a joke and a threat.

'I do not think Anna *was* with Max for the entire night on which he died . . . I believe that she may have missed the moment of final crisis, although perhaps she has convinced herself otherwise,' Harry said ruefully.

'Please explain, sir.'

'Anna and Fraulein Herzen stayed with Lutzow all of that last day and when Fraulein Herzen grew tired, Anna sat with him alone. The final crisis came in the small hours of the morning when poor Lutzow began cursing Fraulein Schwab in the most outrageous manner. His language . . . He called her . . . He was using the language of the gutter. He had quite taken against her. Finally Anna could take no more of it and retired to her hut.'

'Why did he take against her?'

'The unfortunate Miss Schwab was the one who had convinced Max to come out here. Her sister had briefly been engaged to him and they had remained close. She had written to him explaining the nature of the *Sonnenorden* and describing our island Paradise.'

'So he blamed her at the end?'

'Yes.'

'Are you sure that she left him alone that night?'

'I saw her go.'

'So who *was* with Lutzow when he actually died?' Will asked.

'That is the tragedy. No one, I think. The poor fellow must have died alone. Shortly after Anna left, he stopped yelling and shortly after that I went to get a drink of water from the well. I saw August and we discussed Lutzow's case. August wondered if perhaps it would be better to send him to the hospital at

Herbertshöhe. We were talking about the various possibilities and it was I who noticed that Lutzow had gone very quiet. We ran to his hut and the poor fellow was quite dead. I knew that Anna would not be asleep so I went for her while August woke Bethman, who, of course, was previously a doctor.'

Will nodded. 'And then what happened?'

'Anna ran into Lutzow's hut and took the poor man's hand but it was too late. She may have convinced herself that there was still life in him but he was already dead,' he said.

'That's all of it? That's the truth?'

'I assure you that that is everything,' Harry confirmed.

Will considered this. If he had caught Anna in a lie it was not an extravagant one. And perhaps, as Harry said, she sincerely believed that she had held Lutzow's hand while he breathed his last.

'How much time elapsed between Anna leaving Lutzow's side and the moment when you and August found him dead?' Will asked.

'Five minutes, not much more than that,' he said.

They had come through the plantations and had now reached the outskirts of the Augustburg again. The settlement looked empty. Empty except for one of the Kanaks, who was anointing the hideous Malagan totem with grease.

'Five minutes? Are you sure?' Will asked.

'I did not start my stopwatch, but I do not think it was a very long time. Perhaps ten minutes at the most,' Harry said.

'If I may be excused? There is little I can contribute to this discussion and our walk has quite tired me out,' Christian said. And he did look rather peaky.

'Of course, Herr Weber,' Will replied with professional gravitas.

Christian gave him a bow and scurried to his hut.

'Shall we continue this conversation under the gazebo?' Will asked.

'If you wish,' Harry replied unenthusiastically.

Will and Harry sat at the table where Ms Schwab's chess game was still lying undisturbed.

'Do you play?' Harry asked.

Will shook his head. 'May I see your remarkable glasses?' Will asked, to relax the young man.

'Yes!' Harry said, pleased.

Will put on the glasses and examined Harry through them. Like all the *Sonnenorden* he was a little too self-satisfied, a little too confident about himself and his decision to abandon the modern world. Fleeing civilization for this small island of theirs could never be an answer to the problems of the twentieth century and you would have to be a bit mad to think that August Engelhardt could be any kind of a prophet or guide for the masses. A man who had done that to himself . . .

'There you are!' Miss Pullen-Burry said, coming upon them from another trail through the jungle.

'Here we are,' Will agreed.

'I have been looking for you Mr Prior. I am in need of your assistance.'

'What exactly—'

'It is most urgent, you must come at once.'

Miss Pullen-Burry's enormous breasts were swaying from side to side in an alarming manner as she advanced towards him.

'If you would explain—' Will began, but Miss Pullen-Burry gave him a look that he could not read and then, quite suddenly, she reached across the dead air and grabbed his wrist.

'Come, come, there's a good fellow,' she said, as if he were a child or an amiable lunatic. Will was too astonished to object and allowed himself to be led across the piazza.

'My glasses!' Harry protested.

Will returned the specs.

'Come, we must hurry,' Miss Pullen-Burry insisted.

'What's going on?' Will asked.

'Fraulein Herzen requires our help,' she answered.

'How so?' Will asked.

'Fraulein Herzen desires to leave Kabakon on the *Delfin* and she is being held here against her will!' Miss Pullen-Burry said, her face scarlet with emotion.

'Is Klaus down there?' Will asked Miss Pullen-Burry.

'He is.'

Miss Pullen-Burry led him along the short path that led to the south beach. When they arrived there was a scene of some confusion. Fraulein Herzen and August Bethman were in the middle of what in Yorkshire would be described as a 'fair old do'.

Bethman was naked but Fraulein Herzen had dressed herself. She was crying, he was yelling.

Contributing to the confusion were Engelhardt, Bradtke, Helena and Anna. Neither Jürgen or Misha, the big Russian, were present but Will had a feeling that they weren't too far off and could be summoned if needed.

Unhappily, Kessler and the German naval pilot were talking together on the beached *Delfin* and doing nothing whatsoever to help the lady.

'What is the meaning of this?' Will asked Miss Pullen-Burry as they advanced on the party.

'It is as I explained, Mr Prior. Fraulein Herzen has expressed a desire to quit the society of the *Sonnenorden* and leave Kabakon with her baggage. Herr Bethman claims that she is under his authority because of an engagement. Furthermore, the Countess Höhenzollern demands that Fraulein Herzen remain here until the end of her employment contract, which runs until December 1907!' Miss Pullen-Burry said despairingly.

'And Klaus and the German sea officer?'

'Neither Karl nor Hauptman Kessler will interfere. They say it is a private matter and not their concern. Oh Mr Prior, this is a clear and obvious case of a young lady being kept against her will. This would not be permissible in England.'

We're not in England you old bat, Will thought, and said: 'Madam, rest assured that I will take care of it!'

'Good! Come now, Mr Prior, keep up with me.'

When they reached the party on the beach the contre-temps had reached some kind of emotional climax. Fraulein Herzen was sobbing, Bethman yelling, Helena and Anna remonstrating with Fraulein Herzen in fast, incomprehensible German while the idiot Bradtke was taking photographs of the whole thing with his blasted camera. Engelhardt was stroking his beard as if this were a play being put on for his amusement.

'You must tell Hauptman Kessler to put an end to this. He will listen to you,' Miss Pullen-Burry said and she dragged Will over to Klaus who, it had to be said, was letting the side down rather badly.

'Good morning, Will,' Kessler said.

Karl, the young pilot, finished his cigarette. 'Shall I cast off?'

'You are near your tide?' Kessler asked.

'I am,' the pilot assented.

'Then you might as well—' Klaus began.

'You will do no such thing!' Miss Pullen-Burry said in a voice dripping with cold authority and even colder fury. Miss Pullen-Burry poked the young man in the chest. 'You, sir, will remain here until I tell you that you may go, and you, Hauptman Kessler, will assist Mr Prior!'

'My dear Miss Pullen-Burry it is not my place to interfere in the private affairs of German citizens.'

'A German subject's rights are being violated and you, Herr Hauptman, are the representative of Governor Hahl!' Miss Pullen-Burry said.

'Bethman and Fraulein Herzen are engaged. This is a lover's quarrel. It is not within my purview.'

Will was beginning to have doubts now, too. 'Perhaps we should let this play out, Miss Pullen-Burry; often women say one thing but mean quite another.'

Miss Pullen-Burry had turned white with rage now. 'You are cowards!' she said.

'I am not overly fond of violence,' Kessler said. 'And getting betwixt lovers is a fool's game.'

'Mr Prior, you must intervene!' Miss Pullen-Burry insisted.

Just then Fraulein Herzen screamed. Bethman had seized the young lady by the hand and was attempting to drag her back to the settlement.

Will took off his straw boater and handed it to Miss Pullen-Burry. He marched across the sand, tapped Bethman on the shoulder and when the man turned, Will shoved him backwards with two hands. 'That's quite enough out of you, my lad,' Will said in English.

Bethman swung a clumsy haymaker at Will's face, which he easily dodged before cleaning Bethman's clock with an upper cut to the point of his prominent chin. The German fell backwards, poleaxed by the blow.

'I say!' Miss Pullen-Burry cried delightedly.

'What do you think you are doing, sir?' Engelhardt yelled.

'This is not your concern, Herr Prior!' Helena added.

Will walked to Fraulein Herzen, took her hand and marched her across the beach to the *Delfin*.

'You have one passenger for the journey to Herbertshöhe,' he said and handed her to the pilot, who helped her on board.

'Come on, Klaus, let's get the lady's trunk,' Will said.

Kessler shrugged and approached the little band of Cocovores guarding the trunk. None of them, Will noted with amusement, had rushed to help their prone colleague.

Will picked up one handle of the trunk and Kessler the other.

'You are not to touch that trunk, the ungrateful little thief has taken some of my things!' the Countess said.

Will looked at her grimly. 'That's enough out of you too, lassie,' he said.

'This is a question of theft!' Engelhardt insisted.

'Funny that, I thought all your property was held in common,' Will said.

'Theft is theft!'

'Another word out of you and you'll be eating your coconuts with no bloody teeth. Savvy?' Will said and shook his fist an inch from Engelhardt's long, aquiline, sunblistered nose. Engelhardt nodded and slunk back.

'Do not trouble yourself, August. We are better off without people of such low character,' Helena bristled.

Will and Kessler carried the trunk across the beach and loaded it onto the *Delfin*.

'Until tomorrow then,' the pilot said dubiously.

Kessler looked at Will. 'Do you think our business will be concluded by tomorrow?'

'I bloody hope so,' Will said.

Fraulein Herzen was bawling now. She leaned over the deck rail, took Miss Pullen-Burry's hand and kissed it. 'Thank you so much, Frau Burry, I am forever in your debt,' she said in her singsong Plattdeutsch.

'You are quite safe now,' Miss Pullen-Burry said.

'Excuse me, madam, we must away,' the pilot said and pushed the *Delfin* into the surf.

In just a minute he had tacked the skiff three times and was a hundred yards from the shore.

The remaining *Sonnenorden* were quite confounded: the ladies and Engelhardt already retreating sullenly up the beach, Bradtke and a now-sitting Bethman staring after the *Delfin* as if they could bring it back by the power of thought alone.

Miss Pullen-Burry was satisfied. 'Thank you Mr Prior,' she said.

Will gave her a curt bow. 'Your servant, ma'am,' he said.

'You will still be in the book of photographs!' Bradtke shouted after the boat as it cleared the bay.

Will wondered if the man had gone quite mad.

'I must go and make my peace with the ladies, if I can,' Miss Pullen-Burry said. 'Thank you again, gentlemen.'

Klaus bowed and Will nodded. When she had gone the two men were left alone on the beach. 'Could someone have made off with my hat?' Will asked.

Kessler shook his head. 'No, there it is,' he said, picking it up from the sand.

Will plonked it on his head and sat on a large tree trunk that had been cast up upon the shore.

Will lit a cigarillo. 'Maybe this will actually help us,' he said, blowing a line of smoke in the direction of New Britain.

'How so?'

'Their existence here is one of stasis. Breakfast, dinner, sleep, reading, worshipping the sun. Their life is frozen in a routine. At the very least this will shake up the jar full of bluebottles a bit, won't it?'

Kessler shook his head. 'I do not know.'

'I *do* know. Why do you think there are no children here?'

Kessler hadn't considered it before and the question surprised him.

'If you're going to build a civilization wouldn't you want children?' Will asked.

'Go on,' Kessler said.

'It's because they add too much randomness. They're unpredictable. The *Sonnenorden* like things to stay the same. Fraulein Herzen's departure will rattle their nerves.'

They stared after the *Delfin* until it was indistinguishable from the white caps on the sea.

'And I have found out one thing,' Will said.

Kessler looked at him eagerly. 'What?'

'Anna Schwab says that she held Lutzow's hand at the very moment of his passing. She was quite adamant about it and I was tempted to believe her.'

'But you did *not* believe her?'

'She was very convincing. Indeed, if it wasn't for Doctor Bremmer's evidence I think perhaps we would be on the *Delfin* with Fraulein Herzen. But Harry told me that Anna did not exactly tell me the whole truth. Lutzow was raving and abusing her and she stepped away from his bedside for a time, and it was during that period that the crisis reached its climax and he died.'

'Of drowning,' Kessler said.

'Of drowning.'

'Most interesting,' Kessler muttered.

'Tell me Klaus, why did you order the autopsy on Lutzow in the first place?'

Kessler shrugged. 'This was the second death on Kabakon in a year. Malaria is not uncommon, but two deaths in so small a group and neither of them thought to take advantage of the hospital . . . '

'No that's not it. What was the real reason?'

Kessler said nothing.

'It was Engelhardt wasn't it? What's in the Abteilung III files about Engelhardt?'

'There is no Abteilung III, Will. The Abteilung III is a myth invented by English novelists. But you are right in a way. There was something about Engelhardt that I did not like. The one time I met him at the Governor's residence, I was disturbed by his manner.'

'What about his manner?'

Kessler smiled. 'I cannot, as you English say, "put my finger on it".'

'Neither can he.'

'What do you mean?'

'The man's a eunuch. Him and Bradtke. Had their balls cut off in Hong Kong so they could live forever.'

'My God!'

'They're raving mad, Klaus, all of them.'

'But it does not mean that they are murderers.'

'No, but it leaves us in a pretty pass. Either Anna *and* Harry are lying about the night's events or someone drowned Lutzow in an impossibly brief interval . . . Or Doctor Bremmer got it wrong, or our Australian somehow ballsed up his corpse delivery so badly that it fooled Doctor Bremmer into thinking that Lutzow drowned.'

'Either murder or incompetence.'

Will nodded.

'What do we do now?' Kessler asked.

Will considered for a time.

'Half of a military policeman's job is just being present,' he said. 'Merely being there changes things. Puts people under pressure. Be present and keep asking them questions, that's the ticket.'

They sat on the beach for a long time under a sickly, greenish sky.

On their walk back to the Augustburg they met Jürgen – the German–American – and Will vainly attempted to converse with him, but he could not draw the taciturn fellow out.

In the Augustburg itself, none of the *Sonnenorden* spoke of the morning's incident. Their hospitality remained intact and that afternoon they invited Miss Pullen-Burry, Kessler and Will to join them for dinner and partake of the coconut feast and the heroin-laced *arak*.

The talk at dinner was of philosophy and literature.

Will retreated to his hut. The floor was still a red pond of tiny crabs and he kept his shoes on as he climbed into the hammock and adjusted the mosquito net.

After a while Klaus came into the hut and to avoid conversation, Will pretended to be asleep and not too long after that, the powerful Bayer heroin dissolving in his stomach converted Will's pretence into a pleasant reality.

Three buildings over, Miss Pullen-Burry returned from her nightly constitutional to an empty dwelling. Helena had gone to spend the night with Fraulein Schwab and with Miss Herzen safely back on New Britain she was alone in the large timber hut. She lit a candle, scooted an impressive menagerie of insects from the writing table and picked up her pen.

She wrote in Welsh, the language of her nanny in Cumberland, because she was certain that no one on Kabakon would be able to understand it.

> . . . *Of the remaining women I say little. The Countess is vain and foolish. Miss Schwab is the living proof of the adage:* cito maturum cito putridum. *In the morning I shall flatter their vanity a little and fully repair our friendship. The men are quite another matter. August Engelhardt is interesting and charismatic: his conversation polite and engaging. I like Harry a great deal and I certainly do not think him capable of murder. Denfer, Christian and Bradtke have barely exchanged two words with me, but I do not sense any deep malice there. My impression of August Bethman*

is of an intelligent, charming man – at times he is so solicitous of me – but such a temper! Miss Herzen is well rid of him. Of all the Cocovores, Jürgen Schreckengost (if that is in fact how you spell such an extraordinary name) is the personage with whom I have had the most 'to say'. And yet we have actually 'said' very little indeed. He has taken a great delight in showing me interesting mammals and birds on Kabakon and has admired my drawings in this journal. I can confess this only to you, Bessie, my future self, that this is perhaps the first time in my life that I have had the suspicion of an . . . one hardly knows how to put it . . . an interest in me which goes beyond the Platonic. Abyssus abyssum invocat. This, I confess, has excited me a great deal but no doubt I am mistaken and what I take for Herr Schreckengost's latent carnality is mere politeness. I MUST NOT make a fool of myself. A note on the late Herr Lutzow . . . There is little sympathy for the man, here. An irascible, discontented fellow it seems. Miss Herzen says that his 'writings' upset some of the others, which was intriguing to me but alas the unfortunate young lady had little time to elaborate as I was attempting to expedite her departure. A note on the birds. One does not think of parrots as social creatures. One sees them in cages by themselves or in ones or twos in closed aviaries. But here they go in great flocks of thirty and more. They crave company and togetherness as we poor Earth-bound mortals also do.

14

Sunbathing

In the wee hours, shortly after Miss Pullen-Burry had retired, Will awoke suddenly, convinced that someone was in the room with them. He clawed at the mosquito net, but when he struggled out of the hammock and lit the spirit lantern there was no one there. He was certain, however, that someone *had* been there a moment ago. He checked his stuff, checked on Klaus, looked out into the piazza, saw no one and reluctantly climbed back into the hammock.

It was hot, airless and humid and despite the heroin in his system it took a long time for him to fall asleep again. Gradually he became aware of light ebbing into the room. He could not remember his dreams, but the feeling of unease remained like the slime trails of the little crabs who had been washed out of their hut and had now gone. The sun had not yet risen and he lay for a time listening to the ghastly squawking of the parrots and the unnamed arboreal creatures shrieking indignantly at one another through the trees.

He looked at the holes he had made in the mosquito net. It would be foolish to stay here much longer without quinine pills or bark. Would Helena or Fraulein Schwab or Miss Pullen-Burry know how to sew and repair a mosquito net? 'My arse,' he muttered. Doubtless, they would take his request as some kind of affront. He scratched at his fresh bites and looked over at Klaus's bed but the German was already up and gone again!

When Will did get out of the hammock he found a cup of lukewarm Turkish coffee on the writing table and a brief note from Klaus: 'Gone to meet the pilot. Have coffee. Good luck.'

Will drank the coffee, pulled on a shirt and walked into the piazza where he encountered a naked Miss Pullen-Burry drawing in her notebook.

'Good morning!' she said happily.

'Good morning Miss Pullen-Burry. What are you—'

'The birds Mr Prior! Jürgen has been kind enough to lend me a book on the subject. Fruit doves, hanging parrots, imperial pigeons, pygmy parrots, blue-eyed cockatoos, friar birds, black-tailed monarchs, atoll starlings, rare Kabakon thrushes, rarer still, the poisonous singing pithooey! And such colour and variety too. Such diversity of song!'

'If you say so, I'm sure,' Will replied.

'So many more birds than in Herbertshöhe!'

'That's because the Prussian officers shoot all the ones in town.'

'Will, over here!' Harry shouted.

He turned to see Harry and the other *Sonnenorden* heading down the trail into the plantations.

'Hello,' Will said.

'The weather will be fine today. Come with us!'

'Where are you going?' Will asked.

'Sol Island. Come with us,' Harry insisted.

'What are you going to do there?'

'We are going to bathe in the sun all day until night fall. You should come along.'

It did not sound promising, but Harry's enthusiasm was a cure for Will's humours.

'We will swim and bathe in the sun,' Miss Pullen-Burry said. 'I am going too.'

'Sea bathing and land bathing does not sound too onerous,' Will muttered.

'It will be a new experience,' Harry said.

'That it will. Everyone else is going?'

'All of us.'

Will had a sudden dread of being left alone at the camp. 'All right, I'm in,' he said.

'Good. Hurry!'

'I shall leave a quick note for Klaus.'

He wrote, 'Gone to Sol Island, I'll try to do some interrogating, back this evening,' and left it on the writing desk.

Will, Miss Pullen-Burry and Harry joined the others on the trail across the island.

'Ah, you have come to join us!' August Engelhardt exclaimed. 'Excellent. I should tell you, however, that for we *Sonnenorden* this is a sacred journey.'

'Uh?'

'We must ask you to be silent until nightfall. We only talk when necessary on Sol Island.'

There goes the interrogation, Will thought.

'May I draw in my notebook?' Miss Pullen-Burry asked.

'I would prefer that you do not,' Engelhardt said sternly.

'What may we do?' Will asked, beginning to have second thoughts about this trip.

'You may embrace the sun! You may feel the divine light!'

Will almost turned round there and then, but seeing his reticence, Fraulein Schwab and Helena marched on either side of him and put their arms through his, which, he had to admit, was an unexpected and charming experience.

They crossed to the far side of Kabakon and there beyond

the black sand was Sol Island, a small rocky treeless outcrop of coral about a quarter of a mile from shore.

'How do we get out there?' Will asked.

'Most of the men swim. The ladies take the canoe,' Harry explained. 'Which do you prefer?'

Will was a moderate swimmer but he was more concerned about the sharks than drowning in the water. 'I'll join the ladies in the dugout canoe,' he said.

The crossing was uneventful and when they arrived at Sol Island the sunbathing began immediately.

'What do we do?' Will mouthed to Harry. Harry showed him. It was simplicity itself. All one did was lie on the rock with one's eyes closed.

After an hour he began to feel uncomfortable and Fraulein Schwab offered to rub him with coconut oil.

The experience was sensual and intensely pleasurable; but after a further hour, even with all the oil, he had begun to blister and Helena was good enough to lend him her parasol.

The rocks were oven yellow and griddle hard. Engelhardt passed around a bottle of coconut milk and heroin. As usual the heroin had its effect and under the multiplications of the sun Will's mind drifted.

He drifted from the island and his fellow bathers. He drifted above the highest birds. Up through the leagues of cool air. The sky was music. The sun a flute. His body a blank stave on which the sun wrote red ghazals. He could see the Earth as a jigsaw carved up by the Germans, Russians, French, Americans, Japanese and of course that most beneficent of gentle rulers, England. He went further. Like Verne's Michel Ardan he walked among moon creatures and saw wonders . . .

'Will,' Helena whispered and woke him gently.

He rubbed his eyes and sat. 'What is it?' he mouthed.

'It is time to go,' she whispered.

'What? Where—'

'It is dusk. It is time to go back to the Augustburg.'

'We slept the whole day!' Another day gone?

He felt weak. Burned. Exhausted. He tried to get to his feet, fell. 'Someone will have to carry me,' he moaned.

'It is always like this the first time,' Helena explained.

'No, I feel ill,' he insisted.

Miss Pullen-Burry instructed Schreckengost, the big German-American, to carry him gently down to the canoe.

The sea voyage revived him a little. 'Are we allowed to speak now?' he asked Miss Pullen-Burry.

'I think so. Did you enjoy the "sunbathing", Mr Prior?'

'Most interesting,' he said. 'Yesterday's unpleasantness seems to have been forgotten.'

'Yes. I believe I was quite successful in smoothing things over with the Countess Höhenzollern. I told her that one must not be too black-letter when enforcing the contracts of servants. Good companions are impossible to find. I advertised in *The Times* and *Manchester Guardian* and not one English or Irish lady would accompany me to New Guinea.'

'They probably thought they would end up in a cooking pot,' Will said.

'That is exactly what they thought, Mr Prior,' Miss Pullen-Burry said with a smile. Will was too exhausted to join them at dinner and made his excuses and retired to the tranquillity of his hut. The sun had given him multiple blisters but the coconut oil had done wonders for his mosquito bites and for the first time in days he found that he could lie down without having to scratch himself like a tinker. He poured himself a generous measure of the Johnnie Walker and was thus happily recumbent when Klaus came in, dressed in a pair of Nanking trousers, half boots and his uniform jacket – as relaxed as the poor fellow could possibly get.

'Did you have a productive day, Will?' Klaus asked.

'Uhm . . . not as productive as I would have liked.'

'You must have learned something. You were gone with them all for twelve hours.'

'Bethman seems to have forgiven me the blow. Miss Pullen-Burry has repaired relations with the ladies.'

'Did you question the others about Lutzow's death?'

'I had hoped to, but apparently sunbathing is a sacred act and must be endured in silence. I shall interrogate the others tomorrow.'

Kessler sat on the chair and waited for Will to speak further, but Will had nothing to add. At least nothing that could be put into words, although he had the curious feeling that he had come to know more about the *Sonnenorden* in this day of silence than in all the previous days' questioning. He was a little more sympathetic to them now. The *Sonnenorden* weren't mad, they were merely Bohemian, different.

The heroin, the sunbathing . . . he had never experienced anything like that before. And that feeling of contentment, he hadn't felt that at ease with himself since before he went to Africa.

'I had the most extraordinary dreams, Klaus,' he said.

'Oh? What about?'

He suddenly felt embarrassed. Flying? The moon?

'Uhm, I don't remember.'

Kessler lit the oil lamp and almost immediately the hut filled with bright white moths. 'What did *you* do today?' Will asked.

'This and that.'

'Listen Klaus, could Doctor Bremmer have made a mistake?'

Kessler put down his book and looked at Will with uncertain eyes. 'I am incapable of judging Doctor Bremmer's competence.'

'You must have read his file.'

'He is a good doctor. The best that was available. That is all I know.'

'References?'

'Sound.'

'Hmmm. Then I'd say we are no closer to an answer.'

'Things move too slowly. I am impatient to leave this place.'

Will sat up in the hammock and sighed. 'I know what you mean. And if the doctor *was* mistaken this expedition moves from an enquiry to a farce. Our question becomes not "who did it" but "why are we here?"'

Kessler nodded and thumbed through his book. Will yawned and after a few minutes Kessler heard him snoring. He watched him with affection. He liked the English. Perhaps he liked them better than the Germans.

He carefully undressed, hung up his uniform and climbed into the Deutsches Heer bed. Unlike Will, he had had a busy and interesting day. With everyone gone he had taken the opportunity to send the Kanak servants on an errand at the far side of the island. He had then searched the huts, but found nothing incriminating. The Countess Höhenzollern and Fraulein Schwab's locked jewellery boxes contained rings and banknotes and Herr Bradtke's curious locked photograph album defied his pick, although it was clear to Kessler what it contained; all men, even in Paradise, had a weakness for the erotic image. Even apparent eunuchs, it seemed.

After this, Kessler had assembled his secret wireless telegraphy machine, taken it to the beach and communicated in Morse with Leutnant Giessen, his deputy. Unfortunately, after instructing Giessen not to permit Fraulein Herzen to leave Neu Pommern and receiving some rather dull information about Admiral Spee's upcoming visit, the 'battery' on the wireless telegraphy machine had died.

But still, the test had worked and the machine had proven its efficacy. This trip to Kabakon would not be completely in vain. The army taught you the virtue of equanimity and the patience of the Imperial Intelligence Service was geological . . .

He picked up his book, brushed away the most impertinent moths and resumed his contemplation of Heine.

The poet was in melancholy mood:

Ich weiss nicht was soll es bedeuten
Dass ich so traurig bin.

Kessler thought how impossible it was to translate this sentiment into another language. The pain was elusive, it was an anguish that came simply from existing in the modern world. *Maladie du siècle*, the French called it, but the century had turned and the new one had begun and the feeling was still there. Weary, Klaus put down the book and blew out the lamp. He fixed the mosquito net about him and lay in the darkness and after a few minutes of drizzle he heard the heavens open. Another day gone, another circumnavigation of the clock that would never return – these, Klaus reflected, were the doleful thoughts one had on the island of the immortals.

15

The Sausage and the Photograph

Perhaps the naked 'sunbathing' had changed something in him, for the next morning Will decided to go shirtless and shoeless – but not trouserless – as he joined Klaus, the Russian, Misha Denfer, Wilhelm Bradtke and August Bethman at breakfast.

Bradtke was fiddling with the lens of his Eastman-Kodak 'Brownie'. The others were eating in silence. Will said good morning and sat; one of the blacks brought him a bowl of the vile *chanak*. The smell of the porridge and Bethman's scowling face removed some of Will's good feelings towards the Order of the Sun.

'I suppose there's no coffee?' he asked.

Kessler shook his head sadly, as if he had already asked the question, wondered why not, explored the point exhaustively, been given some impolite rebuke, and let the matter drop. 'Klaus, you must have some hidden away?'

'If I had known that we were going to stay here for more than twenty-four hours I would have packed quite differently.'

Bethman looked up from his bowl of *chanak*. Doctor he may have been, Will thought, but he was one without a bedside manner. He was a dour, pinched, broody fellow, good-looking if you liked that sort of thing, which the otherwise unimpeachable Fraulein Herzen must have done at one point. Bradtke was his opposite: haggard, skinny, with narrow, reptilian eyes and a squat pug-nose. The ugliest man in camp, you might have said if you could have gotten a look at the big Russian under his beard. '*Chanak* will restore you, Herr Prior,' Bethman said.

Will nodded and stared at the putrid, white, evil-smelling substance in his wooden bowl, which even the flies would not touch. He looked up to find Bethman's gaze still upon him. Will returned the stare and would have held it until doomsday had not Bethman stirred his spoon and returned to his own porridge. Bethman was a boor, but if he and Fraulein Herzen had really been 'engaged' then perhaps the fellow had some virtues: women were mysterious creatures but they seldom completely misread a man.

'You are a keen photographer, sir?' Kessler asked Bradtke after a long silence.

Bradtke smiled and nodded. 'I have taken hundreds of photographs since coming to Kabakon.'

'How heavy is that device?' Kessler wondered. Bradtke passed him the box camera. It was considerably lighter than Kessler had been expecting. 'German?' he asked.

'American.'

'I see,' Kessler said, passing the camera on to Will, who had no interest in it whatsoever.

'With a German lens,' Bradtke said.

'May I ask what the subjects are of your photography?' Kessler wondered.

'For the most part the flora and fauna of Kabakon.'

'Miss Pullen-Burry is fascinated by the local birds,' Will said.

'My ears are burning!' Miss Pullen-Burry said, walking to them from the hut of Jürgen Schreckengost.

'There are two hundred and fifty species at least on this island, Miss Pullen-Burry,' Bradtke announced. 'I have photographed many of them. Herr Doctor Parkinson is making a book of the fauna of New Guinea and I promised to send him some plates if I was able,' Bradtke added.

'Doctor Parkinson has been making his book for as long as anyone can remember,' Kessler said with a light smile.

'Doctor Parkinson is—' Will began, but was seized by a coughing fit that doubled him over. When he had finished he spat yellow bile onto the ground and gasped for air.

'Let me see your tongue,' Bethman said.

'No thank you,' Will said automatically.

'I am a doctor, come now,' Bethman insisted.

There wasn't a man born yet who could resist free doctoring and Will duly stuck out his tongue.

'Hmmm,' Bethman said. He put the back of his left hand on Will's forehead and then took his pulse at the neck.

'What is it?' Will asked.

'You are running a slight fever.'

'A fever?'

'It is of no consequence,' Bethman said.

Will had seen a dozen men die of fever in Herbertshöhe; no doubt their doctor had also told them that 'it was of no consequence'.

'I feel a little weak too,' Will said. 'And, I have had bad dreams.'

Bethman smiled. 'That is normal. It is the shift from a meat diet to a vegetarian one. In a few days you will feel better than you have ever done in your life. I have seen it with everyone who has come here.'

'Not Lutzow,' Will said.

'If he had truly believed, Max would have healed himself. In a way his death was a . . . '

'A what?' Kessler asked, raising an eyebrow in Will's direction.

'A suicide. He willed it. He brought it on himself. That is what I think,' Bethman said.

Will raised his eyebrows back at Kessler.

'Perhaps he had too much of this heroin we seem to consume in such quantities?' Miss Pullen-Burry wondered.

Bethman snorted. 'Bayer heroin is one of the finest products of German science.'

'I'm sure it is, but—'

'If the world beyond Kabakon is to survive this century it will be because of aspirin and heroin and the new sciences being pioneered within the German and Austrian Empires,' Bethman insisted.

Bradtke stopped fiddling with his camera for a moment, nodded vociferously and pointed at his own temple. 'And do not forget the new German sciences of the mind.'

Kessler could not disagree with the implied patriotism in these remarks; of course the *Sonnenorden* had some odd ways but they had not forgotten that they were subjects of the Kaiser. 'Perhaps you are right, Herr Doctor Bethman,' Kessler said.

Bethman nodded. 'I am right. But Germany has become decadent. The race has become weak. Herr Darwin and Herr Malthus show us the way and no one listens. If Germany is to survive and I say *if* advisedly, we must get rid of the weak before they are even born!'

'I'm not sure this is a fit subject for – there is a lady present, sir,' Will said.

'Oh please do continue, gentlemen, I am late for an appointment,' Miss Pullen-Burry said, excused herself and walked off into the plantations.

'What did you dream about, exactly, Herr Prior?' Bradtke enquired.

'In one of them I was flying,' Will said.

Bethman waved his hand dismissively. 'Oh, that is quite common!'

'Be that as it may, I think it *is* something to do with the diet here. I am not myself. Man cannot live on coconuts alone. Not this man, at any rate. Klaus is all right, with his sausage stashed away, but he's pretty close with that and I have to make do with this muck which I—'

'You have brought sausage here?' Bethman said, aghast.

'Why yes, I—' Kessler began, but was interrupted by Bethman getting to his feet, the colour entirely drained from his face.

'How *dare* you!' he said, barely able to contain his anger.

Bradtke rather less rapidly also got to his feet and began yelling for Engelhardt. The dour Russian, Misha Denfer, neither reacted nor said anything, eating his porridge untroubled by any of this. Engelhardt came running out of one of the huts, his fingers stained with printer's ink. 'What is going on?' he asked, 'I was quite in the middle of something.'

'They have contaminated the camp,' Bethman said, his entire body shaking with fury as he pointed at Kessler.

'Steady on, old chap, it's just a bit of sausage,' Will protested.

Engelhardt looked at Kessler and then turned round to look at the Malagan totem. The furious faces painted upon it looked a little more furious than usual. Engelhardt gestured towards the Malagan and said in an embarrassed, halting, whisper: 'Hauptman Kessler, it is in the constitution of the *Sonnenorden* that the slewn flesh of the lower animals shall not be placed within . . . '

But before he could quite get it out, Bethman interrupted and continued for him: 'We will have no meat on the island! We have made an agreement. We will not consume nor kill any flesh. You have broken one of our sacred laws. You have jeopardized our entire existence here!'

'You hear that, Klaus? They're going to have to move to a different island because of your Bratwurst,' Will said.

'You will, sir, please dispose of all such items, immediately,' Engelhardt said.

'We really must insist,' Bradtke said in a milder voice.

Misha said nothing, but he gave Kessler his finest menacing stare, which in truth, Will thought, wasn't that different from his habitual expression.

Kessler shook his head apologetically. 'I had no idea. I knew, of course, that you only consumed coconuts, but I did not think—'

'Well now you *do* know. Could you please dispose of them at once!' Bethman said.

'Take the outrigger canoe and row beyond the reef where you can get rid of all your poisonous foodstuffs. Please do so before the Countess Höhenzollern returns,' Engelhardt said.

The smile faded from Will's face. The mention of the Countess was, to his mind, something of a threat. *You ticked her off once already, Kessler, – do you really want to upset her again? Who knows whom she might write to in Germany?* Will wondered if Kessler would be cowed. And he was, the poor devil.

'*Natürlich,*' Kessler said, 'I do not wish to give offence to anyone.'

There was something about Bethman and Bradtke's look of triumph that was too much for Will. 'No Klaus. Sit down. If they want our sausages, they're going to have to ask us for them, politely, and let me assure you, Herr Doctor Bethman that neither Klaus nor I are bloody rowing anywhere. I don't think you quite understand what our role is here on Kabakon,' he said.

'And what is your role, Mr Prior?' Bethman asked.

'We are here, sir, conducting a murder investigation,' Will said.

This did not, unfortunately, have the effect he was hoping for. 'A murder investigation? Who are you going to arrest? The mosquitoes?' Bethman scoffed.

Will found that he was clenching his fists and the two men stared at one another uncomfortably until, with a low rumble of thunder, the first drops of rain began to tumble out of the black sky.

'I will have one of the Kanaks get rid of the meat you brought,' Engelhardt said to Kessler with a broad conciliatory grin.

'Thank you,' Kessler said.

'But we must do it now. The Countess has been a vegetarian for ten years. She, in particular, would be quite shocked to have learned of what you have done. Come let us repair to your hut.'

Will watched Klaus and Engelhardt walk across the piazza to their hut.

'No one better lay a finger on my belongings!' Will called after them. And this again was where Siwa would have proved invaluable. She would have come at them with a meat cleaver rather than have them so much as breathe on Will's kit.

Will had wanted to ask Bradtke what *he* remembered about the night of Lutzow's death, but he was suddenly so disgusted with the lot of them that he got up from the table and walked out into the trees.

Will was feeling under the weather and had some difficulty until he found a fallen plane-tree branch which he was able to transform into a serviceable stick.

He walked away from the Germans and the Augustburg and their silly prattle and deep into these wonderful old plantations. He admired the breadth of these rubber trees and coconut palms. Nourished by a hot sun and constant rain, the volcanic soil here was dense and luxurious. This was how he imagined New Guinea was going to be when he read the pamphlets from the German agent in Cape Town. So thick was the canopy overhead that he barely felt the downpour intensify, or when it ceased again.

Soon he found himself at the north shore of the island, where he was greatly surprised to see the three ladies, Miss Pullen-Burry, Countess Höhenzollern and Fraulein Schwab, swimming naked in the sheltered black-sand sickle bay. Surprised not because of the intermittent thunder, rain and prospect of the lightning (that kind of eccentricity had ceased to astound him on Kabakon) but because he had assumed that Miss Pullen-Burry's relations with the other ladies were still somewhat strained. And yet here they were, swimming together, laughing.

Will sat on a massive teak-tree trunk cast up upon the shore. A branch snapped behind him and Will turned to see the goblin face of Wilhelm Bradtke grinning at him. Bradtke also had a walking stick with him . . . or a stick that you would use to brain someone with.

'What are you doing here?' Will asked.

'I followed you,' the man said.

'May I ask why?'

'You wished to speak with me about Lutzow?'

Will nodded. Bradtke put down his stick, sat and smiled. It wasn't a wholesome expression. Several of his teeth were missing and his gums were rotted. He was only about fifty years old, but he looked so emaciated and sick that he could have passed for a hundred. Flat on his back with his eyes closed, he would have made a very presentable corpse. Will remembered what Harry had said about the castration and shuddered.

'Where's your camera?' Will asked.

'I left it inside, it does not do well in the rain,' Bradtke said. 'I am sending to Berlin for a better one. Are you interested in photography? Have you read Herr Joseph Lux?'

'I am afraid not.'

'Oh you must! His book *Künstlerische Kodakgeheimnisse* is a masterpiece. He argues that the camera will become the medium of choice in the twentieth century. Our century will be a visual century in a way no previous era has been. We will understand history and science and ourselves through images taken with the camera.'

'I see.'

'You *will* see. The camera is an agent of democracy. Amateurs will photograph and document the world. Do you understand what that means? No longer must we take our orders from the Church, or the State. We can preserve our own truth and nail down our own reality. A thing of vital importance in this Heraclitan age of ours.'

The women in the water laughed again. They were racing each other to a small island a hundred metres from the shore. Miss Pullen-Burry and Anna were swimming frog fashion but Helena was doing an extraordinary cartwheeling motion with her arms that propelled her through the water at a considerable velocity.

Will watched them and then returned to Dradtke's glum, saturnine face.

'If I can turn to Herr Lutzow's death . . . ' Will began. 'You are a man of some understanding, sir. How do you think Herr Lutzow died?' Will asked.

'Malaria, of course.'

'You've had several previous deaths here on Kabakon from malaria, I believe.'

'No, only one death on Kabakon. Two others died after they left here for Herbertshöhe.'

'The one who died, who was that?'

'Alfred Kuchen. He came out almost a year ago, but he only lasted two weeks on the island.'

'Where did you bury him?'

'Nowhere.'

'What do you mean?'

'We did not want to ritually pollute the island.'

'You buried him at sea?'

Bradtke nodded and then frowned. 'Why do you think Lutzow's death was anything other than malaria?'

'Fraulein Schwab says she was with Lutzow when he died and she seems like a sensible and credible young woman.'

'Yes?'

'But there was a brief period of time when Lutzow was left unattended in his hut. I am trying to ascertain if anything untoward happened during this period.'

'Untoward like what?'

'Oh . . . anything,' Will said vaguely. 'When were *you* informed that Lutzow had died?' Will asked.

'In the morning.'

'This would be Sunday morning?'

'If you say so.'

'Indeed I do. And who told you that Lutzow had died?'

'August told me.'

'Which August?'

'Engelhardt. Although I believe Bethman knew too. August woke him that night to confirm that Lutzow was dead.'

'Yes, because of his doctoring skills, I know,' Will said and sighed.

'I'm exhausted, I'm heading back!' the Countess yelled to the other ladies. Will watched her clamber out of the sea, dry herself with a towel and walk into the jungle.

'My problem is motive,' Will said, with a sigh.

'Motive?'

'Why would somebody murder Lutzow? What is there to gain? Did you ever read Cicero? *Cui bono*? That is what Cicero wanted to know. Who benefits from Lutzow's death?'

'No one on Kabakon.'

'Are you sure?'

'Quite sure. This was no possibility of fiduciary gain, for example. Money is irrelevant here. As you know, our property is held in common. Each of the *Sonnenorden* owns an equal share.'

'The Countess was angry with Fraulein Herzen for taking some of her items.'

'Of course. She was leaving the colony. The property would no longer be held in common. Here we are all equal partners in the island and its surroundings.'

'I see.'

'In any case, Lutzow was penniless. He came to us with no money or assets,' Bradtke said.

Will looked at the little German. The man's pinched face was pinched even more. There was something that Bradtke was not telling him. A thought occurred to Will and he let a half smile ruin the symmetry of his moustache.

'This man you mentioned, Joseph . . .'

'Lux.'

'His philosophy is to document everything?'

'Yes.'

'And you have been attempting to do that, here on Kabakon?' Will asked.

'I try to. All the important events, certainly.'

'So let me ask you something. Did you take a picture of Lutzow?'

'What do you mean? Of course I photographed Lutzow.'

'No Bradtke. *After*. Did you photograph him after he died?'

The little German looked at the soles of his feet.

'I think we both know that you did, didn't you Herr Bradtke?'

'Yes,' he admitted.

'I'm sure there were very good scientific reasons.'

Bradtke's face lightened. 'Not for science. For posterity. To document the history of the community,' he said.

Will leaned in confidentially. 'I don't really need to know why you did it. But I do want to see the photograph.'

Bradtke shook his head emphatically. 'I, I, I did not develop it, I . . . ' he said.

Will leaned in towards Bradtke. 'You see, Bradtke, this is the kind of thing that makes me worried. Why would you lie about something like that? What else have you been lying about? What else have you got to hide?'

Bradtke's face had taken on a panic-stricken expression. He fumbled for the right words and then in a whisper said: 'It was for the history that is to be written. A hundred years from now. To make a complete record of our community . . . '

'A noble idea. So why keep it a secret?'

'The, uh, the ladies in particular may not, perhaps have thought it in the best of taste. Fraulein Schwab, Helena . . . I think that perhaps they . . . '

Will put a big paw on the German's shoulder. 'We'll keep it between us, I promise. Now, let's look at this photograph of yours.'

Bradtke saw that protest was useless.

They walked back together through the plantations, Will still feeling vulnerable, careful to keep Bradtke slightly ahead of him. When they reached the settlement Will followed Bradtke to his hut. It was identical in all respects to the other prefabricated dwellings, but for an additional little windowless room off to one side, which Bradtke called a 'dark room'.

Bradtke kept his developed photographs in leather volumes on a shelf bordered by waxed arsenic. He took out a little red album, numbered XXI and with due solemnity handed it to Will. Will took it and thumbed through rather dull pictures of plants, birds and strange beetles, until suddenly he came upon the post-mortem visage of Max Lutzow.

'This is the only one?' Will asked.

Bradtke nodded.

It was hard to examine in the dim light of the hut so Will removed it from the album and took it outside. It had obviously been taken in a hurry, a close-up of Lutzow's waxy yellow face. His eyes were closed, his lips on the turn from red to blue. Shades of grey, of course, in the photograph.

But it gave Will no additional information. Lutzow looked virtually the same as the corpse he had seen in the ice chamber in Herbertshöhe. No blood on the scalp, no overt signs of strangulation or drowning.

'When you did take this?' Will asked.

'The morning after he died.'

'Before the Australian came for him?'

'Yes.'

Will passed the picture back. Bradtke returned it to the album and set it carefully back on the shelf.

He was disappointed.

'Did the photograph help you with your investigation?' Bradtke asked.

'Perhaps,' Will said.

'Is there anything else I can assist you with?' Bradtke asked.

Will shook his head. 'I don't think so. I will bid you a good day, sir. Oh, and Herr Bradtke?'

'Yes?'

'I carry a revolver, so if I were you I'd think twice before sneaking up on me again in the jungle. I was a soldier, sir, and if I were surprised or alarmed I would be tempted to shoot first and deal with the consequences afterwards. Do I make myself clear?'

And without waiting for an answer Will left Herr Bradtke and walked back across the piazza to the hut belonging to the Countess Höhenzollern.

16

The Countess,
the Russian and the American

Will entered the Countess's hut without ceremony. She was at her writing desk, working on a letter. 'Herr Prior! May I help you?' she asked, startled.

'I would like to ask you a few questions about Max Lutzow's death.'

'This is most inconvenient.'

'It will only take a moment. Do you mind if I sit down?'

'Very well then.'

He sat on the ottoman next to the writing table. 'Let me take you back to the evening of Lutzow's death. What do you remember of that night?'

'I was asleep but Fraulein Schwab was with Max when he died and she was so upset that she woke Fraulein Herzen and myself.'

'Did you see the body?'

'No. I comforted Fraulein Schwab in here.'

'Did you leave your hut at all that night?'

'Why would I?'

'Do you recall who was awake at that time? That night?'

'Fraulein Herzen, myself, Fraulein Schwab, the two Augusts and I think Harry too.'

'Everyone else was told in the morning that Lutzow had died?'

'I believe so, yes.'

'And they were told he died of malaria?'

'He did die of malaria.'

'That's one possibility.'

'What other possibility could there be?'

'Murder.'

'But why would someone murder poor Max?'

'Why does anyone murder anyone? Money? Hatred? A *crime passionnel* . . . '

'All of which are impossible here. Money is irrelevant on Kabakon and our passionate natures have been curbed.'

'Bethman seems to be quite a passionate fellow.'

'Our base instinct compels us, sometimes against our will. Bethman is working on controlling himself. He has made much progress on Kabakon. That is why he and we have come here, far from the dying lands of Europe where individual apotheosis and self-mastery is impossible.'

'And yet one passionate slip is all it takes to kill someone.'

The Countess frowned. 'You clearly do not understand our ways yet, Herr Prior.'

'I would like to ask you some questions about your family situation. You are of the Höhenzollern?'

'It will have to wait until another time, Herr Prior! I am busy with my correspondence! The departure of Fraulein Herzen, which you aided, has caused me considerable inconvenience,' the Countess said.

'Madam I merely—'

'Please do not make me raise my voice, sir!'

Will thought about insisting, but he was feeling poorly again and it would surely keep. He stood and bowed. 'Another time then,' he said.

He exited the hut and walked across the piazza.

He found Kessler snoozing inside their hut. He sat down at the writing desk and tried to organize his thoughts.

The picture had been an apparent dead end. And yet . . . And yet, things were not quite right. He could not escape the feeling that he had missed something.

He stared out of the window at the rain. He wondered what time it was.

One o'clock. Two? How long until dinner? What did one do to pass the time around here? He had a glass of whisky, put on his straw boater and walked outside again. He must see this through until the end of the enquiry. Whom hadn't he spoken to about the particulars of Lutzow's death? The American, the Russian, August Bethman.

He marched to the hut two along from his own, which belonged to Misha Denfer and Jürgen Schreckengost. The men were playing whist. Will wondered what immortality would be like playing whist with these two all day long while it rained and rained and rained. Some fates really were worse than death.

'Good day gents,' Will said cheerfully.

Neither man looked up from their cards but Schreckengost grunted 'Good afternoon' in English.

'What are you playing?' Will asked in German.

'A private game,' Schreckengost said and Misha gave Will a look that was either cosmic boredom or contempt – Will couldn't quite decipher which.

'Gentlemen, I'm going to have to ask you to stop for a moment. I have come here at the direct request of the German government to ask a few questions about the death of Max Lutzow.'

Schreckengost nodded and then translated what Will had said into Russian for Misha's benefit.

'He speaks no English or German?' Will asked.

'Very little,' Schreckengost replied.

'You speak Russian?'

'My mother was a Volga German,' Schreckengost said. Will had no idea what a 'Volga German' was but he did not press the matter.

'I would like to know where you gentlemen were the night Lutzow died,' Will said.

'I was sleeping,' Schreckengost said. 'I did not learn of his death until the morning.'

'And him?'

Schreckengost translated the question and Misha said that he also was sleeping.

'In the morning Engelhardt told you what happened?' Will asked.

'Yes.'

'What exactly did he say?'

'That Lutzow had passed. He had been ill.'

'No one was surprised?'

'No.'

'Who did he say was with Lutzow when he died?'

Schreckengost asked Misha and the Russian shook his head and said something which made Schreckengost laugh.

'Well?' Will asked.

'Lutzow was not well liked. He did not embrace our ways. At least not without a great deal of complaint. Likely no one was with him when he died,' Schreckengost said.

Will nodded. 'I was told that Anna, Fraulein Schwab, had held his hand at the last.'

Schreckengost switched from German to English: 'I think she tries to help him but he begins calling her the most outrageous slanders and she leaves him. So we are told.'

'What names?'

'Whore, prostitute, things of this nature.'

Will looked at Misha, who was stroking his thick red beard thoughtfully, as if he was about to contribute some vital piece of information. Will waited but Misha said nothing and after a time went back to studying cards.

'How did you end up here on Kabakon?' Will asked Schreckengost.

'By boat.'

'No, I mean why did you come here? How did you hear about this place?'

'That is a long story.'

'We have plenty of time.'

Schreckengost sighed and smiled. 'What do you do with your life if you are not good at the thing you love?'

Oh Christ he's an artist, Will thought.

'What is the thing you love?' he asked.

'My brother Ossee plays baseball for the Philadelphia Athletics. Do you know baseball, Herr Prior?'

'American cricket.'

'You have it. This is why I left America.'

'You left America because of a game?' Will asked.

'I left because of my brother.'

'How so?'

'Ossee was better than me. He was paid well for this and I was apprenticed to a bicycle maker. He was married. I could not afford to have a wife.'

'So you decided to jack the whole thing in and run away?'

'I took passage to Hamburg and in Hamburg I read one of Engelhardt's pamphlets. I worked my way to Singapore and came here. I met Misha on the way and we came together. We had nothing to offer Engelhardt and the others but our labour, but they did not hesitate to accept us. They took us in with open arms. They are our family. They have given us everything we need. Do you see? I think this is why Lutzow died.'

'Oh?'

'His heart lay on the other side of the Bismarck Sea. He was not with us.'

I'll give the buggers this, Will thought, *they all pipe the same tune.*

Schreckengost pointed at the ground. 'This small, insignificant island, this is all that matters to us, to all of us. The world out there can go hang!'

Misha nodded in agreement, not quite catching what Schreckengost was saying, but appreciating the depth of his feeling.

'It was you and Misha that carried Lutzow to the beach the morning after Lutzow died, am I right?' asked Will. 'You're the biggest and the strongest.'

'Misha and myself, Harry helped also.'

'And how long was he left lying there before Clark, the Australian, came to take him away?'

'No time. We carried him straight to Clark's boat.'

'Clark was there to deliver letters, I gather.'

'Yes.'

'And if Clark hadn't been there, what would you have done with the body?'

'We would have buried him at sea more than likely.'

'Do we play or not?' Misha grunted in broken German.

'We will play,' Schreckengost said. 'Do you have more questions about Lutzow, Herr Prior?'

'It was Fraulein Herzen wasn't it? It was her idea to send Lutzow to Herbertshöhe?' Will asked.

Schreckengost did not appear nonplussed. 'I think so.'

'Did anyone object to that idea?'

'Perhaps Engelhardt did.'

'But Miss Herzen insisted. She insisted in front of Clark.'

Schreckengost shrugged. 'No one made a strong objection. Lutzow was more of that world than our world. No doubt his family will approve of his Christian grave. He is buried as a Christian, yes?'

'They haven't buried him yet. He's lying on a block of ice in a basement in the hospital.'

'He is not buried?'

'No. Not until my investigation into his death is concluded.'

The two men looked at one another for five good seconds, Schreckengost's big gormless face like that of a Boer farmer of whom you've just asked directions.

Denfer grunted again impatiently.

'If you will excuse me, I must get back to my game,' Schreckengost said, regaining his composure.

Will stood. 'Of course, and perhaps you can show me the finer points of baseball at some point. I was a useful cricketer back in the day. I'm sure the games have much in common.'

Schreckengost nodded animatedly. 'Bessie . . . Miss Pullen-Burry speaks of cricket!'

At the mention of the English lady's name Denfer grunted and shook his head. Will put on his straw boater and walked back out into the piazza. The sky was black and the rain coming down in buckets.

Sonnenorden! What a joke. Hardly ever see the bloody sun, Will thought.

The next course of action was obvious, if he could hack it. It was time to visit the ladies again.

He rapped on the Countess's closed door.

'Come in, Herr Prior,' Helena said with resignation.

Will opened the door and went inside. He found the Countess in bed with Fraulein Schwab. Anna was curled into Helena's body, nestled against the older woman's left breast, her hand resting on her belly.

'How can we help you?' the Countess asked.

Her cheeks were flushed, her lips red, her eyes a deep green. Her expression hovered between idle curiosity and annoyance. She was an intimidating woman and she knew it and she was used to command. Used to having her way, even here in utopia. Fraulein Schwab was thin and somehow insubstantial in the foundering light.

Will was determined to show that he was not shocked.

'Well?' Helena asked.

Will sat on the chair at the writing table, where green ants gnawed at the Countess's sealing wax.

'Where's the redoubtable Miss Pullen-Burry? I saw that she was swimming with you earlier,' Will babbled.

'She is still swimming. "To clear her head", she said,' Helena explained.

'I should go swimming too, to clear my head,' Will said. 'In fact everyone could do with a bit of head-clearing around here.'

'What do you mean by that?' Anna asked.

'Your brains seem fugged by heroin much of the time and by starvation for the rest.'

'We have all done much deep thinking here, sir,' Anna said.

'I see little evidence of deep thinking on Kabakon,' Will said. 'I see many half-baked notions that skim the surface of philosophy. I doubt that any of you would last five minutes in the Oxford Union.'

'You are ignorant of our ways, sir, and of much else. If you have no questions I would rather that you go,' Helena said.

Will stood and walked towards the bed. 'I have come to ask about Fraulein Herzen. Do you have any idea why she wanted to leave Kabakon?'

Helena's eyebrows raised and Fraulein Schwab turned her head slightly to regard him. 'She had become less enthusiastic as time passed,' the Countess said icily. 'She was a bourgeois *Haus Frau*. One cannot get travelling companions of quality these days.'

'Why did Fraulein Herzen want Lutzow to be buried in Herbertshöhe?' Will asked.

'What do you mean?' Helena asked.

'The morning that Lutzow died, Clark came to deliver letters. It was Fraulein Herzen who suggested that he take Lutzow back to Herbertshöhe for burial, wasn't it? I was wondering why she insisted upon that? Do you know?' Will asked.

'What are you implying?' Helena asked, sitting up so suddenly that Anna almost tumbled out of the bed.

'I imply nothing. I was wondering why Fraulein Herzen insisted that Clark take Lutzow in his boat.'

'She was bourgeoise, she fixated on niceties. A burial by a priest in so-called consecrated ground.'

'A bourgeoise whose will was stronger than all the rest of you put together.'

'I do not catch your meaning,' Helena said.

'She made Clark take the body in his skiff over the objections of your leader. I wonder why? What were you going to do with poor old Lutzow? Or were you afraid of what the authorities might discover in Herbertshöhe?'

'You go too far, sir!' Helena said.

'Do I madam?'

'Please leave.'

'Or you will do what?'

'Sir, your vulgarity does your already poor reputation no credit,' Helena said.

Will held her gaze and then stood. 'Have a good afternoon ladies,' he said, put the straw boater back on his head and walked back into the rain. A grinning black face was watching him beyond the trees.

'You there!' Will said and the face vanished.

When he got back to his hut Kessler was awake and reading. Will sank into his hammock.

'Ah, Will, I was looking for you,' Klaus said. 'Another day has almost gone and I will be seeing the pilot tomorrow. He seems irritated to be travelling back and forth each morning and I was wondering if perhaps we should . . . '

'We should what, Klaus?'

'Return with him.'

'Don't you want to know the truth about Lutzow?'

Kessler's face remained expressionless. 'It seems to me, on the balance of probabilities, that there has been some sort of error. These people are eccentric but I do not think that they have broken any laws.'

Will shook his head. 'There's been an error all right. And it's these fools that have made it.'

Kessler looked at him intently. 'But the navy—'

'You can't be intimidated by a naval rating nearly ten years younger than you. You're a German officer for Christ's sake!' Will said, slapping his fist into his hand.

'This investigation cannot go on endlessly, Will. I do have other responsibilities.'

Will lit one of his precious cigarillos with a sulphur match. 'Give me a little more time, Klaus. Let me at least interrogate the two Augusts: Bethman and Engelhardt.'

'Do you think you are making progress?'

'I think I am starting to see the beginnings of a pattern. A little more time, Klaus.'

Kessler nodded and they smoked and played backgammon until Will had lost so many theoretical Marks it would take him nine lifetimes to win them back. When it looked like everything was ready for the communal meal, Will revived a little and he and Klaus walked to the long table where they were met by a jolly and content Miss Pullen-Burry.

'An agreeable day?' Kessler asked her.

'I must have swum for twelve hours,' she said ecstatically. 'Herr Schreckengost joined me in the late afternoon and showed me the sharks in the reef.'

'Oh dear, you must be careful, Miss Pullen-Burry,' Kessler said. 'I would get in all sorts of trouble with Frau Forsayth were you to be eaten by a shark.'

'Where *is* Herr Schreckengost?' Will asked. 'In fact, where are the lot of them?'

Harry came walking in from the plantations with a yellow umbrella above his head, but none of the others materialized until the door to Engelhardt's hut opened and they filed out one by one like schoolchildren from the headmaster's office. A conference?

Engelhardt sat down at the head of the table and with no ceremony whatsoever everyone began eating their mashed coconut meat. The talk was diffuse and of normal things. At least, normal here on Kabakon; Schoponhauer, Nietzsche, the decline of the West, the coming apocalypse. Will listened and said nothing. He found Fraulein Schwab's gaze upon him and when he nodded at her she smiled at him.

'Apparently you may be leaving us soon?' Fraulein Schwab asked.

'Who told you that?' Will asked.

'Oh, one hears things,' she said.

'Perhaps,' Will replied cautiously.

'So you finally agree with my diagnosis, regarding the late Max Lutzow!' Bethman said.

'That he died of malaria?' Will said.

'Call it what you like. Lutzow would be alive today if he had more faith!' Bethman replied.

'I've been meaning to ask you Bethman: when you examined Lutzow, did you find a pulse?'

'A pulse? On a corpse! Even in the Augustburg I would like to see such a thing!' Bethman exclaimed.

'When Herr Doctor Bethman examined Lutzow, the poor man was beyond our aid,' Engelhardt added. Then he rose from the table and explained that he had to go and prepare their heroin drink.

'May I accompany you?' Will asked, 'I am curious about the process.'

'Of course,' Engelhardt said.

They walked to Engelhardt's hut, which Will discovered was rather less tidy and more cluttered than the others. Engelhardt opened a jar of *arak* and added the heroin from another jar. The heroin was in its powder form direct from Bayer. Engelhardt carefully mixed the *arak* and heroin. 'Now we add coconut milk, some cane sugar . . . This next part of the process will perhaps seem odd.'

Engelhardt went outside, took the laudanum to the Malagan totem and laid it in front of it. 'It is a sort of offering,' he said. Engelhardt closed his eyes and said a little prayer. Then he brought it to the table. In spite of it being a drug that had no addictive properties, Will found that he was anxious to have his turn, and when the wooden bowl appeared in front of him he took it greedily and drank his fill. After a while his breathing became deeper, his heart beat slowed and a tremendous calm overcame him. It was still raining and his aches and fever had never quite gone away, but none of that seemed to matter much now.

Even his mosquito bites ceased to itch quite so much. The voices grew distant and soon Will found himself sitting on the river stones of the piazza a little away from the table. He watched the others eat and talk. He watched the Malagan statue watch them. Tiredness finally drove him to the dubious safety of his torn net. But the mosquitoes wouldn't harm him here. He yawned and sank deep, deep down. Nothing would harm him here on tranquil Kabakon, one of the safe, forgotten islands that lay between New Britain and New Ireland in the deep and ancient waters of the Bismarck Sea.

17

Engelhardt

Dreams again. Bayer heroin dreams. He was in a place of sweet scents: lavender, poppy, cut grass. He was dreaming of Yorkshire: spring flowers on the moors and a line of black-faced men outside his father's surgery.

But then he dreamed he was walking in the jungle: hideous masked faces watching him from the trees. Finally, he dreamed of Africa: the war, the camp, the men wanting to know what to do.

'Fire! Kill them! Kill them all, sergeant, kill every one of the bastards!'

A hand on his forehead.

'It's all right, Will, it's all right.'

'What?'

'You were having a nightmare.'

'Uh . . . I feel – everything aches.'

'What is the matter?' Kessler asked.

'I'm ill, Klaus,' he groaned. 'I'm ill. Not well. I should never have come here without my quinine.'

'I will get Bethman.'

Will closed his eyes and when he opened them August Bethman was standing there with a stethoscope around his neck. His beard was soft, his hair golden, like a Kraut Jesus.

'He has a temperature of 101 degrees. It is not that serious. I will give him aspirin and heroin.'

'Klaus,' Will groaned.

'I am here, Will,' Kessler said.

'It's never serious with this one. I'll be dead and in my grave and he'll still be saying that it is not serious.'

'Make sure he takes these Bayer aspirin and heroin pills with a little water,' Bethman said to Kessler.

'Tell him to take his Bayer aspirin and his Bayer heroin and shove it up his arse,' Will muttered.

Bethman got up to go, but Will grabbed at his wrist. 'How much heroin did you give Lutzow over the course of his final crisis?' Will asked.

'He was in great pain.'

'Too much opium can kill a man, is that not so?' Kessler wondered.

'We did not kill Lutzow with too much heroin powder or pills, Herr Kessler. Engelhardt is cautious with the supply and I am, or rather I was, a physician. Now is there anything else?'

Will shook his head and Bethman turned to Kessler. 'Make sure he takes those.'

Bethman left and under Kessler's relentless glare Will took his medicine. An hour later he was sitting up in the hammock and he had to admit that his head was starting to feel much better.

Kessler was dressed and looking at Will with affection.

'How do you do?' Kessler asked in English.

'Middling,' Will admitted reluctantly.

'That is German science at work!'

'German science,' Will muttered. 'Where are you going anyway?'

'To talk to Karl, our pilot.'

Will grunted, and as Kessler stared at him he answered an unspoken question. 'Tell him tomorrow will be the last day he has to do this. I think I have nearly everything I need now.'

'Are you sure?' Kessler asked.

'I believe so. And if I can get off this godforsaken island alive, I will tell you all about it in the safety of Governor Hahl's residence.'

'Not here?'

'I think not.'

'Are we to make an arrest?'

'I need to ask a few more questions today. But you and I will not be doing any arresting. If necessary we will return with a troop of soldiers.'

'Nonsense! All German nationals will—'

'Let us hear no more idle talk of that, Klaus, rest assured that Germans murder their neighbours in as great a quantity as everyone else.'

'You can be certain, Will, that the Germans here on Kabakon will cooperate with us.'

Will let him talk but he didn't listen to the predictable string of words that formed into one of Kessler's predictable sentences. Klaus did not understand, but he would. When his lips stopped moving, Will said: 'Maybe you're right.'

'Take your time getting up,' Kessler said, giving him a fey little continental salute, before walking out into the piazza.

One more bloody day, Will thought.

An hour later he was in his cricket flannels and straw boater. The shirt and shoes again seemed unnecessary in the oppressive heat. He found his 'walking stick' and went out into the piazza.

He avoided Harry, Christian and Schreckengost, who were loitering at the breakfast table, and made his way to Engelhardt's hut: the one that was closest to the statue of the Malagan.

'Come in!' Engelhardt said.

Will entered. Engelhardt was wearing clothes, which surprised Will. He had on a kind of coverall made of thick blue cotton, cotton that was stained nearly black by printer's ink, for in this tiny space Engelhardt was running off a series of bills from a hand-cranked press.

'Ah, Herr Detective Prior!' Engelhardt said cheerfully.

'Good morning,' Will said and glanced at one of the drying bills. He read it and translated it in his head thus:

THE SOCIETY OF SONNENORDEN ON THE
TROPICAL PARADISE OF KABAKON ARE SEEKING
A SMALL AND LIMITED NUMBER OF ENTHUSIASTIC
HELPERS TO LIVE THE IDEAL OF NAKED
COCOVORISM IN GERMAN NEW GUINEA.

WE HAVE DISCOVERED THE SECRET TO
ETERNAL LIFE THAT HAS BEEN LOST TO MAN
SINCE HIS EXPULSION FROM THE GARDEN
OF EDEN! IT IS A SECRET NO LONGER!
'SUNBATHING' AND A STRICT 'VEGETARIAN'
DIET ARE THE KEYS TO ETERNAL LIFE!

ON KABAKON, OUR NEW EDEN, WE DO NO
LABOUR AND WE ARE FREE TO PURSUE OUR
INTELLECTUAL PASSIONS! RID YOURSELF OF
THE TYRANNY OF DESIRE. RENOUNCE THE
PRESSURE OF THE WORLD! COME TO KABAKON
AND ALLOW YOUR SPIRIT TO GROW!

Engelhardt saw Will's eyes on the handbill. 'What do you think?' he asked.

'Interesting,' Will said.

'We are going to post them up in Herbertshöhe and give them to travellers throughout the German Pacific. Tell me, in all candour, how do they seem to you, as an outsider?'

Will rubbed his chin. 'Well, I do not think you should say the word 'helper'. That sounds too much like there's going to be hard work and contradicts what you say in the next couple of paragraphs. Maybe 'follower' would be better, or 'disciple', and you should mention that there are ladies here. Naked women will be a big selling-point in Herbertshöhe, believe me.'

Engelhardt frowned. 'We do not wish to attract the wrong type of people,' he said.

'Do you mind if I sit down?' Will asked. 'I am feeling a little under the weather this morning.'

'Not at all,' Engelhardt exclaimed, far too loudly for Will's fragile condition. In a more civilized tone he added: 'You do not look well, Herr Prior.'

'That is what I have been trying to tell everyone.'

Engelhardt had no conventional chairs in the hut, but there were a few awkward-looking stools. Will sat and breathed a small sigh of relief.

'Would you like a glass of water? Or a few heroin pills?'

'No thank you.'

Engelhardt nodded. The silence grew from a few seconds to an uncomfortable half minute, which did not bother Will in the slightest but Engelhardt was keen to get back to his printing. 'As you can see, I am quite busy,' he said.

Will nodded and cleared his throat. 'I am curious how you chanced upon this secret to eternal life,' he said.

Engelhardt shrugged. 'It is no secret. It was known to the ancients. The myth of Eden is a reflection of a truth buried within the consciousness of all mankind. Do you read Doctor Freud?'

Not another bloody doctor, Will thought. 'He too advocates the coconut?'

'He urges us to listen to the voices in our dreams. I have listened. Bradtke listened. We went where our heart told us to go. Without the sun there would be no life anywhere in this solar system. The sun is everything!'

'Fraulein Schwab says that Schopenhauer is the key to understanding your—'

'Fraulein Schwab is a novice in our philosophy! Schopenhauer has been quite exploded. His ideas are irrelevant here.'

'Oh? Yes?'

'Nietzsche has taught us how to live. Nietzsche teaches the doctrine of the Superman. We must cultivate our passions, not reject them. That was the error of the Greeks, as I am sure you know.'

'Uhmm . . . '

'The late Herr Nietzsche desires us to return to the days of the Pre-Socratics, of Dionysius, when the heart did the bidding of reason, not the reverse!'

'In the Bacchanal, if I am recalling correctly from my hazy school days, men were sometimes torn to pieces by followers of the Dionysian cult,' Will said.

'Yes.'

'Do you also believe that sacrifice is necessary to achieve apotheosis?'

'What a perfectly revolting idea. We are vegetarians here, Mr Prior. Have you learned nothing of our ways since your arrival? You still looking at us through the eyes of that world. That world where man can barely keep up! Flying machines, telephones, motor cars. New art, new books. But here we have something more important than all of that: new men! The Romantics had a word for it: *Geistesgeschichte* – the evolving history of the human spirit. You must try and understand, Herr Prior!'

'What I must try and understand, Herr Engelhardt, are the events surrounding the death of Herr Lutzow,' Will said.

'In case you are labouring under a misapprehension, Herr Prior, I must inform you that Lutzow was not torn to pieces by anyone,' Engelhardt said.

'When did *you* first hear about Lutzow's death?' Will asked.

Engelhardt sat on the edge of his bed and shook his shaggy head. 'I do not know the precise hour.'

'Was it on Saturday night? Early Sunday morning?'

'One or two o'clock in the morning, I suppose,' Engelhardt said dubiously.

'Who told you?'

'Harry.'

'He woke you?'

'Yes.'

'Then you went to Lutzow's hut?'

'Yes.'

'And what did you find there?'

'He was dead.'

'Who else was there?'

'No one.'

'What about Bethman?'

'I sent for him.'

'None of the others were awake?'

'Fraulein Schwab came immediately. Later I heard Fraulein Schwab talking to Fraulein Herzen and Helena.'

'Lutzow was dead but you didn't think it necessary to tell any of the others?'

'What good would that serve? They could do nothing.'

Will nodded. Although Engelhardt looked like a tuppenny Don

Quixote, complete with cadaverous countenance, odd uniform and ink-stained beard, his blue eyes were steady and he did not seem troubled or evasive.

'What made you change your mind about the burial arrangements for Max Lutzow, Herr Engelhardt?'

'What do you mean?'

'You were going to bury him here or at sea, but when Clark appeared with a sack of letters, you changed your mind and asked Clark to transport the body to Herbertshöhe.'

'*I* did not ask him.'

'No, *you* did not. Fraulein Herzen did. Fraulein Herzen insisted. Why do you think she did that, Herr Engelhardt?'

'I have no idea.'

'You have no idea why she insisted that Clark take Lutzow's body to Herbertshöhe?'

'None.'

Will paused until he got Engelhardt's full attention. 'I think you made a mistake granting Fraulein Herzen's wish.'

'What do you mean?'

Will smiled. 'We conducted an autopsy on Lutzow in Herbertshöhe. Do you know what an autopsy is, sir?'

'Yes.'

'We have a very good, patient and observant doctor there.'

'Doctor Volker, I know of him, he—'

'Doctor Volker's dead. A new doctor. Bremmer, a diligent, careful young man.'

'A Jew?'

'A Jew, yes.'

'I have known intelligent Jews and unintelligent Jews.'

'Bremmer is of the former type.'

Engelhardt nodded. The room was oddly silent now, as if the inanimate objects were holding their breath and both men could feel the tension being generated by this exchange, a tension as palpable as the electric current or a change in pressure.

'What did your new doctor discover?' Engelhardt asked.

'I think you know what he found,' Will said.

Engelhardt shook his head and looked Will square in the face. 'I assure you that I do not,' he said, his voice as steady as a Colour Sergeant on parade. It was a nice act, Will thought. A very nice act. You could get a run at the Theatre Royal with an act like that.

'Lutzow did not die of malaria,' Will said.

'Oh?'

'Our doctor found water in Lutzow's lungs. He was drowned.'

Will let that sink in.

'Drowned?'

'Drowned. That is peculiar, is it not? How does a man drown in his own bed in the middle of the night, by himself?'

Engelhardt's smile had faded, but he was not bereft. 'I have no idea,' he said.

'Think on it,' Will prodded.

'I have no explanation.'

'Think of one.'

Engelhardt rubbed his inky fingers through his beard. 'Perhaps I too should approach it like a policeman,' he said.

'Be my guest.'

'You have four witnesses who say that Lutzow died in his bed of malaria, but your doctor in Herbertshöhe says that someone drowned him. That does not make any sense, does it?'

'No,' Will agreed.

'Obviously your doctor has made an error.'

'And what about Fraulein Herzen? Why was she so insistent that Lutzow be taken to Herbertshöhe? Why did she wish to go there herself? What do you think she is telling the governor right now?'

'Nothing. I assure you of that.'

'Why?'

'Because there is nothing to tell. Lutzow died in his bed . . . of malaria. Your doctor has made a mistake, doubtless. He will gain notoriety if this becomes a cause célèbre, rather than what it transparently is – a simple case of a man in the tropics dying of a common tropical disease.'

Will nodded to himself. He was cool as a cucumber, but perhaps his eye had twitched just a little at the mention of Fraulein Herzen . . .

'Of course we will interview her thoroughly when we return.'

'I am sure you will do your job with consummate professionalism,' Engelhardt said coolly.

Will felt the ice and it unnerved him.

He took a step back. Literally and figuratively. He did not want to push the thing just now. Engelhardt was a rum cove and no mistake. It was perhaps better to let the bones rattle around in the soup for some more hours.

'Of course,' Will said. 'If the doctor *has* made a mistake then this whole investigation has been an utter folly.'

'I am amazed that someone of your perspicacity could be taken in. Let our own doctor, the esteemed Bethman, conduct your "autopsy" and I assure you he will find no drowning mark upon Lutzow.'

Will nodded slowly. 'You may be right, sir.'

Engelhardt began a reply but a coughing fit from Will stopped his flow.

The smile returned to Engelhardt's face and he put his arm about Will's shoulders. He was a tall man, taller than Will by two inches, but so *very* thin and the coverall seemed to extenuate his thinness. A moderate wind could blow him over.

'I like you Herr Prior and I trust you. I am certain that you are not going to let a little middling Jew doctor come between us,' Engelhardt said.

Will nodded. 'Do you have a glass of water by any chance? As I said earlier I am really not feeling myself today,' he asked.

Engelhardt poured him water from a covered pewter carafe. 'Here,' he said.

Will thanked him and drank.

'*Also*,' Engelhardt said.

'*Also*,' Will agreed. 'I must go.'

'To Herbertshöhe?'

Will set down the cup. 'We have missed our chance today, but perhaps we shall go back tomorrow.'

'And what will you tell Governor Hahl?'

Will's head was thick. He took a minute to gather his wits. 'I have uncovered no actual evidence of foul play. As you say, Doctor Bremmer has likely made some sort of error.'

'I am happy to hear it!' Engelhardt said delightedly. 'But if this is your last night we must have a feast in your honour.'

Will shook his head. 'That is not necessary. Neither Hauptman Kessler nor I wish to put you to any trouble.'

'Nonsense. It will be the ceremony of the new moon tomorrow. It is an occasion for a feast on Kabakon.'

Will swayed a little on the stool. He touched his forehead. His fingertip came back hot and clammy.

'If you will excuse me, Herr Engelhardt, I think I will lie down. As I say, I am rather . . . '

'I will send for Bethman.'

'I have already seen Bethman. He has prescribed aspirin.'

'You must take it!'

'I will. Good day, sir.'

'Good day to you.'

Will left, but instead of going to his hut he walked with his stick as fast as he was able to the beach. The journey was not far but he had to stop several times to catch his breath.

Kessler was standing on the sand gazing out to sea.

'Good morning, Will,' he said.

'Has he come yet?'

'He has been and gone.'

'Damn it.'

'What is it?'

'We should have gone with him.'

'What is the matter?' Kessler asked, with concern.

'I fear I may have overplayed my hand.'

'With Engelhardt?'

'He may want to do us a mischief.'

Kessler shook his head. 'Engelhardt will not harm us.'

Will sighed. 'I suppose we could not have gone anyway, could we? Not without Miss Pullen-Burry.'

'She may not go with us.'

'Indeed not?'

'She is quite enamoured with the place. And I believe she has formed an attachment with the American.'

'Schreckengost? You astound me. I would not have thought it. He is as dumb as a post. As dumb as a baseball club, I should say,' Will said.

'Miss Pullen-Burry is no beauty.'

'For shame, Klaus, I wonder that you can speak so of a lady!'

'You are quite right. It was ungallant.' Kessler examined his friend. 'You look pale, Will.'

'I feel awful.'

'Come, let us return to the "Augustburg" and prepare our sea bags. That young pilot will be here tomorrow with the flood, whenever that is. But oh, my goodness, here comes a vessel now!'

It was, however, only the dugout canoe Will had seen on the north shore. It was being paddled by Schreckengost, Miss Pullen-Burry, Christian and Harry. All were naked, though Miss Pullen-Burry had taken the precaution of carrying a parasol.

The sky was darkening in the east - a prelude to yet another storm. The Germans and Miss Pullen-Burry paddled into the little bay. The canoe landed and Miss Pullen-Burry stepped from it, radiant with pleasure. 'Two sharks and a ray, Mr Prior!' she said.

Will was almost used to her nakedness now, but he couldn't resist. 'You could put them in your book if you had a place to put your book.'

'Salt-water crocodiles also. Thirty feet long, Herr Schreckengost says,' Miss Pullen-Burry exclaimed.

'I shiver in horror, Miss Pullen-Burry,' Kessler said.

While they were standing there next to the canoe on the glittering sand Bradtke wandered in from the plantations with his box camera and asked to take a photograph of them. Will smiled and wondered when the last time was that he had had his photograph taken. Years ago, probably on campaign.

Click went the action and the light bouncing off him was preserved on film.

Half way back to the Augustburg, Will stopped to take a breather.

'My dear fellow, you are quite unwell. You must return to bed at once,' Kessler insisted.

'Where do you think I'm going?' Will replied, sweat dripping from his forehead.

'We shall carry you!' Harry said.

'You shall do nothing of the sort,' Will protested, but carry him they did. Schreckengost, Harry and Klaus making a chair between them.

Thunder was rolling across the strait and it was raining again.

'We must go faster,' Kessler said.

When they made it back to the hut Kessler and Harry helped Will lie down in Kessler's bed.

'I shall take the hammock tonight,' Klaus said.

'Pour me some whisky, please,' Will asked.

Harry poured him a measure of the Johnnie Walker.

'How is your investigation going?' Harry asked, handing him the glass.

Will took a sip of the agreeable spirit. 'Our main problem, Harry, is that Lutzow did not die in his sleep.'

'Oh?'

'He was drowned. Someone drowned him here on Kabakon. Who do you think would do a thing like that?'

'No one!' Harry said.

'I think Fraulein Herzen knew who did it. I think that's why she wanted off this island.'

'Stuff! Fraulein Herzen was weary of the Countess – that is why she wished to leave. Especially after Bethman was such a bully to her. Drowned? How could anyone tell if Lutzow had drowned? It is absurd,' Harry insisted.

'Doctor Bremmer found water in his lungs,' Kessler said.

'Lutzow died in his sleep. I was there!' Harry said.

'I thought no one was there.'

'Your doctor is mistaken,' Harry insisted.

Pain wracked through Will's chest and he coughed and groaned. Kessler hurried Harry from the room. Will rolled over on his side and dozed for a while. When he came to, Kessler was sitting next to the bed with a look of infinite concern on his face.

'They were lying, Klaus,' Will said.

'Are you sure?'

'Somewhere in this camp there's proof of it,' Will said.

'I doubt that.'

'Why?'

Kessler smiled. 'When you all went sunbathing I searched the entire compound. There was nothing.'

'Nothing at all? Nothing suspicious?'

'Nothing at all that I could find.'

'Did you search Bradtke's hut?'

'Yes.'

'And?'

'Nothing.'

'What about among his photographs?'

'Ahh, well.'

'Yes?'

'A locked album of photographs which I took to be . . . uhm, indecent in nature.'

'A castrato looking at dirty pictures?'

'I have heard of stranger things.'

'Me too, but still . . . ' Will groaned.

'You must sleep, Will. Here, open your mouth. Take these pills,' Kessler said.

'Yes.'

When Will opened his eyes again it was dark. The hut was empty but he could hear the Cocovores at their dinner. He was cold. He put on a shirt, found his shoes and walked unsteadily into the piazza.

He joined the table in mid conversation. Klaus looked at him with concern.

'Please continue,' Will said, trying not to draw too much attention to himself.

'I was asking the Countess how she is related to the Kaiser. I have been consulting my charts of the Royal lineage and I am at a loss to know,' Kessler said.

'He is a third cousin, twice removed. From the inferior Prussian branch of the family, I am sorry to say,' Helena replied. 'You, I take it, sir, are a subject of the mad princeling in Bavaria?'

Klaus did not take the bait and merely nodded.

'How are you feeling now, Will?' Miss Pullen-Burry asked, touching his forehead after he had sat down.

He was touched that she had used his first name. 'I'm not sure,' he told her.

It was raining heavily and between his feet Will saw that the little scarlet crabs were back. He was offered food, but he couldn't eat. *But it was a special food to celebrate the new moon*, he was told. He tried a little, but it was no good. His head was on fire again. He got to his feet.

'You must excuse me, I'm afraid. I should have remained in bed.'

'Shall I assist you back?' Klaus asked.

'Sit there! I'll be all right.'

As he was walking back to his hut he caught sight of Fraulein Schwab on her knees before the Malagan totem. She looked pale and lovely in the moonlight. It was an arresting scene.

The truly astonishing thing happened next.

One of the black servants came out of the jungle, grabbed Fraulein Schwab by the hair and with a little screech from her, he dragged her away.

'Ye Gods!' Will said, and followed them as quickly as he was able.

He found them two hundred yards away, under the trees deep in the plantations. Both Kanaks were there and Miss Schwab was kneeling before a white man wearing a hideous wooden mask that concealed his eyes and face.

Will crouched low behind a wild patch of river orchids.

'Do you still object?' the man asked.

'I cannot say,' Fraulein Schwab said.

One of the Kanaks slapped her face and Anna burst into tears.

'Do you still object?' the man asked again. Will edged closer and recognized Engelhardt's ink-stained beard peaking out at the bottom of the mask.

'No, I do not object,' Anna said between sobs.

Engelhardt muttered something to one of the blacks and he lifted Fraulein Schwab onto his shoulder and carried her bodily back to the camp.

Will shambled as fast as he could back through the plantations. When he made it back to the hut Kessler was waiting for him anxiously.

'Ah there you are—' he began, but stopped when he saw Will's face. 'Is there something wrong?' he asked.

Will began rummaging in the German's trunk.

'What are you doing, Will? Those are my things!' Kessler said.

'The game's up, Klaus. They mean to do us in. Where's your pistol? Ah, there it is! Now we're talking!'

Will grabbed the gun, but as he stood up suddenly, his head began to reel.

'Give me that!' Klaus said.

Harry was in the doorway. Behind him the rain was pouring down in great sheets.

The hut was spinning. Klaus's face was spinning.

What was a gun doing in his hand?

Harry was coming towards him. Will heard Helena's voice: 'My God he has a gun, he will kill someone!'

'Give me that!' Harry said.

Will pushed him backwards and pointed the shaking gun at Harry's ribcage. 'Now, my friend, we are going to get some answers.'

18

The Murder of Max Lutzow

Will swayed forward and righted himself. He blinked slowly. The floor was swimming. Crabs, flower petals. A sea of indigo and vermilion. A perfume river.

He shook his head and called himself to attention. 'Why did you kill him, Harry? Why did you kill Lutzow?' he demanded.

'Lutzow killed himself.'

'How?'

'He did not believe.'

'He talked himself to death,' the Countess added from the doorway.

'He talked himself to death?'

'He said we were all going to die. He convinced himself, he had a big mouth,' Helena said.

'And, no doubt, a bigger pen,' Will said, with a sudden flash of insight.

Harry looked at the Countess. The look explained everything.

'Christ! It was all of them, Klaus. They all killed him. They killed him because he wanted to leave. He wanted to write about what he had seen. He wanted to condemn them. They feared his words!' Will said, ecstatically.

'Utter nonsense,' Harry murmured.

Will pointed the Luger at the Countess. 'It was Engelhardt, wasn't it? He gave the order.'

'What about Fraulein Herzen?' Klaus asked.

'Who? Fraulein Herzen? Oh yes. Fraulein Herzen. He let her go because he knew she wouldn't talk. Won't talk. But had we not been here, they would have killed her too! Wouldn't you?'

'She is harmless,' Harry said.

'How is she harmless? She was more of a risk than Lutzow. Yes, more of a risk . . . she knew about the murder,' Will said. 'Unless . . . unless she was compromised, somehow. What did you do to her?'

'You're raving, Will,' Harry said.

'What did you do to her? How do you know she will keep silent? There must be something . . . some hold over her. Blackmail. Yes! Something, a letter, a document . . . A photograph. Bradtke! Yes! That's it!'

Keeping the gun pointing at them, Will motioned Helena and Harry to Klaus's bed.

'Will, can you explain what is happening?' Klaus asked again.

'Bradtke took more photographs! The locked album!' Will said.

'What?'

'Keep them here, Klaus, don't let them leave. If they try to leave shoot them!' Will said, handing Klaus the Luger.

'Where are you going?' Kessler asked.

'The album, Klaus. That's why they let Fraulein Herzen go. They knew they could blackmail her. All of them did it. They all did it! Do you see? How many bullets in that thing?'

'Seven.'

'Plenty. Wait here, Klaus!' Will barked and hobbled outside.

Rain. Heavy rain. Cold, head-clearing rain.

He looked over at the diners at the long table, but none of them were paying any attention to him. He darted to Bradtke's hut and started rummaging through his albums. He pulled them off the shelves, and out spilled photographs of frogs, trees, marsupials and, of course, the Cocovores going about their daily business.

He found the locked album. No, not a photograph album. *A confession.* He knew what would be in there.

They would have taken Lutzow to one of the lava rock pools on the south shore. He would not have been bound, because Bethman had dosed him heavily. His eyes would be rolled to the back of his head. The pictures would form a story. Each of the *Sonnenorden* looking solemnly at the camera. Each showing his hands, palms up. Lutzow lying on the ground in front of them. All of the *Sonnenorden* there, lifting Lutzow to the rock pool, save Bradtke taking the photographs. All of them shoving him face first under the water. They would be expressionless. But they are not drugged. They know what they are doing. Each one of them a discreet entity murdering their fellow Cocovore.

We do not eat meat, we renounce the tyranny of the will, we do no violence. Fraulein Schwab's hollow words echoed in Will's ears.

He banged at the lock on the album. It didn't break. He needed a knife to cut through the leather.

He looked out of the window. Dawn was a long way off.

When did the *Delfin* come? When was the flood?

A knife, I need a knife.

He looked through the shelves and under the bed. Nothing. He had to see the photographs. He had to see the proof! Finally, he found a pair of scissors and began cutting and sawing through the hard leather.

He lifted the leather skin from the cover.

A shadow on the book.

He looked up to see Bradtke standing in the doorway. 'What are you doing!' he yelled.

This was the moment. This was it. Why Will was here.

I am the vector of this story. I am justice. I am redeeming myself for my sins by bringing law to this island and justice for this one dead man.

'What have you got there?' Bradtke said, his face contorted with rage.

'Proof. Proof that you murdered Lutzow,' Will told him, his voice breaking into a triumphant higher register.

'What is your proof?' Bradtke demanded.

'These photographs,' Will said, shaking the book.

'You are deranged! No doubt it is the first flush of the malaria. Let Bethman take a look at you,' Bradtke replied calmly.

'Get back!' Will snarled, slobber drooling from the corners of his mouth.

'Herr Prior—'

'Out!' Will said grabbing a candlestick holder. 'Out or I'll smash your murdering skull in!'

'Herr Prior, you are making a—'

Will brought the candlestick holder down on Bradtke's head and he crumpled to the ground like a collapsing concertina.

'That'll teach you!' Will said and walked into the plaza with the book and the candlestick holder. He shuffled to his hut, where Kessler was still keeping the gun pointed at Helena and Harry. Will took the Luger from him and handed him the sealed book of photographs.

'Please tell me what is going on, Will,' Kessler said.

'They murdered Lutzow. They took photographs of the actual crime. That's why they let Fraulein Herzen go. They knew she wouldn't say anything. She was implicated along with the rest of them,' Will said.

'You are hallucinating, Will. It is the heroin, perhaps,' Harry said.

'You have taken leave of your senses,' the Countess declared.

'Klaus and I are the only sane men here,' Will countered.

'What are you going to do, Will?' Harry asked.

'Klaus and Miss Pullen-Burry and I are going back to

Herbertshöhe with this book and then we are going to come back with the navy and lift the lot of you.'

'You are such a fool,' Helena said, her eyes wide. 'I knew you were an idiot from the moment I set eyes on you.'

'Shut up or I'll put a bullet in you,' Will said.

'What is going on in here?' Miss Pullen-Burry asked from the doorway.

'They murdered Lutzow,' Will replied. 'They murdered him and took photographs of themselves doing it. It was a kind of initiation. The thing that bound them together. The proof is in this album.'

'Are you quite sure?' Miss Pullen-Burry asked.

'What should we do, Klaus?' Will asked. 'We must not let them escape.'

'We must lock them in one of the huts until the pilot comes in the morning. I will send him back for a troop of soldiers.'

'I will not permit that,' Engelhardt said from behind Miss Pullen-Burry, with an air of menace in his voice and a grim look on his face.

'Your days of permitting are over, Engelhardt. I saw your game with Miss Schwab. I know everything. Back up! All of you outside!'

'Put the gun down, Will,' Harry insisted.

'It's over, Harry. Finished. Do not move!'

Will forced them outside into the plaza. 'Nice and slowly. I want you all to walk to Bradtke's hut, where I'm going to lock you in.'

Fraulein Schwab offered Will her hand. 'Give me the gun, Will, you are beside yourself.'

'You don't think I won't shoot you? Watch me. Now, I want all of you to go over to the hut, I want everyone inside!'

No one moved.

Engelhardt reached over to the communal table where he had been cutting up bananas and grabbed a large steel machete. 'Put down the gun, Herr Prior,' he said. 'This has gone beyond a joke.'

'Do you want to lose the number of your mess? Understand me, Engelhardt, I am giving the orders! I've got a magazine full of bullets in here, more than enough to take care of the lot of you. Miss Pullen-Burry: escort the ladies to the hut, if you please.'

'Stay where you are Miss Pullen-Burry!' Engelhardt said and began marching towards Will. 'Put the pistol down, Herr Prior. Weapons from your world will not work here on Kabakon,' he insisted.

'Oh no?' Will replied, and to dispel any creeping doubt, pointed the gun in the air and pulled the trigger.

Nothing. He pointed the gun at Engelhardt's chest and pulled the trigger again.

Click.

Another click.

'What did you do?' he asked, looking at the Luger in panic.

'I told you that your weapons would not work here,' Engelhardt replied.

The others looked at Engelhardt wide-eyed. Harry and Anna fell to their knees.

'It's a trick! He must have found the gun and filed the firing pin.'

But it was too late. Engelhardt had his machete. The big Russian had an iron skillet. Jürgen Schreckengost had an axe handle. Bethman had grabbed a knife. Even Christian was advancing on Will with an adze. Will raised a defensive arm.

The blows came. A crash into his ribs. Another one in his neck.

They knocked him to the ground. He curled into a ball.

Kicks, punches, hands tearing at his hair. Searing pain along his spine.

Blood in his mouth. A hard kick in his testicles that sent a screaming funnel of white-hot lead into his brain.

'The *coup de grâce*,' someone said, and the skillet came down on his head. And then –

Nothing at all.

19

Bethman and Engelhardt

Void for an indeterminate time. Void. And slowly, *slowly*
awareness of self.

Breathing.

Pain.

Voices.

He was being dragged by the hair.

His skin was alive with hurt.

He felt like he was being flayed.

The dragging stopped.

More voices.

An argument.

He opened his eyes.

Swarms of mosquitoes about his face. Ants of every phyla
crawling over him. He had been tied hand and foot. He was next
to Klaus in the centre of the plaza. Tied to the Malagan. An
argument was in progress between Bethman and Engelhardt.

'He is dead anyway of the malaria,' Bethman was saying. 'It
will be quicker and more merciful for him.'

'There are ways of solving this without further violence,
Bethman!' Engelhardt said.

'We must act at once.'

'We must consider this!'

'We must act! They are a cancer that must be cut out if we are to live!'

'Bethman is right,' Harry agreed.

'No!' Engelhardt insisted.

Will saw the blade hover before his eyes.

'We must do it!'

'No!' Engelhardt yelled.

Fraulein Schwab screamed.

Engelhardt grabbed Bethman by the arm.

Will's head was throbbing.

His ears were ringing.

A knife flashed.

A machete blurred.

Will closed his eyes.

A thud of metal on bone.

A collective gasp of horror.

Bethman staggering backwards, trying desperately to remove Engelhardt's machete from his neck.

Screams.

Bethman stood there for a moment and then fell sideways, blood pouring from an artery in a jet of frothing crimson.

He looked at Will in bafflement.

He looked at Will until his legs stopped kicking.

Helena was yelling hysterically.

Anna slapped Will on the face.

'Look what you've done!' she screamed. 'Look what you've done!'

More slaps.

Nails tearing at his cheek.

More voices.

More pain . . .

20

The Peace that Passeth all Understanding

An ellipsis of time. Engelhardt's face. 'Speak to me, Will, unburden yourself.'

'I have nothing to unburden.'

He gave Will something to drink. He spoke of Doctor Freud. Will listened, understood.

'Talk to me, Will, tell me why you are here.'

'I am here to put you in prison.'

'For what?'

'For murder.'

Engelhardt shook his head. 'You were wrong, Will. Quite wrong.'

'I was right and you know it! I've got the proof!'

'What proof?'

'Bradtke's photograph album.'

'Herr Prior, here, let me show you.'

He showed Will the album. Opened it. Ladies in various states of undress. Ladies in bloomers on bicycles.

'Lies!'

'It is the truth.'

'Bradtke's a eunuch!'

'He is not.'

Will looked at the photographs, at the album. How could this –? But he was so sure . . . 'Another trick!'

'No trick. You have deceived yourself.'

But that would mean. All this . . . Bethman's death . . . for nothing.

He shook his head. Tears were rolling down his cheeks.

'Unburden yourself. Tell me everything. Talk. Everyone here talks to me. Everyone unburdens themselves. What is the evil that hounds you?'

Will thought about the evil.

The *great* evil. He named it.

'Louder.'

'Africa,' he said and sobbed.

'What about Africa?'

'I shot them. Dozens of them. Men, women, children. I shot them down.'

'Tell me, Will . . . '

'They were trying to escape. I was a guard. They were starving. That's all. Hungry. Watching their children starve.'

'You were the guard of a prison camp?'

'A *concentration* camp. A guard. They gave me a medal. For killing them. For killing them all.'

'I'm sure you did what you thought was best. You had no choice.'

'We all have a choice. The law does not allow . . . does not allow . . . '

'What?'

'The law does not allow duress as an excuse for murder.'

'You were at war, Herr Prior.'

'War . . . yes.'

Engelhardt's bony hand on his forehead.

'It's all right, Will, it's all right.'

He chanted a blessing.

Om shanti om.

Om shanti om. Om shanti, shanti.

The peace that passeth all understanding.

'Join us, Will. Leave your troubles back in the dead world.'

'I can't join you.'

'Consider it, Will. That world is dying. That world is dead. "Cunning is the water and the rock. On that black coast there is no walker and no voice." They are all doomed. Only we shall live. Consider it.'

Will looked at him.

Ink-stained beard. Gaunt cheeks. But his eyes were gentle, kind, sincere. The sun was down behind the coconut grove and from the east the sky was a darkening purple.

'No. I won't do it.'

Engelhardt sighed. 'Think on it.'

'No!'

'I must tell you that you can expect no help from your navy pilot. We flew the quarantine flag and he understood, and scampered back on board his ship.'

'More lies!'

'The truth. Here, Will, drink this.'

'What is it?'

'It is for your own good. It will help you sleep,' Engelhardt said, and left.

The sun sinking into the plantations.

The sun under the Earth's curve. Dusk. Night.

Will riding into the dark on the broom of a night witch.

'Out there, Will, God has abandoned man,' Fraulein Schwab said.

'But here we see him along the backbone of the sky,' Harry said. 'We read his numbers in the quipu of the Inca, in the

Parikarma of the Jain. A paper in the new *Annalen der Physik: Ist die Tragheit eines Korpers von seinem Energieinhalt abhangig?*

'Now that we have uncovered God's secret, *we* may become gods.'

'Energy and matter are one.'

Harry gave Will rainwater from a coconut husk. 'Do you see, Will? We can live on the sun alone. We have always known it. We have merely forgotten how.'

'The navy will come for me.'

'No one is going to come for you. The Malagan watches out for us. Protects us. Gives us eternal life. We have been poor devotees. She cannot have been content with the blood of mere animals . . . '

'It is no use, Anna, he's a fool. I saw it from the moment he stepped onto our beach.'

Night.

The yellow moon.

Stars.

Orion, crazily inverted.

Must stay awake. Concentrate.

A conversation on the far side of the piazza.

'Miss Pullen-Burry, you are either with us or you are against us.'

'You must do as you see fit, it is not my affair,' Miss Pullen-Burry said.

Miss Pullen-Burry! Will thought, suddenly remembering her.

Only one eye would open. He struggled against the rope but he was still tied fast to the Malagan.

Jürgen and Miss Pullen-Burry were standing next to one another, holding hands like bride and bridegroom. Schreckengost said something to her in a whisper. She nodded and stroked his arm affectionately.

'You will help us?' Engelhardt asked in a murmur.

'I am content to watch, sir. Ceremonies of these kinds have always been fascinating to me. I saw something similar in Jamaica, long ago,' she said, and then for emphasis she raised a finger. 'But I will take no part in violence. That is not my way.'

Bradtke looked at Engelhardt but that, apparently, was good enough for him.

They would make her play her part when the time came. All must be complicit here.

'Miss Pullen-Burry! You can't let them kill us!' he yelled at her.

Everyone turned to look at him. Miss Pullen-Burry shook her head. 'This is not my concern, Mr Prior. I am a guest here on Kabakon and as such I respect their ways and local customs.'

'They will never let you go! You will have to stay here forever!' Will said desperately.

'Why would I want to go, Mr Prior? Why would I want to go when I found here everything that I have been looking for in all my travels?'

Jürgen smiled and put his arm about her.

'No! Go and get help!' Will croaked.

Miss Pullen-Burry walked over to him. Her face was pitiless. 'You have got yourself into this pickle, Mr Prior. It is not for me to get you out. You will have to bear the consequences. You have abused your position as a guest on this island. Abused it most severely. I am sorry for you. But there is nothing that I can do or indeed would do to help you.'

She shook her head and walked out of his eyeline.

'You've all gone mad! Eventually the authorities will come. Are you going to kill the whole German Navy?' he said.

'They will believe what we tell them,' Harry said.

'They're going to kill you, Miss Pullen-Burry! They're going to kill you, too!'

'Be quiet, you have caused enough trouble! Silence him!'

They hit Will with bamboo canes until he was cowed into silence.

The voices were fading.

He was fading.

His body ached. His forehead burned with fever.

Rain. Terrible rain.

Will looked in the puddle. He sobbed in its mirror. He went through the mirror to the other side.

'Siwa!' he sobbed. 'Siwa! I need you!'

He and Kessler were dragged into a hut.

There were drums.

Will opened his one uninjured eye.

'Someone please help us! Get the militia, get the police!' he croaked, but the nearest German police officer was in distant Samoa, two thousand sea miles to the east, and as he sobbed into the darkness, he knew that there was no help coming.

21

South by the Sickle Moon

Lemon sea. Golden sea. Sleepwalkers come! Quickly now. Between the acts. We will go on the sweet waters. We will ride the black waves. We will escape the shadow and the copper knives.

Star fish, chiagra spider shells, wet, volcanic sand between your toes.

Twenty quick steps and finally the surf. Surf like a drummer, like a highland drummer proudly leading the Argyles into some surrendered frontier town.

The tide reaching its apogee. Sea around your ankles.

A thrill of early memory – the bathing huts at Brighton: the big ungainly girl swimming beyond the boldest men, free in the Channel, free for the first time.

The outrigger and the paddle are where you left them and beginning to lift.

You look out. New Britain is not far. Nine or ten miles.

The lights twinkling in the distance may even be Queen Emma's house.

Now is the time. Now or never. You take a breath. The smell of sea birds. Rotting fish. Now is the time. But you are afraid. Afraid for your life. Mr Darwin and Mr Spencer have convinced all right-thinking people that there will be no reward for virtue; both just and unjust will be extinguished for all eternity by cruel death. And these men will surely kill you if you attempt to thwart them. Just as they killed Lutzow and Bethman and who knows how many other Kanak and Europeans.

You're trembling. You feel tears. You bite your lip.

The memories come unbidden. Stifling schoolrooms. Miss Thackeray beating the lesson into you with the willow cane.

England expects every man to do his duty . . . And woman too.

You shove the canoe over the sandbar. It moves more easily than you were expecting. Of course it will be heavier with you and a passenger, but by then the tide will be at its maximum.

You turn and walk briskly back over the sand and lava rock.

You have a momentary doubt. Perhaps you should just save yourself. Now.

No. No, you can do all of it. You have power. The island has made you strong. It has given you the combination to your embryonic lock. You must at least save Prior, an Englishman, a fellow subject of the King.

You walk into the settlement of the immortals. The Augustburg.

The moon in its first quarter peers between the clouds. Your body covered in clothes and clay and black soil is invisible in the dark, but you wait anyway for the satellite to hide herself.

Drums, real now, and a fiddle. In the huts people preparing for the ad hoc ceremony. Daubing themselves with paint, drinking *arak*, sharpening knives.

There has been blood spilled and there will be more.

Two figures (Helena? Fraulein Schwab?) near the altar in the midst of frenzied copulation. You ignore them and walk to the hut you now share with Jürgen.

He is lying on the bed, exhausted from his work harvesting coconuts with Denfer and from the heroin he consumed at dinner.

You lie next to him.

'Ah, Bessie, my own dear Bessie,' he says, and kisses you.

There is no easy way to bring it up, but bring it up you must.

'Jürgen, I've been meaning to ask you something.'

'Yes?'

'Lutzow.'

'Yes?'

'It was Bethman wasn't it?'

'Bethman what?'

'It was Bethman who killed Lutzow. You helped didn't you? You and Misha, but it was Bethman's plan. You wouldn't do something like that of your own volition would you?'

'Of course not, Bessie! All we did was turn him over and hold him down while Bethman forced his head into the bucket of water. It was over very quickly. He was dying anyway. It was a mercy.'

'But people have been known to recover from malaria, haven't they? Bethman couldn't risk that could he?'

'No.'

'Why not? Because Lutzow was threatening to go back to Germany and write bad things about the *Sonnenorden*?'

'Bethman was worried for himself, not us. As usual!'

'Why? Some scandal in his past?'

'It doesn't matter, Bessie.'

'Something about his doctoring?'

'Yes, I think so.'

'Was he . . . ?'

You suddenly remember Bethman's conversation at breakfast that morning. The look on his face when he talked about Malthus.

'He was an abortion doctor, wasn't he? Did he flee some scandal in Germany and fear that Lutzow would bring the authorities down on his head?'

'It was something like that, but it—'

'More than a scandal! A crime! A woman who died after Doctor Bethman's ministrations?'

'Abortions! Crimes! What does it matter if that whole world is aborted, or if a million Lutzows die? We have left that world behind, Bessie!'

'It wasn't Bethman's original plan, though, was it? He wanted to inject Lutzow with heroin, didn't he? But Engelhardt kept the heroin in his hut and *he* did not believe in euthanasia.'

'Why do we talk of these sad events? It is the past! It has gone!' he says brusquely.

'You're quite right, Jürgen,' you say, slipping under his arm and getting out of the bed.

'Where are you going?'

'Just a brief walk. The night is so lovely. I shall be back presently.'

You run to the hut next to the forge.

You find Will, naked, half asleep on the floor. His eyes are yellow, his lips blue. There are cuts and bite marks on his arms and back. They have bound his hands behind his back with hemp rope.

You examine the knot. It is not one of those your father taught in his periods of lucidity. You pull at it but it is tight and secure.

The only solution is Alexandrian.

'A knife,' you mutter to yourself.

Will wakes, whimpers a little, but does not recognize you.

You look around the hut but with Teutonic efficiency they have removed anything that can be used to cut bonds.

He looks at you. His eyes are like those of an intelligent dog who senses something is not quite right.

'It's all going to be all right,' you tell him. You stroke his hair. He starts to cry. 'There, there,' you say and kiss his forehead.

You lay his head gently on the floor and look for anything sharp at all.

You hear voices coming this way. What would the Germans do if they found you in here? There would be every chance that they would see through your pretence. They would have no choice but to add you to the sacrifice.

The voices are coming closer. Engelhardt and two others.

There is nowhere to hide in here. You look out through the doorway. Three of them, yes. Engelhardt, Harry and one other. Perhaps you could make a dash for the trees, circle back around the camp through the jungle, and run for the beach.

There is no point wasting your strength thinking about that.

There is only Captain Kessler's Deutsches Heer bed up against the wall. In a libretto by Mr Gilbert that is where you would hide yourself. Heart pounding, you run for the wall and crawl under the bed. It is utterly absurd. It doesn't cover your arms or your feet and if they look directly at you all is lost . . .

The men enter. 'He has moved,' Harry says.

'Or someone has moved him,' Engelhardt says suspiciously.

'Get back over here,' Engelhardt mutters and you hear Will being dragged away from the door.

'He does not look well,' Harry says.

'I will remain here with him,' the other man says. Christian?

'If you wish,' Engelhardt says. 'Come, Harry.'

Engelhardt and Harry leave the cabin. The third man sits on the edge of the bed and begins humming to himself. You lie underneath him. Waiting.

He yawns and drapes himself on the bed, his head inches from your own. You can feel his weight on you.

You hear his breathing. You hear *everything*. You are alive in the rich tropical night among the vampire bats and moths and flying squirrels and tree kangaroos and army ants. You are alive and you too are part of the web of life and death. You too are a predator.

You feel a cough rising in your throat.

But you are not afraid.

Once you lived in fear, but no longer.

You crawl out from under the bed.

And cough.

Christian Weber does not look up. He appears to be dozing.

'Christian!' you whisper to be sure.

He does not reply.

You walk to the entrance and look outside. Engelhardt and Harry are walking across the clearing. They stop at the old well to discuss something and then disappear into the jungle.

Yes your senses are awake to everything now. The wind. The distant sea. In the other huts: motion, conversation, laughter. Everyone is excited. This new ceremony of Engelhardt's will shortly begin.

And time is pressing and the high tide will not come again for twelve more hours.

You stand in the doorway. No one is watching the beach. *You* could escape easily. Attempting to get Will away could even be construed as a form of suicide. Like the Light Brigade – a foolish, gallant act.

You step outside and walk briskly to the Malagan.

'Excuse me, ladies,' you say, stepping over Helena and Fraulein Schwab. You take a long bone-handled ivory knife from the feet of the Malagan.

'What is that?' Fraulein Schwab asks.

'It's just the knife, darling,' you tell her, holding it up in the moonlight.

'Come here,' she says in English. 'Join us.'

'I'm rather busy.'

'You are afraid,' Helena says.

'Perhaps that, too,' you say and walk quickly back across the clearing.

In the hut Will is awake now. A little more cognizant than he was before. Unlike laudanum, the heroin in its raw form apparently peaks and dies off quickly. 'Will, are you all right?' you ask him.

'Water,' he says.

You look around the hut. 'Will, there's no water. Now please stay still, I need to cut your—'

'The well, please, I'm dying,' he replies.

'Let me cut your ropes first.'

The sharpened ivory blade slices through the bonds. He rubs his wrists and groans with relief.

'Can you stand?' you ask.

'Water,' he insists.

'Yes, yes,' you tell him.

You put your hand under his elbow and pull him to his feet. The blood rushes from his brain and he sways there like a young sapling.

'Come, we must go. Now.'

'I need water,' he says.

'I'm going to get you water,' you assure him. You help Will to the entrance and peer outside.

The moon. The trees. You lead Will a few steps, but it's like dragging a corpse. You can't possibly do this all the way to the canoe.

'Wait here, Will, I shall bring you the water,' you tell him and sit him at the bench in front of the hut.

You run to the well and lift the grating and plunge the bucket into the water. You fill it and as you are bringing it back you notice Engelhardt walking to a large pile of sticks at the other side of the camp. You follow him with your gaze and you realize to your horror that the bundle of sticks is a pyre, with a stake in the middle of it. You duck behind a hut. Engelhardt doesn't see you and he fusses for a moment by the pyre then disappears into the jungle to gather more kindling.

When you get back to the hut, Christian Weber is outside, staring stupidly at Will.

'I must raise the alarm!' he tells you.

You quickly grab a long, broad palm-frond from the side of the hut and shove the stem end hard into his face, so hard it almost certainly breaks his nose. He staggers back against the hut but before he can raise the alarm you strike him again in the temple, knocking him off his feet. He falls heavily to the ground with a loud grunt. You check the piazza, but no one has seen you. Not yet. 'Let us go, Will,' you say, pulling him vertical.

'I want to sleep now.'

You set him down again, lift the water bucket and empty it on his face. You force his mouth open, making him drink. He blinks and shakes his head.

He looks at you with recognition.

'Will?'

'I'm all right,' he says.

He seems more lucid.

'Then we shall go,' you say, and help him up again.

'Where?' Will asks.

'We're leaving here,' you whisper.

'When?'

'Right now. I believe that they are going to do you mischief, Will. Killing Bethman has unhinged the *Sonnenorden* from good sense. We must get out of here.'

Talking to him is like chattering to your horse; he doesn't understand the words, but perhaps gets the tone. He sways forward and then back again like a palace guard on a hot August day.

'Will?'

His eyes close.

'Will! We have to leave immediately!'

He nods and then shakes his head. 'I won't go without Klaus.'

You try to explain. 'We cannot bring Klaus. The attempt to bring him would be dangerous and I cannot heave the dugout over the sandbar with the two of you on board.'

He pushes away your arm and sits down.

'Will, it is the high tide, we must away,' you say, and you pinch him for emphasis.

He shakes his head. 'The ceremony . . . If they can't kill me, they will kill Klaus.'

'They will murder all of us if we don't leave this instant!'

'Not without Klaus. He is my friend. It is your duty, Miss Pullen-Burry.'

'He is German. He is of their camp.'

'Never! He is with me and I am not going without him. They'll kill him!' Will insists.

There are tears in his eyes.

You take a deep a breath. Smile at him. Nod.

'Very well. Wait here, in the shadow, I will attempt to bring Hauptman Kessler. They are holding him now in Bradtke's hut.'

'I'm coming with you.'

'You can barely walk.'

'I'm coming.'

'You are a most vexing person.'

'So are you, Miss Pullen-Burry. That is what's going to save us.'

The pair of you walk to Bradtke's hut, where Denfer is on guard. Will grabs an axe handle and slips into the shadows.

'*Wer ist da?*' Denfer challenges from behind a cloud of blue pipe smoke.

'It is I,' you tell him.

He is still angry that you lie with Schreckengost and not him.

'Be gone from here,' he says, and blows the smoke at you.

Will approaches from the side and hits him with the axe shaft. It is a vicious crack and the man crumples to the ground unconscious. Will almost falls on top of him. The axe handle is cleft in two.

'How about that!' Will says.

'Ssshhh. Quietly now,' you tell him. 'Wait behind me, Will. Who knows who might be inside with Klaus?'

You go inside the hut. Kessler is lying in the hammock, drugged, dozing, his hands bound.

Bradtke is sitting next to him mulling over a position on Anna's chess board.

He lifts his head and is surprised to see you. 'Miss Pullen-Burry, I thought you were resting.'

'No.'

'You have put on clothes.'

'Yes.'

'You are carrying a palm tree frond.'

'Yes.'

'Surprise!' Will says, appearing behind you.

You strike Bradtke with the palm frond before he can raise the alarm. You knock him off the chair and hit him hard on the side of the head.

Will slaps Klaus on the face and wakes him.

'We're getting out of here, Klaus, they're going to kill us.'

'There is no way off this death island,' Klaus groans.

You cut his bonds and look into his face. He is conscious but not very alert.

'The redoubtable Miss Pullen-Burry has got the canoe,' Will says, and helps him to his feet. When you exit the hut you see that Denfer's pipe has set fire to a pile of straw bedding. Smoke is billowing from the straw and the side of the hut is beginning to catch fire.

'We must leave!' you say to the men.

'Take Klaus, I'm going to see if I can find that photograph album,' Will says.

'We don't have time!' you hiss at him.

He ducks back inside Bradtke's dwelling just as a sheet of flames rushes up the side of the hut. Helena and Fraulein Schwab wander towards you from the Malagan.

'What are you doing?' Helena asks dreamily.

'It is not your concern,' you inform her.

'You're leaving!'

'Why would you want to leave Paradise?' Fraulein Schwab asks.

'We are going to go now. Please do not try to prevent us,' you say.

'Go if you must,' Helena says scornfully.

'We shall,' you tell them.

They walk away, seemingly indifferent.

You almost clobber Will as he appears next to you. 'Did you get your book?'

'No. The whole place is on fire. The roof nearly fell on me.'

'Help me with Hauptman Kessler.'

Will takes the German's left arm and you drape his right over your left shoulder. You walk a good twenty-five paces before Kessler stumbles and all three of you fall. You struggle back up. You must keep off the trail at all costs.

Behind you, the roof of Bradtke's hut collapses in a deafening clang of corrugated iron. There are cries of panic all over the settlement and someone starts ringing a hand bell.

'How far is the canoe?' Will asks.

'It is only a short way to the beach,' you assure him and lead him on a diagonal through the coconut plantation. You see a long piece of bamboo lying on the ground with a one inch diameter, about the length of a hockey stick. This will serve even better. You drop the palm frond and pick up the bamboo.

Behind you there are screams and shouts of consternation.

You look back to see embers from the hut streaking into the air. You put your arm under Kessler and help him walk.

'You are doing very well,' you tell him.

You've only gone ten feet more when you see the ursine, startled face of Misha Denfer again. You hook the bamboo stave behind his legs and trip him hockey fashion. He falls backwards, banging his head off a coconut palm and crashing to the ground. Before he can attempt a warning you crush the bamboo pole into his temple.

'Well done Miss Pullen-Burry,' Will says.

'Hurry,' you say urgently.

There is a slight rise and from here you can see the moonlight scattering on the Bismarck Sea.

You are safe now. You feel the cool atramentous sand beneath your toes.

You drag the two men towards the canoe. A commotion comes from behind you. *Faster*, an instinct tells you.

Something whizzes above your head and plunges into the sea.

'The Night Witches!' Will screams.

Another object whistles above you to the left.

You turn to see Engelhardt, Harry and a revived Bradtke running along the beach towards you. Every few moments, they stop to throw bamboo spears.

'Into the canoe!' you command the men.

All three of you wade into the surf. The salt water stings the cuts on your toes and the undertow pulls you laterally.

You heave Kessler into the canoe. He is not heavy. In his few days here he must have lost a stone. Will attempts to help, but slips underneath the hull.

You grab his matted hair and pull him to the surface. 'Get in!' you order him.

'They're coming for us,' he says, his eyes wide, his lips ashen, his whole body trembling. 'What shall we do?'

'You shan't be able to help me. You will only get in my way,' you tell him and with one almighty shove you push him into the dug out.

'Halt there!' Engelhardt screams. 'That is our property!'

'Start paddling if you can,' you tell Will.

'What about you?'

But before you can answer a spear comes hurtling out of the darkness and embeds itself in the side of the outrigger.

'Christ!' Will shouts.

Anna and Helena are walking down from the dunes.

Five of them. Five against one.

You start shoving the canoe into the deep water but with two men aboard it resists stubbornly.

Engelhardt comes running towards you through the waves, brandishing his remaining spear. 'That is our property, get out of it at once!' he shrieks.

'Stand aside, sir,' you tell him.

'Miss Pullen-Burry, I demand that you return our property immediately!'

He thrusts his spear at you – the long bamboo stave silhouetting against the stars as it flies towards your head.

The way you watched the kendo masters do once in Japan, you parry his spear and thrust your own bamboo cane into his throat. Engelhardt drops his weapon and falls backwards into the water. He is weak. What the heroin has done to these wretches is appalling.

Harry wades into the surf now, beard bristling, hair wild. He is laughing. He is carrying a machete and a bamboo pike.

'You must give this up, Miss Pullen-Burry,' he says and clumsily swings the pike at you.

You step backwards and allow the sharpened bamboo to carry itself in an arc past your body. Bradtke wades towards you with a machete. You cannot deal with both of them at the same time. Harry first. Bradtke does not look that keen to tackle you again.

Before Harry can react you prod him hard in the face with the tip of the bamboo. He screams as you break his nose and in a sideways motion you thrust the bamboo at Bradtke. The old man is too fast, however, and he chops the bamboo with the machete, snapping it in two.

Engelhardt is lying on the water but he is groaning now and he will soon be up.

'You must give it up, madam,' Bradtke says.

Engelhardt fumbles for his weapon.

Harry wipes blood from his eyes.

Three of them.

Three of them in the dark.

Your grandfather – that old hound from Ebbw Vale – told you that in ancient Erin to become a member of the Fianna a warrior had to parry the blows of nine men with spears while flawlessly reciting lines of verse.

Harry swings at you again. Bradtke's blade glints.

You can't remember any verse.

But you will fight.

'Put it down, woman,' Bradtke says.

'I will not,' you reply and smack the broken bamboo staff into his ribs. He attempts to slash it with the machete but he isn't fast enough and the blow hurts him. You hit him again and again in quick succession: in the ribs and jaw and smack in the middle of those rotten teeth.

Helena and Anna are advancing into the surf now and behind them, on the sand, Misha Denfer. These creatures are as resilient as the creations of Mr Stoker.

Harry climbs into the canoe with his machete. Will is standing up, holding the obsidian knife. 'There are no two ways about it. Harry, get out of the canoe or I'll kill you,' Will says.

'Put down the knife, Will, my weapon outmatches yours,' Harry replies.

'Get out, Harry, or we will have to kill you, sir,' you tell him.

Will lunges at him and loses his balance and almost falls out of the canoe.

'Ha!' Harry laughs, and jumps from the canoe and lands on you and knocks you down.

You go under the waves, swallow water, come up again.

The machete comes swinging through the air.

'Hold her, Harry!' Fraulein Schwab yells from the shore.

But you can tell that he means to kill you. You take a breath and dive deep down under the water and find his ankle and tug him off his feet. You hold him under until he is lost in panic.

As you surface, a spear from the shore passes over your head.

You wait for Harry and when he surfaces you strike him in the face, hard, with the bamboo staff. Engelhardt is trying to get into the canoe. You bring the bamboo down hard on the top of the head.

Moonlight. Blood. Bradtke floating face-down in the surf, Engelhardt and Harry on their backs.

The tide has lifted the dugout. You start shoving it off the sandbar.

'Bessie!' Schreckengost calls, from the top of the dune. 'Come back!'

You heave with all your might while Will paddles.

'Come on Klaus!' Will says, and despite their wounds and exhaustion the two men paddle for all they are worth.

The canoe lifts up and you push it further and when the water is at your neck you climb aboard, take the paddle from Kessler and begin stroking like a woman possessed.

A fusillade of spears and stones.

A wave breaks over you. The going is rough.

'That is our property!' Engelhardt shouts. 'We are coming after you!'

Will looks at you. 'Do they have another canoe?' he asks.

'I do not know,' you tell him.

'I can't paddle anymore; I'm wrecked,' he says.

'It's quite all right, Mr Prior, I will take us.'

I will take us.

You sit in the rear of the canoe and paddle on both sides. It begins to rain.

'We must go back for my wireless telegraphy set!' Klaus moans.

'Do not excite yourself, sir,' you tell him firmly.

The rain is heavy, the sea black and violent. A dozen more strokes.

And then another dozen.

No sign of pursuit, but the tide will soon be setting against you.

Kessler is barely awake and Will is hunched over in a swoon.

'It's down to you Bessie,' you say to yourself.

When you look back there is, as yet, no sign of pursuit.

You paddle and put out your tongue to catch the rain water.

Minutes become an hour. The land seems no closer.

It is less than ten miles across the sound to Herbertshöhe, but the north-east trades are blowing and the powerful current heads out, out into the south Pacific . . .

All you can do is paddle harder.

The wind blows, the sky clears and there above you are the southern Constellations.

The navigators cross, Gemini, Centares.

Your arms ache, but still you must paddle.

You are being carried east. To that place Queen Emma told you about in the ceremonies of the taboo: Tingenatabaran, where souls go at sunrise into the vast, empty aquamarine ocean. Your hands blister. Blood pours down the wood.

The drift is increasing and you realize now that you must paddle across the current. You must head for Simpsonhafen at the western edge of the Gazelle Peninsula if you are not to be carried away from New Britain into the vast Pacific.

You can only imagine what would happen under the tropical sun without food or water; and you paddle, ignoring the fire in your arms.

You close your eyes and count strokes. One left, one right.

Ten, a hundred, a hundred and fifty.

You open your eyes, but the land seems just as far away as ever.

Ten, a hundred, two hundred, three . . .

When you dare to look, New Britain does seem a little closer! Perhaps the current has eased, or your plan is working.

You continue along the diagonal.

And close your eyes again. Ten, a hundred, another hundred, another.

Yes, it is closer.

Ten, a hundred, two hundred, three . . .

And a furtive light in the east.

Lemon sea. Golden sea.

Ten, a hundred, two hundred, three hundred, four hundred, five hundred, a thousand . . .

You can see Herbertshöhe and Queen Emma's massive warehouses around the docks.

Ten, a hundred, two hundred, three hundred.

The lamps on the pier. The windows of the Governor's mansion.

Ten, a hundred, two hundred, three-

'Where are your running lights?' someone shouts.

A young German naval rating yelling at you from a little steam launch.

'We are in need of your assistance, sir,' you tell him and drop your paddle and swoon backwards, utterly, utterly spent.

A rope.

A tow.

Questions.

Astonished faces.

'*Wasser . . . wasser. Bitte!*'

'*Wasser, schnell!*'

Movement. Someone lifting you.

You are on dry land, on a stretcher.

'Take them to the hospital!'

Faces.

Female faces.

A fan turning above your head.

'Sleep now,' a voice says.

Sleep.

Daylight. White sheets. Overhead fans.

Voices in French. Nuns who feed you and give you tea.

Doctor Bremmer takes your pulse and seems satisfied. 'Try to rest,' he says.

Rest.

Yes.

By the evening you are sitting up reading a newspaper from Australia when you see Governor Hahl walking towards your bed. He is alone. Dressed rather formally.

'My dear Miss Pullen-Burry, how do you do?' he begins.

'I am feeling much better, I find.'

'I am so glad! Doctor Bremmer says that you are making excellent progress.'

'Yes. I am quite on the mend. And Will? And Hauptman Kessler?'

'Hauptman Kessler discharged himself from the hospital and is recovering in his own home.'

'That is excellent news. And Will?'

'I'm afraid Herr Prior has the malarial fever, but he is in good hands with Doctor Bremmer.'

'I hope so.'

'Miss Pullen-Burry?'

'Yes?'

'This is a delicate matter.'

'Proceed, sir.'

'In light of what Hauptman Kessler tells me of the extraordinary events on Kabakon, I wanted to ask you if you still feel that you are able to keep your promise not to write about what you have seen and heard there?'

You raise your hand. 'Allow me to put your mind at ease. Rest assured that I will not write about this. I have given my word and my word is sacred, sir.'

'Miss Pullen-Burry, I knew that we could rely upon your discretion,' Governor Hahl says. 'Of course, when you are quite recovered you shall stay at my residence.'

'I shall be leaving here, as soon as I am able,' you tell him.

'Then I shall place the servants of His Imperial Majesty at your disposal; wherever you wish to go, the Kaiserliche Marine will take you.'

'A most generous offer.'

'I will bid you good day madam,' Governor Hahl says with a bow.

'Good day, sir.'

When he has gone you ask for your journal.

'No, I will not write about this,' you tell yourself. 'I will spare my friends embarrassment and I will spare myself indignity and I will trust Governor Hahl to deal with the wretches on the Cocovores.'

You tear out the pages of notes you have made on Kabakon. You hold the pencil in your bandaged fist, planning maps, gypsy routes and sea lanes to strange new lands that should provide the local colour which Mr John Murray requires to make into a book.

22

The Night Witches

On the day of Gan, the kingfisher, Siwa learned that a navy steamer had towed a canoe onto the beach of Herbertshöhe. There had been consternation on the Strand with men yelling in native languages and in German.

'Your man is alive, but not well. He coughs blood. His eyes are caked with salt,' a boy told her.

She went to the hospital but the nuns would not admit her. She returned in her church dress and carried a Bible and still they would not admit her because she was no blood relative. She went to the new doctor and told him that if she was not admitted to the ward then some night while he was sleeping she would steal into his house by the ground-floor window and cut his throat with an obsidian blade.

She was admitted.

Will was shivering under the sheets. He had been beaten. He was very sick. 'It is malaria, of course,' Doctor Bremmer said. 'Rather an advanced case, I'm afraid. It is in his liver.'

She took his hand, dismissed the doctor and hissed at the nuns.

He was cold. 'Am I on the block of ice?' he asked.

'No, Will, you are with me.'

'If this is death? Where is the box and the earth?'

'You're with me. You're safe.'

'Siwa. Oh God!'

Under the bandages he wept.

An hour passed.

Siwa knew this because the ward had a loud grandfather clock that marked out the fever hours.

Will's forehead was burning up.

Another hour. Another unwelcome visitor. 'How does he do?' a woman asked.

'He is doing very well,' Siwa told this English lady who was also bandaged and a patient here.

She knew that Siwa was lying. There was a croak in her voice that carried no conviction.

'Miss Pullen-Burry!' Will groaned. 'Thank you!'

'That's quite all right,' the lady replied. 'You are in good hands, now, Mr Prior, I can see that, you must do your best to get well.'

The nuns helped the lady back to her wing of the hospital.

'She saved me, Siwa,' Will said.

The saving, Will, has not even begun.

She squeezed his hand and leaned forward to kiss his brow. She saw that his blue eyes were bleached almost white. His breath reeked of death.

The sun advanced slowly across the sky.

He gazed at her like a man overboard looking back at the ship. She was a shade to him. The whole world was like this. A shadow play with shadow puppets.

'Who are you?'

'Oh, Will.'

Doctor Bremmer came to administer a purgative.

Siwa seized his wrist and squeezed. 'He is too weak.'

'We must clear his lungs with cigar smoke.'

'You will do no such thing.'

'This is my patient.'

'This is my man.'

Their eyes met, and again Siwa did not waver.

She took Will's hand. She watched him breathe. She watched the blue in the ship-filled sea. She watched the yellow in the hospital garden.

'Where are we? I need to know where I am.'

'We are in the hospital, in Herbertshöhe.'

'We are in the canoe. They are after us. There are sharks!'

'There are no sharks. You are safe. You are in the hospital.'

'They're going to kill us. They're mad! A conspiracy.'

'No, Will, you are safe.'

'Where's Bremmer!' Will screamed. 'Bremmer!'

Doctor Bremmer came. 'Tell them about the water in his lungs. Tell them!' Will said.

'Do not agitate yourself, Mr Prior, you must rest.'

'Tell them about the water!'

Siwa bathed his head.

The late afternoon heat. Ice from Queen Emma's machine. The whirring of a mechanical fan . . .

Bremmer was about to retire for the day. Siwa sought him out. 'Tell me.'

'I'm afraid he has reached the final crisis. He will either recover or die in the next day. Of course no one ever truly recovers from malaria, but this will be the apex.'

'What must I do?'

'Stay with him. Talk to him. Keep him from the coma if you are able.'

'I shall.'

Dusk. Her hand on Will's forehead.

The domain of the other. The world of the Dreaming.

She bathed his temple and observed carefully as the sun dipped below the pelagic rock.

Red sky.

Blue sky.

Black sky.

Moths banged against the screens. The last of the nuns went to their convent in Simpsonhafen.

Will opened his eyes. It was night, when the witches took to the air . . .

He could hear them coming across the Bismarck Sea. Over the wave and swell. To this world of machines and concrete and oil. A world they hated. Along the Wilhelm II Strasse and through the graveyard. Sniffing at the Lutheran headstones and the Celtic crosses. Past the Forsayth warehouse. Up Bismarck Strasse and Hanover Strasse. And finally:

The hospital steps.

The brass lock on the front door.

The entrance hall, the fever ward.

'The witches!' Will said.

'You are safe, Will,' Siwa replied.

Safe within the circle of salt and orchid petals with which she had surrounded the bed.

She held the coral at her neck. She spoke the old words. Not Welsh hymns, but an older wisdom by far, a string of words that were as old as man's first march from the West, when the Dreaming willed her people across the sea and along the coasts and into these wild, remote lands.

Words from when all the languages were one.

Thunder rolled down from the highlands. Lightning stabbed at the conductors on the hospital roof.

The spirits tested her.

Again and again they tried and were repelled.

Her glyphs and incantations were powerful magic and they knew that she was not to be bested.

'You're too strong for them,' Will murmured.

'Yes,' she soothed, and she bathed his forehead.

Around two o'clock, Siwa saw the change under the oil lamp: Will's breathing deepened and his fever broke. But still she watched and waited until dawn was the golden rumour in the east.

Parrots.

A dog cart.

Men talking in Cantonese.

Will's eyes fluttered. This was not Kabakon. Or the dugout.

It was morning in Herbertshöhe, in the German colony.

And there beside him on the bed was Siwa, exhausted, drenched in sweat, curled like a question mark. He sat up, took the bandages from his face.

'Siwa,' he said and kissed her.

'How are you feeling?'

'A little better. You fought the witches.'

'Yes.'

Later that afternoon.

Siwa pretending to sleep.

Will sitting up in bed reading the German papers.

The click of a walking stick. Siwa opened one eye. Hauptman Kessler, dressed in a baggy uniform.

'Klaus!'

'They told me you were at death's door.'

'On the contrary,' Will croaked.

'You do not look well.'

'Look at you. You're skin and bones.'

Kessler sat. 'How are you, Will?'

The men examined one another and a secret seemed to pass between them.

A party of German soldiers walked past beyond the hospital wall.

'New men?' Will asked.

Kessler nodded. 'Engineers from Samoa.'

'A new road?'

'For a new harbour – Simpsonhafen to become the largest German base in the Pacific.'

Will nodded and sighed.

'Are you all right, Will?'

'What are you going to do about the *Sonnenorden*, Klaus?'

'Do not concern yourself with that now. You must take time to—'

'What are you going to do?'

'Probably nothing.'

'Nothing?'

'There is no proof of any wrongdoing.'

'Fraulein Herzen! She's the proof! She'll tell you everything!'

'I interviewed Fraulein Herzen earlier today. She knows nothing of a murder. She was sleeping when Lutzow died.'

'The photograph album?'

'Obscene pictures of women.'

'The autopsy?'

'A mistake, perhaps.'

'No murder? No murder you say! But they killed Bethman,' Will cried.

'Self-defence, Will. I saw it. You saw it. It is not worth the scandal of a trial.'

'They were going to sacrifice us.'

'We have no proof of anything, Will.'

'For God's sake, man, they attacked us in the canoe!'

'*Their* canoe. I imagine that the German laws regarding defence of property will protect them there, too, I regret to say.'

Will shook his head. 'It's you, isn't it? You and Governor Hahl. You are going to cover it up. To avoid a scandal! If I tell Doctor

Parkinson what I have seen he will have them evicted from the island for piracy!'

'You will say nothing to Herr Doctor Parkinson, Will. *Nothing happened on Kabakon.* Do you understand me?'

Another secret look between the two men.

'Oh, I understand you only too well.'

A nurse slid open the screen door to the veranda, where one could sit among the dahlias and crimson anthuriums and the palms full of butterflies.

'Well, I must away,' Kessler said. 'I am late for an appointment with Governor Hahl.' He walked to the swinging door that lead to the general ward and stopped with a fingertip on the door's brass handle. 'Have you ever been to see the birds at the zoological gardens, Will?' he asked.

'Yes.'

'That is what Kabakon will become. An aviary for our more exotic Deutsch-Neuguineans.'

As Will considered this, his face tightened. 'A closed aviary, Klaus. No new specimens. We will insist upon that.'

Kessler stood utterly still for an instant and then smiled. 'Yes,' he agreed.

Siwa watched him walk through the general ward, exit by the side entrance and go into the hospital flower beds to sniff the moth orchids.

'You must rest now,' she said to Will.

'All right,' he agreed.

She curled next to him. His breath was sweet. His skin no longer like parchment.

They lay in the bed together like prayer books in a vestry. She closed his eyes. And their breathing syncopated. And their heartbeats syncopated. And in that state of natural asepsis they slept the sleep of restoration.

AFTERWORD

In early 1907, the colonial authorities in Herbertshöhe concluded their official investigation into the deaths of Max Lutzow and August Bethman. No action was taken against Engelhardt or any of the *Sonnenorden*, although no more Europeans seem to have been given permission to live on Kabakon, and the community began to shrink by emigration and its alarmingly high death rate from malnutrition and malaria.

In 1908, Bessie Pullen-Burry published her New Guinea travelogue, *In a German Colony*. A generous portion of the book was lavished upon the hospitality of 'Queen' Emma Forsayth, Doctor Parkinson and Governor Hahl. The Cocovores were mentioned only briefly.

In 1909, Doctor Richard Parkinson, Emma Forsayth's man of business, died shortly after publishing his own well-received book *Dreissig Jahre in der Südsee*. Following Doctor Parkinson's death, Emma Forsayth sold her estates in New Guinea for a staggering 3.57 million Marks, moved to Europe and married a German playboy several decades her junior. She succumbed to diabetes in Monte Carlo in 1913. Her ashes were sent back to New Britain and buried in a lavish ceremony near her mansion, Gunantambu, in Herbertshöhe.

Later the same year, the capital of German New Guinea was moved a few miles up the coast from Herbertshöhe to

Simpsonhafen which was then renamed Rabaul – 'mangrove' in the native Kuanua language. Rabaul's harbour was deepened for the German Navy and a coaling and radio station established. Governor Albert Hahl was on a visit to Berlin in August 1914 when World War I broke out. He did not return to the Pacific but he, too, wrote a lively memoir about his time in New Guinea.

The capture of Rabaul was the first successful action of the Australian armed forces in the Great War, the town falling on 13 September 1914. It remained under Australian administration for the next twenty-eight years, until 1942 when it was taken by a marine detachment of the Imperial Japanese Navy. Rabaul became the primary Japanese staging-post for the entire Southern Pacific region, with up to 120,000 troops stationed there, including a garrison on Kabakon Island. The mastermind of the Pearl Harbor attack, Admiral Yamamoto, was on an inspection tour to the port when he was shot down and killed shortly after taking off from Rabaul Air Station on 18 April 1943.

In 1944, the United States First Marine Division landed in New Britain, in the Cape Gloucester area, and elements of the US Army occupied the southern portion of the island under the auspices of Operation Cartwheel. The Japanese ultimately abandoned Rabaul in August 1945. Australia resumed its Trustee Mandate over New Britain in 1946 and governed the province until the independence of Papua New Guinea in 1973.

On 19 September 1994 the population of Rabaul was evacuated shortly before the Tavurvur volcano erupted with devastating consequences. The town and much of the surrounding district were utterly destroyed and the regional capital was moved back to Herbertshöhe (which had been renamed Kokopo) where it remains today.

The strange history of the Cocovores is little known outside academia. The sole reference to August Engelhardt and Kabakon in *The New York Times* Index leads one to a 1905 article that is almost entirely fallacious in content and ends with the claim that Engelhardt died mad and alone on Kabakon in September 1905. In fact, Engelhardt lived with his few remaining followers on Kabakon until 1915, when they were interned by the Australians for the duration of World War I. After the armistice, Engelhardt returned to Kabakon and died there on 5 May 1919, followed four days later by Wilhelm Bradtke, the last surviving member of the *Sonnenorden*.

In the summer of 2013, as research for this book, I spent several days on Kabakon Island, camping in a clearing under the palm trees and eating only coconuts. The experience, even for so short a period, was not an entirely pleasant one. At that time I appeared to be the island's only human resident, although I found ample evidence of previous occupation. There were a number of plantation buildings, several concrete pillboxes, a ruined jetty and other detritus from the Japanese World War II defences. I had been told that there was a small German colonial-era graveyard on Kabakon but this too had been obliterated by Japanese military structures. A century after their heyday, no traces at all remained of the 'immortals' and their Order of the Sun.